CLOSE ENCOUNTERS OF THE OLD WEST

By Logan Hawkes

LOGAN HAWKES

ISBN-10: 1461089859
ISBN-13: 978-1461089858

DEDICATION

To the ones I love the most: Carla, who makes life an adventure and fills my soul with the flame of hope and passion; to Jason, Shane, Ryan, Regan and Kyle, my five offspring who bring joy and pride to the heart of a father that could hope for no better sons; and to Norma, Don, Joan, Jim and all their crew who have also supported my wild ideas down through the years, even when they thought me crazy; to Bob and Jean for their support and the inspiration they provide with their kindness and love, and to my loving parents who never put limits on my imagination, may they rest in peace forever; and, last and not least, especially to you Grandmother, who taught me the Cherokee spirit without ever trying. *U-ne-qua a-da-do-li-gi*

Cover Art: Carla Land/Kyle Landwalker

"Life, for ever dying to be born afresh, for ever young and eager, will presently stand upon this earth as upon a footstool, and stretch out its realm amidst the stars."

H. G. Wells, *The Outline of History*, 1920

"I believe it is in the power of the Indians unassisted, but united and determined, to hold their country. We cannot expect to do this without serious losses and many privations, but we possess the spirit of our fathers, and are resolved never to be enslaved by an inferior race, and trodden under the feet of an ignorant and insolent foe, we, the Creeks, Choctaws, Chickasaws, Seminoles, and Tsalagi (Cherokees), never can be conquered..."
~ *Stand Watie, Tsalagi (Cherokee)*

FORWARD

Since the summer of 1947 volumes have been written and millions of hours of discussions and debate have taken place about whether extraterrestrials have piloted spacecraft and visited the earth and, by accident or design, interacted with the human race. There are those who embrace that idea and those who deny such a thing could possibly take place. The skeptics are quick to point out that the vast majority, if not all, of called sightings of unidentified flying objects, or UFOs, are nothing more than misidentifications of military and/or civilian aircraft, weather balloons, or some other terrestrial object or event. With thousands of satellites and aircraft in the sky at any given time, their arguments are difficult to counter.

But some of the most credible sightings and reports of encounters with off world objects or creatures come not from the present, but from our past, specifically our near past, the nineteenth century, when America was experiencing great growing pains and the nation was determined to expand westward, driven by concepts like 'Manifest Destiny'.

When a cowboy out on the range sitting on his pony singing a lullaby to his cows looked up and saw a strange shiny object speeding across the sky or hovering over the herd, you can bet it wasn't a jumbo jet or weather balloon; it couldn't have been a satellite or falling military flares or sky divers. The only thing he expected to see in the sky was a bird or a cloud, perhaps a rare falling star in the night sky, so you can bet chances are good he was witnessing a very strange anomaly, quite possibly an airship of extraterrestrial origin, something, perhaps, from another world.

Adding to these 19th century mysteries are Native American legends and myths about star beings and strange creatures; origin stories of how star beings transported the early Americans of earth from distant systems like Pleiades or Sirius or Ursa Minor. There are native stories that tell how some of America's early Native cultures ascended from the underworld through sacred holes in the ground, their *sipapu*, as half-animal, half human creatures, leading some to speculate that alien intervention and genetic manipulation may have been involved in the evolution and population of our planet.

In this book you'll read about many strange sightings of the 19th century and explore a host of ancient myths and legends, each enhanced for the purposes of this fictional tale. But at the beginning of many of the chapters in the novel you will find historical notes referencing real published newspaper reports from the 1800s that you can explore in more detail in the comprehensive appendix at the back of the book, events and encounters that were as perplexing in their day as they remain in modern times.

Keep in mind that in the novel, as true with any work of fiction, I have taken the liberty of embellishing these historical accounts to give them what I hope is entertainment value with an intentional speculative spin, especially as it relates to Native American culture and mythology. Inheriting my Cherokee bloodline from my grandmother, I have taken the liberty of using many stories from my youth and enhancing them for fictional presentation. They are not to be construed as factual events or representations of Native American beliefs, especially as it relates to the Cherokee Wolf Clan, but simple interpretations of myth and legend.

Whether you are reading this book for the "thrill of the adventure" or have picked it up specifically to read about the historical and documented reports found in the appendix, I wish you a "good read" and hope the material will serve to open your mind and expand your interest in the subject.

Hi-tsa-tv-da-s-da Ha-tv-da-s-da

CHAPTER ONE
DEATH BY DECREE

The seaside villa didn't look particularly presidential, though Jonah Montana didn't really have any idea what 'presidential' should look like. He expected more, a home much larger perhaps, and decorated with furnishings and grand adornments like those you would expect to see in a museum or in a palace of kings.

But James Garfield wasn't a king. He was raised in a log cabin in Ohio, worked his way through college, and was by any stretch of the imagination an ordinary man. His simple seaside home seemed to fit his modest beginnings, and Jonah could relate to that. What was bothering him more than the simple surroundings of this meeting was why he had been summoned to the President's home in the first place, especially considering Garfield had a lot more to worry about than calling for a mysterious meeting with a man he didn't even know.

Jonah quickly glanced around the parlor room before his eyes came to rest on a door he assumed led to the President's office. That's where the tall, stoic secretary had disappeared behind after greeting him and leaving him on an uncomfortable set`ee´. Like his Cherokee grandfather, Jonah was gifted by "the sight", as his Gray Wolf called it, an innate ability to sense things before they happened. He watched the brass door knob turn and quickly Jarvis, the President's secretary, called his named and motioned for him to follow. Collecting his wits, he approached as Jarvis stepped aside to allow his passage.

"The President will see you now," he said.

He was led down a short hallway with several doors to each side and coming to the last was greeted by yet another man, a tall fellow and rather pale he thought, who extended his hand by way of introduction.

"Alexander Bell Mr. Montana, right this way."

As he entered the room he was surprised to realize he was entering a bedroom, not an office. At one end of the room stood a large brass bed and upon it lay the President appearing anything but Presidential. He was dressed in a nightgown and half covered with a bed sheet. His hair was unruly and his face unshaven, his skin rather pallid and his voice slightly cracked when he spoke. But his eyes were clear and grey and wise and strong.

"Jonah Ten Killer Montana," the words stung Jonah like sleet on a cold winter's night. Garfield feebly pointed to a chair on the other side of the bed. "Nice to make your acquaintance son. You'll have to come closer."

Garfield looked him over, sized him up, as crossed the room to take the seat nearest the bed.

"You're surprised I know your birth name." It wasn't a question, but a statement. "I'm afraid I know a lot more than that about you. Sit, sit down."

Garfield waved in the direction of the other man, Bell, who followed Jonah into the room and who was assuming a chair beyond the foot of the bed.

"Mr. Bell here is going to join us Jonah, if you don't mind me calling you that?"

His deep Grey eyes never blinked. In spite of his humble background, Jonah immediately decided the President was a man of great strength, this in spite of his frailness.

"Of course not sir...Mr. President."

"Good. Now, about why I called you here," Garfield paused as if considering his words carefully. Jonah uncomfortably fidgeted in the chair. Garfield coughed and winced with pain before continuing. It was then Jonah noticed the thick bandages that were wrapped tightly around his chest just underneath the bed gown. Faintly he could see blood stains.

"You're a patriot Jonah," Garfield collected his strength. "I know this because I am very thorough in qualifying men with whom I have an interest. You're name was brought to my attention by a long time advisor, Professor Ridley Willard. I believe he was your tutor at the University."
Before Jonah could answer, the President continued.

"Now son, as you can see, I find myself in quite a predicament. An assassin's bullet has found its way to my heart," he glanced at Bell at the end of the bed. "Or somewhere near it I think. And the truth is I haven't got a lot of time left."

Jonah wasn't certain how to react. He knew Garfield had been shot. It had been well publicized. But according to newspaper reports, the President was recovering in his home by the sea, not dying.

"That's what makes this meeting so important son. So humor a dying man and I'll make this as short as I can. Bell here can fill you in on the details, but in short, I am recruiting you – I should say commissioning you – to take a very thankless and important job on behalf of the future of this great Republic. The task I lay before you requires the greatest confidentiality. If you accept, you will report directly to this office, the Office of the President, or his designated officer, and to no one else. It will involve the serious business of investigating the most unusual mysteries that exist in this world of ours, many which are believed to threaten the well being of the country. In service to this Nation you will travel down many rabbit trails, be led down many blind alleys. You will face the unknown, the unexpected and the impossible, and all the while you must keep an open mind, a pure heart, and a dedication that goes beyond reason."

He paused to clear his throat, displaying his extreme discomfort and visibly fighting back the pain.

"I understand you're a reader. You like the Frenchman's work, Jules Verne I believe, and you've read that new writer, Arthur Doyle. And I know you're well versed in the stories of George Gist – or should I say *Ssiquoya*, one of your relatives I believe?"
Jonah was surprised. How could he know of Sequoyah or his family history?

"I'm gonna make this short. You see Jonah, I know a great deal about you, about your family. I know you were an honor graduate at the Cherokee Seminary and the protégé of Professor Willard. You excelled in

9

astronomy, history and language arts. I know your Grandfather is a respected spiritual leader, an *A-ni-ki-tu-wa-gi* – a man who knows answers to many mysteries. And your grandfather's eldest brother served as an Indian officer under General Washington. You're the right man for this job. If you accept, you will be bound in the service of a great nation," Garfield looked expended. There was another fit of coughing, blood visible on his lower lip, and the look of pain on his brow. "You have been selected because they say you have a keen sense about things, an uncanny ability of reason and deduction, and your heritage makes you an acceptable representative among the Native People where, I might say, many answers to many mysteries lie. The task before you, should you sign on for this job, requires an open mind and the wits to the get to the bottom of a good mystery. This nation can not exist while there are so many things out there we do not understand. We need answers Jonah, about strange lights on mountain tops, haunted canyons, strange flying airships, perplexing legends about skin walkers and the like. And of equal concern, there are individuals and societies out there that would undermine the great destiny of this nation if they aren't stopped. We need to know about them. We need answers. And I believe, in time, you might get them for us."

He sighed heavily. The meeting had reached its conclusion. He feebly waved a hand at the door.

"There's so much to tell you, to explain, but Bell here will provide the details. I'll need your answer in the morning."

Jonah hesitated, then slowly rose. He couldn't believe the meeting was over, that he had been called half way across the country for a five minute meeting. He nodded at the President though and started for the door. The man named Bell rose in unison and eyed Jonah curiously. Before he could leave, Garfield offered a final comment.

"My days are terribly numbered son. Your prime contact will be your old friend Ridley Willard. Bell will be assisting you as he will explain. Give him your final answer and it will be conveyed to me. This will be our first and last meeting. Future communication will be with a man named Cleveland, and stay away from Arthur Hill. That upstart knows nothing about any of this, and he can't be trusted. This conversation is to never be discussed with anyone outside a very small circle. Is this clear?"

Jonah was perplexed, but nodded, and Garfield painfully lay back on his pillow and closed his deep troubled eyes. It was the last time Jonah would see him, but not the last he would wonder about this strange and unexpected encounter.

Walking through the hallway and parlor he was shown the front door by secretary Jarvis and stepped into a bright, late summer morning. He found himself standing near the low white fence of the President's New Jersey home staring at the blue Atlantic. A carriage with a pair of well groomed Morgans was waiting for Bell, who had followed him. He turned to face the other man, but before he could ask one of a hundred questions that were racing through his mind, Bell smiled.

"That didn't go as well as I hoped Mr. Montana. The old boy is suffering I should say, and to me, apparently, falls the task of explaining the details. I'm staying at the Orchard Hotel. I took the liberty of securing you a room there as well. If you'll tie your horse behind the carriage, we can proceed to the next phase – that is, if you haven't been frightened away already."

Jonah wasn't frightened, but his curiosity had been sparked. Garfield was right, he loved a good mystery. One thing he knew for certain, he had to know what this was all about and how he came to be selected as - how did the President put it -- the "right man for the job". He chose to ride his own horse to the hotel and as he followed the carriage he relived those short moments in Garfield's bedroom. How in the world did he get involved in this he wondered. It was a most unusual and perplexing development. Ten days before this meeting he was riding across Indian Territory of the Five Civilized tribes, a tribal deputy who enjoyed the outdoors and the solitude of wide open country. Suddenly he had been summoned to a meeting with the President, and he knew, by intuition perhaps, that his grandfather must have had something to do with it.

After stashing his saddlebags in his room and splashing water on his face from the ceramic basin he crossed the hall and knocked on the door of Room 13. He half smiled and wondered if Bell had taken that room by design. Almost immediately the door opened and Bell motioned him in.

"I should start by explaining who I am and my role in this affair I suppose," Bell motioned for him to take one of the two chairs in the room and quickly sat down in the other.

"I know who you are. Alexander Graham Bell, the inventor," Jonah said matter-of-factly. Bell looked mildly surprised. "I do read the newspaper Mr. Bell. Tell me, did you really invent the talking device?" Bell laughed half-heartedly.

"Some don't seem to think so, and call me Alex will you. May I call you Jonah?"

Jonah nodded.

"The truth is Jonah, I think several of us had the same idea about the same time. The talking machine I mean. But I like to think I had my invention working before the others. But that's neither here nor there, not really relevant to the business at hand," He paused, and took a deep breath allowing time to gather his thoughts.

"As you might imagine, as an inventor, a scientist, communicating the desires of others is not really my main suit. I too, you see, have only recently been enlisted into the service of the President," he paused again, as if struggling to find the right words.

"I read you had invented a machine to find the bullet in the President's chest," Jonah offered.

"Well...yes, but not exactly. A man named Newcomb actually had invented an electrical device that when passed over an object with magnetic properties would create an audible hum – a sound you could hear. But in the case of a bullet inside a man, the hum wasn't loud enough to detect by the human ear alone. I teamed with Newcomb by offering to use my talking device to amplify that sound. But that's a long story. You see, it was the result of our efforts, Newcomb and I, that we became involved in Garfield's big plan. That's what I call it. A brilliant man, actually, and a brilliant mind. His wheels never stop turning, not even on his death bed – as you just experienced. But to the point. What do you know about the Culper Ring?"

"You're referring to the spy ring organized by Tallmadge and active during the first war with England," Jonah had read about the Ring, it seemed to be one of Professor Willard's favorite stories.

"My, you are an educated..." his words trailed off and he blushed.

"Indian? That's alright Alex, I'm used to it, and yes, I am well read and highly educated – for an Indian."

"I am sorry about that Jonah. I myself am not a prejudiced man. To be honest, you are as close as I have come to having a real conversation with a, uh, a first American," Bell smiled at his choice of words. "I like that term. They should use it universally I think."

"No offense taken, but I think I prefer Indian. The truth is, many do not realize I am a Cherokee. My mother is Irish, and even my father's people look at me as if I were *unega*...white."

"None-the-less, I must say it is rather unusual for an...an Indian...to be so well educated, or so I was always led to believe – and I'm sorry for that. But nothing pleases me more Jonah. I have a fascination with the whole Indian, Cowboy thing. Under different circumstances, I think I might have traveled West myself for a taste of life on the great prairie as they say. But back to the Culper thing, I must admit this was a bit of history I was not familiar with being a Scotsman. It has been explained to me of course, a bit of an interesting piece of historical development I might say. Are you aware that the Ring remains very active in modern times?"

This Jonah did not know.

"Are you telling me that is what this is all about, that I am being recruited as a...spy?"

"Well no, not exactly. As I understand it, the Culpers are concerned with international affairs...affairs of the state I mean. But you would be right if you said this assignment you are being offered is somewhat related. Willard is your old professor, right? He is a Culper you know, and it was he who suggested your involvement in this new branch of service. Not the Ring mind you, something new," Bell read the look of surprise on Jonah's face. "You didn't know Willard was a spy did you. No...I suppose you wouldn't. The Culpers, of course, are a top secret organization; they don't go around announcing their existence. Jonah, most of the men and women who serve in the Ring are very powerful and often very influential individuals. Your old professor for example, a Harvard graduate, was probably recruited because of his association with the indigenous population – through the Seminary, a special project of his. And before you ask, yes, there has long been a secret government interest in the native cultures of this New World. They – your people I should say – harbor many myths and legends nearly as old as time itself I am told, and these things have captured the attention of our Nation's most powerful decision makers. To be honest, the way I see it, they are very afraid that the Indians know a great many things that they do not know. There is concern that this knowledge could prove to be an advantage to certain international adversaries should they come to discover this knowledge before we do. But that is but one of the things that concern the top people in Washington you understand. There are some, Jonah, that fear proverbial 'bumps in the night' – you know, to put it like a frightened boy, the stories of ghosts and creatures ten feet tall that walk the mountains of the West. There are tales of an ancient race of people that live under the mountains out West that pre-date your own people, and it is said these subterraneans may harbor technology beyond that of modern men. There are also rumors of flying machines on the plains and down in Texas, and little people four-foot tall that fly them," he paused and studied Jonah's blank face. "Is it too much to swallow sir, these most strange stories?"

Jonah wasn't sure how to answer. As the grandson of a Cherokee spiritual leader he was familiar with many stories that would frighten the strongest of men. But some of the things Bell was talking about sounded utterly fantastic. He was beginning to understand why Garfield referenced the writings of Verne and Doyle, and then the talk of being open minded and confidential.

"You are being serious, aren't you Alex?"

"As serious as the wound in Garfield's chest I'm afraid. There have been fantastic stories, even reports of some very strange things going on down in Mexico; the kind of things people scoff at, laugh at, but down deep they find them troublesome, so troublesome, Jonah, they want you to start investigating and find out how much of it is truth and how much is not."

Jonah let the words sink in, tried to see the reasoning behind it. After graduating from the Seminary his life had taken many turns. Fulfilling a vow he made in his early years, he had traveled to New York, more for the exposure he would get to the White man's way of living than for the lowly job he managed to find unloading crates at the dock, just enough wage to live on the streets and put food in his belly. A year later he headed to Boston where he found a slightly better paying job as a clerk in a ginning mill. He began to study the ways of the affluent and wealthy, watched them as they conducted their business and took mental note of their social interactions. If he ever hoped to succeed in their world, for which he had been educated, he would need to understand such simple things as knowing proper fashion and how to dress, how to speak and address associates and friends, and how to interact in the business world. His years of education at the Seminary had provided the raw academia, but he needed to see how it worked for himself.

Five years of inferior jobs and a pauper's existence among the whites was time enough for him to learn all he felt he needed to know however. It wasn't bad for a boy born and raised on an Indian farm. He had come a long way from his years in Indian Territory. But soon he found himself longing for the forests and the hills again. He wanted to ride the open country and be free of the smells of the city, and it wasn't long before he found himself back in Indian territories and, perhaps because of his grandfather's influence, was quickly recruited as a young officer of the Cherokee Lighthorse Guard, a tribal police force that upheld the laws of the tribe from southern Missouri and northwest Arkansas to the far west boundaries of western Oklahoma territory, even down to the piney woods of eastern Texas. His time as a horseman gave him opportunities to hone his skills as a warrior, and also to study and practice the 'civilized method' of justice. Most of all, it allowed him to live beneath the open skies.

But it wasn't long before he caught the attention of U.S. Deputy Marshal Abe Adams who appointed him a Special Officer of the Indian territory. They were being pressured by the oncoming surge of settlers from the East that were moving West in large numbers, and the civilized tribes needed to prove their independence was an orderly and law abiding operation in order to protect their lands from encroachment. It was a real government job, one he was glad to get, where he could make a fair wage and serve both his own people and the growing U.S. government.

All of this, he reasoned, may have been good training for this new opportunity he was being offered. In fact, he was beginning to think he might actually be the perfect candidate, at least in the eyes of the President. After all, he was still considered by those who knew him a mixed blood. Who better to put in a weird position that most respectable lawmen would scoff at? Chasing ghosts, looking for little flying people and investigating ancient legends - it might be just the kind of job you would hand to a lowly half breed.

Well, he thought, it was better to have a job chasing rainbows than to live his life as a social outcast trapped between the world of both the Indians and the Whites. It's just the type of thing Bell might tell him was "Manifest Destiny'.

Alexander Bell had been lost in his own thoughts, namely, the unusual developments of recent weeks that had brought him to this room on this day under these most unusual circumstances, Alex had not had a lot of time to think, and while Jonah chased his ghosts, Alex considered his own - the events that had brought him to this point in time.

His life had taken many turns in recent months. He was the inventor of the talking machine, only to become the subject of debate, doubt and ridicule in the newspapers that claimed he may not have been the first to invent it, and worse, that he may have stolen the idea from a fellow inventor. And then, by chance, Alex read of Newcomb's machine that might save the life of a President and saw it as a great opportunity. He boldly stepped forward to assist in the cause, using his talking device as the "great piece of invention" that, in the end, could save the day - or so he thought. If he could locate the bullet in Garfield's chest, the newspapers might be forced to cease their doubt about his invention skills, and he might even become a national hero. If he failed – well, that wasn't suppose to be an option.

Newcomb had invented an electro-pulsating device that promised to be a proficient instrument for finding metal objects embedded in all types of material. During testing it performed well, first by detecting a metal bullet buried six inches in the ground, then by locating old embedded bullets in Civil War soldiers.

The problem was that the faint electrical "hum" the device emitted, indicating it had detected the metal object, wasn't always strong enough to detect with the human ear. But by using his talking machine's amplification components, Bell created a way to increase the volume of the hum. If the two inventors could examine Garfield and locate the bullet in his chest, then surgeons might be able to perform their skillful procedures to remove it without disturbing vital organs, provided the bullet was clear of those organs and the surgery was a success. If it worked, Bell could effectively counter the criticism he had received; he could reclaim his right as a brilliant scientist.

By fate or misfortune, however, Alex and Newcomb were unsuccessful in finding the bullet inside of Garfield; their device had failed to locate it when they examined Garfield in the White House – not once, but twice. The entire experience had been frustrating and more devastating to Alex's career.

A week after Garfield was transferred to his New Jersey seaside villa to live out his remaining days, Bell and Newcomb finally discovered why the device had failed to work. It turned out that a specially designed mattress sporting metal springs had been designed for and was a presidential gift from a New York inventor. These metal springs interfered with Newcomb's metal detection device. Instead of 'humming' when passed over an area of Garfield's body where the bullet was lodged, the "hum" was constant, reading the spring coils instead. After discovering the problem, of course, Bell and Newcomb tried again at his New Jersey villa. This time the device worked perfectly. The problem according to the surgeons, however, was that the President's condition had deteriorated greatly by this time and surgery was no longer an option. The President's condition and forthcoming death, however, was being treated as a national secret and Bell and Newcomb were prohibited from telling the world that their invention had succeeded in the end. They were prevented from applying for a patent, and once again the two inventors were blasted by the press. Effectively their careers had been damaged beyond repair.

Garfield was sympathetic with the damage to their reputations and Alex was fed the crumbs that fell from the table. He was offered the job as "scientific advisor" to the new secret government project that no one would ever know about as Garfield attempted to take steps that might help restore Alex's public image. He genuinely liked the young Scot immigrant, considered him a brilliant inventor, and did what he could to even the score. While Alex's pay was generous, it would be some time before his reputation would be overhauled.

Bell suddenly became aware that silence had fallen between them. Time had passed while both were lost in their thoughts, and as their eyes met, Jonah broke the silence.

"Well, Mr. Bell. If I go back to the reservation empty handed now I won't even be able to tell them why I had a meeting with the President, some might actually think I had something to do with the his death," Jonah managed a rare smile.

"So...this means you'll take the job?"

"Well, I suppose it does. But I would like to know a little more about what I will be doing."

Bell fumbled through a file on the table before them and rifled through a number of official looking documents.

"First things first Mr. Montana," looking over one of the documents, he laid a single sheet of paper before Jonah on the table. At the top it was marked 'Top Secret'.

"I assume you will find this form perfectly legal. This is your guarantee that what has transpired since you first stepped foot in the President's home and everything that follows thereafter – for the rest of your life I might say – is classified information. You must agree not to discuss this or anything about your commission to anyone – ever – not even in a court of law. This ensures that your work as a special White House agent remains confidential, and that any and all matters related thereto must be handled with discretion, and will remain confidential."

Bell slid the ink bottle and quill across the table in Jonah's direction. Taking the quill and dipping it into the bottle, Jonah asked "And that would make you my boss?"

Bell chuckled.

"Heaven's no Jonah, not I. I am your scientific advisor, your team mate. You do the investigating and I examine any technical evidence you may collect. Plus, it falls to me to develop a few new tools of modern technology to assist you along the way."

Jonah scribbled his name across the bottom of the form.

"Well. I have my own Colt Peacemaker and a good knife, and I have my own horse. Not sure I'll be needing much else."

Bell fumbled in his chest pocket and produced a small, golden five star badge surrounded by a cluster leaf of olive branches. Printed in raised letters around the star read "Special Agent of the United States, Department of the President".

"You will need this, but understand you would only use that in instances where local law enforcement attempt to interfere in some way with your investigations."

Jonah picked up the little badge and rolled his thumb over its face, admiring its shine. Putting it in his own pocket he said, "Well, that might help considering most local law men aren't going to like a half breed snooping around their territory."

Bell produced a second document, this one on a smaller piece of paper with few words on it. He handed it to Jonah.

It simply read: CADOTTE CREEK, GREAT FALLS, MONTANA, FLYING OBJECT CRASHED, ARTIFACTS OF UNKNOWN ORIGIN: SEARCH AND RECOVER.

"Well. I suppose this means this is my first assignment? There's not a lot to go on here," Jonah wondered how a crashed flying object in the middle of the wilderness could be a threat to the U.S. government. Maybe the government boys didn't know that objects fall from the sky all the time, like the one that made that huge crater in Arizona territory. He always wanted to see that. Just maybe this job would prove interesting. He had never been to Montana, but he heard it could be really cold there - and he wasn't fond of cold weather. "And it's going to take a few weeks to get there. By then the winter will be settling in."

"I have a few supporting documents for you, including a map of the area where they think you might find this...artifact. And the trip should actually take you only about three days to make it far as Denver because you're taking the train," Bell could see the surprise on Jonah's face. "Don't worry my good man. You're taking your horse on the train with you. You'll need to ride from Denver north through Wyoming to get to Cadotte Pass I'm told, I'd say maybe five days north. But the mountains are cold anytime of year I'm afraid."

"Yeah. So how much did you say I will be making in this job?"

"Well you're a lucky one Jonah. You will be paid $90 a month for your work, plus expenses provided you stay out of New York eateries. Your hotel rooms, train tickets and such will be paid by voucher – no need for cash. If you're near a telegraph office, simply wire for more vouchers," he paused. "One of these days, perhaps, you might actually be able to use the electrical speech machine for such things. I'm working on that you know. As far as a ticket to Denver, I have one already. We just need to add your horse."

Jonah raised an eyebrow.

"How did you know I would take the job?"

"Well, we didn't. But you weren't the only candidate, only the preferred one. If you didn't, well, let's just say I am happy to be working with you instead of the President's second choice."

Jonah looked at Bell and wondered.

"And who might that have been?"

"I'm not sure I can tell you that, but let's just say she's not going to be happy she didn't get the job," Bell said.

A woman? Jonah figured Bell must not have liked her very much. He appeared a bit nervous at the thought.

"You'll need to ride over to Trenton in the morning. I must inform President Garfield of our arrangement. You leave out the following morning on the Philadelphia and Trenton Railroad. I'll meet you at the depot two hours before noon to provide you with vouchers and an advance to get you started, and further written instructions. Well," rising, he extended a hand toward Jonah. "This begins a new era for the both of us. Fate – it's a funny thing I might say. But all is well that ends well. May I suggest you enjoy a restful night before your adventure begins?"

Jonah accepted his hand and nodded, wondering what Bell meant by a restful night. For Jonah, the nights would be better once he could escape the city and was back beneath the stars.

CHAPTER TWO
AN INDIAN, A PULLMAN, AND A LADY

I t was raining hard as Jonah watched Alex scurry across the depot wiping water from his brow with the back of one hand and toting a carpet bag in the other. He rushed across a crowded depot busy with travelers saying their last goodbyes to loved ones or associates as the steam rose slowly from the big black engine waiting at the dock outside. As if an omen of days to come there was a chill in the morning air that accompanied the rain, the wind whipping inside the depot doors that had been swung open by porters who were busy collecting baggage from some of the first passengers to board. Alex managed a smile as he spied Jonah.

"Sorry I am running late. The dreadful weather proved to be an obstacle. I think you'll find all things are in order," he raised a bound satchel and patted it with his free hand. "Everything you'll need is inside. It's your advance pay and assorted vouchers you can use on your journey. The President sends his regards by the way, said he's glad to have you on board. The old boy is not doing so well I'm afraid. Honestly, I don't believe he has much longer Jonah. He did wish me to convey that he is most pleased you have accepted this commission. And…uh…to make it official, I must read to you an oath of office of sorts, so raise your right hand and simply say I do after I complete the short version of this: I solemnly swear to uphold the...so forth and etcetera...to the best of my ability...and so forth...to defend my country and...etcetera...well you get the idea...right?"

"I do?"

"That's it old boy. That will work. Inside the satchel you'll find a copy of the oath if you'd like to read what you have sworn to do." As if on cue the big locomotive sounded a high-pitched boarding whistle. "But do read it, and then I suggest you destroy it. Let's not forget your service as a federal agent is an arrangement not to be openly discussed. Officially, you understand, you are an agent of the Office of the President, Special Investigations. To the outside world, if required, you are a deputy U.S. Marshal assigned to Internal Affairs. That should throw them off. And, oh yes, you'll be pleased and disappointed to hear that Professor Willard was at the Old Man's home when I left last evening. He wished me to tell you he was sorry to not see you off in person, but he and the President are planning your future today. Affairs of State I'm afraid. But he did want you to know that he looks forward to your return, whenever that might be, and a full report on your discoveries in Montana. Great sense of humor, your professor. Hearing of your first assignment he called it most fitting, 'Montana goes to Montana' he said. He seemed to like the sound of it. Never-the-less good man, boarding time and all, so off you go. Your steed, he's loaded and all?"

"Yes, and not liking the cramped rail car he's sharing with other horses, no more than I am looking forward to so many people stuffed into such a small place either."

"Yes, well. You have a Pullman car I believe, so when the walls close in, you might find solace in a place to lay your head. That's first class travel, Jonah," extending a hand, he nodded at the train as the final boarding whistle blew, followed by the roar of the steam horn that hurt his ears. He couldn't hear Alex's final words as they were drowned out by the sounds of the depot and the train, but Jonah nodded, picked up his saddlebags and headed out the double doors. Glancing back as he handed the conductor his ticket, he nodded again and Alex waved from boarding dock.

When Jonah found his assigned sleeping compartment in the Pullman he stashed the satchel beneath the bed coverings as the big train lurched forward and began to slowly pick up steam. He quickly settled into an open seat in the adjacent passenger car and settled down to watch the rain beat across the glass window. The New Jersey countryside was gray and wet and he was glad it didn't take long to reach the Philadelphia train station. A number of passengers unloaded and a few more boarded at the first stop on his long trip west. It lasted only a few minutes, but it was just the first of many stops along the way. The train was heading south to Baltimore then west to Louisville and on to Kansas City and eventually Denver. Jonah didn't look forward to so many long hours on board the metal bullet. He spent the first daylight hours watching the rain dance across the window and thought about the rapid developments of the last twenty four hours.

Finally the big train outran the weather and the late afternoon sun was peaking over the Appalachians when he finally retrieved and fumbled through the contents of the satchel Alex had provided. True to his word there was $90 in currency and several official-looking government vouchers inside, more than he thought he would need. As he shuffled through the papers that accompanied the cash and vouchers he came across the document with the Oath of Office scrolled across it and smiled to himself. He reasoned this very strange but official sounding job may prove the easiest one he had ever had. This, he supposed, was the fruit of his labor, that labor being three long years in the Seminary instead of riding the countryside, which he much preferred had the choice been his to make. But his Mother was pleased about his White man's education and this job was turning into something he would have never achieved otherwise. Things have a way of working out, he thought.

The last rays of the sun flickered through the window and Jonah realized he was getting hungry. The dining car was just a few cars ahead and he slowly made his way forward to find out what people ate when riding on a train. It was, after all, his first time. After several stops down the eastern seaboard to Washington and Alexandria, there were now fewer passengers on board and a number of empty seats. But the dining car was busy, apparently a popular place for socializing, an audible roar of conversation rising to greet him as he stepped through the door and spied an empty table a third of the way into the car. Taking a seat, a porter almost immediately appeared by his side.

"The evening meal today sir is a beef stew, still warm I would say, with biscuits and coffee, if the gentleman pleases."

Jonah nodded, happy to put anything in his stomach for his appetite had been growing. He had never acquired a taste for coffee, foreign to his native upbringing, but the other choice was warm Champagne, and he didn't normally partake of strong drink.

When the porter brought the meal a few moments later Jonah fumbled for a voucher in his breast pocket but was told the meals were included in the train's ticket price. It might have been a good deal to an average traveler, warm stew without having to pay for it, but the truth be known, he would have preferred the open trail and a string of jerky to chew.

He finished the stew, not at all unpleasant, and was enjoying a second cup of rather strong but bitter coffee when a remarkable looking woman walked through the door of the forward car. There were a few open tables but spying Jonah, not at all a bad looking man with his full head of shiny black hair and strong facial bone structure, she headed towards him. Jonah would have been considered a handsome man by most, a chiseled sort perhaps, but not all unpleasant to look at in spite of a tinge of ruggedness to his features. There was a subtle hint of nobility about him.

Pretending to look at other tables as she neared, the woman eventually addressed him.

"Is this seat taken?"

She was a fanciful looking woman, perhaps in her late 20s, a little younger than Jonah, with a touch of red in her rather full hair. She wore a lady's dress that was neither fancy nor cheap, but Jonah thought she looked more capable than her fashion suggested. By any description, she was a pleasant sight to see. Her face was soft but not like the high society women he had met in Boston, and her smile was contagious. Her greenish blues eyes were alert and accented the red in her hair.

"No." Having enough social grace to rise from his seat, he offered her a chair.

"Molly Langtry," she offered as she settled down. "Riding as far as Denver and terribly famished. How's the food Mr…"

"Montana, Jonah Montana, and the food is passable I suppose, but the coffee leaves much to be desired."

She smiled.

"Well Mr. Montana, I'll stick to the food. Where are you headed?" she asked.

Jonah thought her a little bold, forward, but he appreciated the distraction and enjoyed the way she looked.

"I also am headed to Denver," Jonah offered. "And I wish we were already there."

She flashed that smile again.

"They say getting there is half of the adventure Mr. Montana, but I must admit I'm not accustomed to these horrible machines myself. I'm still a Missouri girl at heart. I'd rather be straddle of a good horse personally. But then this is the modern way to travel is it not, and I admit much faster, if you have the stomach for it."

"Yes. I suppose." He was surprised. A lady who preferred to ride. There was more to this lady than appearances suggested.

"You've been in the East obviously Mr. Montana, but that's not where you're from is it?" she asked, sizing him up

"No. It was a – a business trip."

"And Denver is your home?"

"Actually not. More business I'm afraid."

She studied his dark eyes.

"Well, I am on an adventure Mr. Montana. My first time to Denver actually. And you? Have you been out West?"

He thought about it. As a deputy with the Light Horse Brigade he had been in New Mexico territory, and in Ute country along the Arkansas River, which was technically southern Colorado. But when he thought of the West he thought of California, and he had not ventured that far yet.

"Parts of it. But the West is a big place, always more to see," he offered.

"Have you ever been up the mountains? I mean, far up, removed from civilization and such?"

It was strange question, but it so happened that he had briefly, in the Rockies and the Sangre de Cristos chasing down a renegade Comanche wanted by Indian authorities.

"Once or twice I suppose."

"Might I inquire, what is the nature of your business? Forgive me for being so forward, but you do seem to be an outdoors man, and curiosity has the best of me."

He took a moment to answer. He remembered the oath he had taken, not suspecting to be bound by it so early in the performance of his duties. He didn't really have an answer prepared for that question.

"I am a representative of a tribal government, an agent" it was the first thing that came to his mind, and not completely untrue. He had been serving as a tribal deputy before heading to New Jersey. In fact, he was technically still on extended leave. Given a choice he would have returned to Oklahoma territory to officially resign and put his house in order before venturing out on this first assignment. But he wasn't expecting to be offered a new job when first summoned to the East coast. In fact, the entire matter had been shrouded in mystery.

It was Gray Wolf, his Grandfather, who encouraged him to visit with the President, explaining he had received word through an Indian agent, Thomas Blue Bell, that government officials had 'an offer to make'. In spite of his questioning, grandfather had simply said the nature of the business was to remain private until he met the president, and told him 'one can not refuse a presidential summons grandson'. And Gray Wolf told him he had 'prayed' about this meeting and had a vision that confirmed it was the right choice to make. Jonah didn't like the idea, but grandfather was not one with whom you could argue, and he respected the old man's wisdom and his ability to know things before others. Obediently, and reluctantly, he had complied.

"An Indian agent? Well that's a bit unusual. I mean, you are a..." Molly blushed.

"Yes, a half breed."

"I was going to say of Indian lineage."

They were interrupted as the porter returned to take her order. Shortly he scurried away to fetch another bowl of stew and a glass of champagne for the lady. She had encouraged Jonah to join her in a glass of his own, as if she might be stalling for time, but he politely denied the offer.

An uncomfortable moment of silence followed. He was enjoying her company, though he had always been a bit awkward when it came to women. It wasn't that he didn't like them, just that most of his experience had been limited to girls he grew up with, and socializing wasn't his best suit. But now something else was going on inside of Jonah. His senses were tingling slightly, something that happened to him often when he felt something was about to happen. It was a 'little voice inside' as grandfather explained it. He had been plagued by the condition since a very young age. His mother called it intuition; his father said it was a family thing. Grandfather simply called it 'the sight'.

The porter returned and Jonah watched her as she ate. He wasn't offended by her question. She was a handsome woman, and a nice diversion from the constant drone of the chugging engine and the rhythmic cadence of metal wheels running over the cross ties of the track beneath them. But he wondered why his senses were sharpened. The tingling was a sign he should be on guard.

She finished the stew and was holding her champagne glass in one hand now, twirling a lock of long red hair as she studied the strong lines in his face. He knew she had more to add to their conversation, but he thought she seemed hesitant, perhaps considering her options.

He was right.

"Mr. Montana, I'll just get to the point" she began, more seriously. "I am going to tell you something that may surprise you. But when I spied you from the door, I headed to your table to join you for a reason," She was right. Jonah wasn't surprised. She raised her glass to the porter, an indication she was ready for another. "You look like a man that knows his way around the wilderness. Would that be right?"

He hesitated a moment, then nodded.

"I suppose you could say that."

The tingling heightened.

"And you know a lot about Indians I suppose"

"You could say that."

"Well I need just such a man, and I would be willing to pay for his services. You see, I'm on a mission Mr. Montana and frankly don't know where to turn. I was raised on a ranch so I know my way around, as good as any wrangler on the ranch back in Missouri. I can ride and rope, brand like a man and shoot as straight as anyone. I don't get lost in the woods and can shoe a horse faster than most can turn around twice. But I'm headed into unchartered territory, a place high in the mountains and far from civilization as I know it. I'm betting you could be someone that might be of assistance, provided you have an interest."

He certainly hadn't expected this turn of events, and he wasn't certain how to respond. Her looks were apparently deceiving. A woman who could ride and rope and shoot straight as a man? It sounded like trouble.

"No offence Miss Langtry. But I have a job. And I must tell you, I wouldn't recommend heading deep into the Western wilderness. It's not all that friendly of a place."

"Yes. My point exactly. I'm headed to the middle of Cheyenne country Mr. Montana, and thought a man of your heritage might be a real asset. If you can't take the job – I understand. But I don't need a lecture about what I should or shouldn't do. I am aware of the danger, the challenges. I thought perhaps the nature of your job might be taking you into the same general area. Perhaps, at least, you might know someone you could recommend for the job, seeing that you seem to be a trustworthy man – or am I wrong?"

"Cheyenne territory? Miss Langtry, you don't want to head into that part of the country, especially…"

"Since I am a woman? "

"Since you are a woman, yes. But more importantly because they are having some trouble up there at the moment. What's so important that you would travel alone, unprepared, to such a place anyway?"

The tingling feeling just became a chill.

"I'm not unprepared, but I am in a bit of a hurry. I don't have the privilege of time on my side Mr. Montana. If I had more time, I wouldn't be asking a stranger to guide me, and need dictates my apparent lack of caution. Now I understand sir if you are not available for the job. But surely, in your line of work, you must know someone in Denver that might satisfy my requirements?"

He knew he would regret asking, but couldn't stop himself.

"And what did you say was the nature of this expedition?"

She looked him over carefully, pondering her response.

"I'm looking for something that fell from the sky Mr. Montana. You could call this a scientific expedition. I am not really comfortable discussing the specifics," She quickly changed the direction of the conversation. "What I need is someone that might be able to help me in communicating with the Native people of the area effectively, as they represent my best hope in locating that which I seek."

Jonah couldn't believe what he just heard. It was becoming evident that this new job was going to be a rollercoaster ride of surprises. He was less than twenty four hours into his first mission as an agent of the U.S. President and already it had taken an interesting turn. Who was this woman and how did she, by chance, walk up to his table, on this train, on this night, in search of what sounded like it might be the very object he was dispatched to investigate and recover? No wonder his senses were tingling.

"Miss Langtry." He struggled to not look surprised. "Why me? How did you decide, of all the men on this train, I would be the one to single out to provide assistance?"

"That should be obvious Mr. Montana. You look like the only half breed on board as far as I can tell. Look, no offense intended, but my father's ranch in Missouri is not far from the Arkansas line. I grew up around the Cherokee, half the wranglers on the ranch were *a-ni-tsa-la-gi*. I spotted you from a mile away and knew at first glance that you were either Cherokee or Choctaw. Which is it? *hi-tsa-la-gi-s?*"

She had nailed him alright. In his own language, with a slightly different dialect perhaps, she had asked him if he was Cherokee.

"A-si-hi. Yes."

"Call it providence if you like. It was my intention to find an Indian – no offence intended – to serve as a guide once I arrived in Denver. If I am to travel into Indian territory it would make sense to take along someone that understands the culture, someone that can communicate on my behalf – does it not?"

That did seem reasonable to Jonah.

"When I spotted you here in the dining car, I allowed my enthusiasm to get the best of me. And after talking to you briefly, a man of intelligence and skill I would judge, it seemed a perfect solution to my problem – the right man for the job. I apologize for any inconvenience that may have caused. Perhaps you know someone in Denver that might be able to satisfy my requirements?"

He took a moment to answer. It would seem that this meeting was, perhaps, by chance and not design. But maybe it was good fortune, at least for him. If someone else is searching for the artifact, might it not be prudent to keep them close until he determined why? Until he knew more, he decided he should stick close to this woman and find out what she knew and what her intentions were. How did she even know about the fallen artifact? And what did she want with it if it was the one and same thing he was after? There were far too many unanswered questions.

"I'll tell you what I think Miss Langtry."

She sat forward putting her elbows on the table and waited for his reply.

"I think you're crazy for even thinking about heading into Cheyenne country. And I think this talk of an artifact that fell from the sky is…well, a little unusual to say the least. But as you guessed, I am Cherokee, and I suppose you know how curious that can make me. Perhaps we should discuss this expedition of yours and then, perhaps, I could find a way to re-arrange my schedule to accommodate your requirement, or in the least help you find someone that might."

She smiled, and then insisted on champagne for the both of them. This time he didn't object, knowing somehow she wouldn't take no for answer. Before long, after small talk about her father's ranch and her experiences with Cherokee in Arkansas, she excused herself to retire too her own Pullman compartment, saying the champagne had made her 'silly'. She suggested they continue their discussion the following day.

"After all, it's going to be a long trip to Denver Mr. Montana," she giggled.

Three long days passed and still he failed to discover any substantial details about her expedition. She was very protective about whatever it was she was up to. Each time he tried to question her about it she simply would say they could talk about it in Denver, and quickly direct the conversation to other things. She did question him about what he thought she might require on such an expedition, horses, food supplies, warm bedding and the like. And she particularly wanted to know about his experience navigating the mountains. On the last day of the train ride she slept late in her compartment and surfaced only an hour before the train pulled into the Denver station.

The Denver, South Park and Pacific Railroad Depot was a bustle of activity. Denver was a popular destination these days after the recent discovery of silver in the nearby mountains.

Molly said she had a reservation at the new Gilman Hotel not far from the depot and Jonah promised he would "be right behind her" after he stopped at the telegraph office for "business reasons". It was true, he needed to pick up a telegram he learned was waiting when the conductor met him at the rail car where he was unloading *u-di-yv-li*, - Shadow – the coal black mustang that was quite obviously pleased to be getting off the cattle car.

While Molly was escorted to the nearby Hotel by a Chinaman with a push cart, he slid into the office and retrieved the telegram, slightly flustered he was unable to get any substantial answers from the woman.

Claiming the telegram, he read it with his back to the wall.

JONAH MONTANA STOP REGRET TO INFORM YOU GARFIELD HAS DIED STOP PROCEED AS PLANNED STOP NEW CONTACT IS CLEVELAND STOP WILL MEET IN DENVER OCTOBER 18 STOP BELL

The telegraph had arrived just that morning, so the news of the President's death was fresh. Bell coming to Denver was a surprise, but not the news of the President's demise. Jonah half way expected it before he ever made it out of New Jersey. He read the message one more time, then crumpled it and stuffed it in the saddlebag he carried hung over his shoulder. One thing for sure, things could change quickly in this business. Oct 18 gave him a few weeks to ride deep into northern territories, find the artifact in the mountains, complete his investigation and return to Denver. That should be enough he reasoned.

Claiming his saddle and bridling up Shadow he mounted and headed up the rail yard boulevard. He had taken the time to change his clothing and already felt more like himself sporting his favorite buckskin shirt, denim britches and calf high leather moccasins. He patted the saddlebags, which were now draped over Shadow's flanks, making certain his Peacemaker was stowed safely inside. The Winchester he carried was seated in its saddle harness.

Even in Denver, a frontier city of a thousand different faces, he was garnering a lot of stares from the merchants and miners and travelers that strolled down the broad wooden walks on both sides of the street.

Shadow pranced instead of walked, shiny black except for his white face and stockings and Jonah Ten-Killer's handprint tattooed in white across his rump. Looking at the sun, Jonah reckoned it must be near the noon hour. He wasn't looking forward to spending another night indoors. The warm sunshine made him more anxious to start his northward trek, but there was a chill to the air.

He thought about the developments of the last forty eight hours. The train ride in the company of Molly Langtry had not provided a lot of clues about her so called expedition. He was able to gather that she wasn't as well informed about its whereabouts as he, something he felt might be an advantage until he could find out more about why she wanted to find it.

He thought about the woman. She seemed a pleasant enough person, he thought, and he admired her independence. She was tough beneath that feminine shell, and she seemed determined - for whatever the purpose. He had no designs on her, though. This was strictly business he told himself. There were too many unanswered questions for him to altogether trust her, so he kept his secrets to himself and decided it best to remain patient and figure out why she was so headstrong and intent about searching for this rock that fell from the sky – if that was what she was after as he suspected.

Heading to the nearest general store he wanted to gather what supplies he thought they would need on the trail. He was also in search of information about the territory up north, what trail was best to take and what areas to avoid. It had been over three years since Crazy Horse, the Sioux War Chief, had fallen, and Sitting Bull was living on the reservation now. But rumors were that Dull Knife, still alive in spite of reports he had been killed in a skirmish with the cavalry, and other Cheyenne renegades, were stirring up trouble again. Add to that the unsettling news of a young Paiute named Wovaka, who was drumming up support for a new movement known as the Ghost Dance religion. Converts from many tribes, including the Sioux and Cheyenne, were being rallied to the cause, and Jonah knew the northern territories would be wrought with dangers. A half-breed was often an unwelcome sight among these plainsmen, especially one that didn't speak the local language. Too many times mixed bloods worked with the Calvary as spies or scouts, and he was sure gaining their trust would be no easy task. Right now tensions were running high throughout the region, and he knew many of the remaining free-tribesmen would never accept the hoe or the plow as a way of life, and dying on the battlefield was their only reason for living.

Outside the trading post he encountered a Ute scout serving the 4th Calvary stationed on the outskirts of Denver who offered invaluable information about the northern territories and the latest movements of the renegades across the north. If the information was right, he figured his best move would be to catch the train further west to Ogden and take the North Line to Montana. Given the short time before having to meet Bell back in Denver, and considering the hostilities of the northern territories, it seemed to be the best choice, though he didn't like the idea of another day and a half on the iron horse. Perhaps it was best though. Molly may not be the rider she claimed to be, and taking her into areas controlled by renegades was a dangerous prospect.

A few hours slipped by before he made it back to the Gilman Hotel. Molly was in the Lobby and none-too-pleased when she saw him walk through the doors, more than a few hours tardy. Twilight was chasing away the sun and she looked a little short on patience.

"Well Mr. Montana, I trust you have completed your business?"

"Yes Ma'am. I also took the liberty of supplying our journey north and managed to find a Ute scout that provided some much needed information about the hostile country which we will be traveling. I trust your riding skills are up to a young and spirited mare."

She looked a little surprised.

"Well, I think I would have preferred to have been present for the selection of a horse I am to ride. But that's one less thing for me to worry about I suppose."

Jonah studied her.

"I hope it has not angered you that I made what preparations I might. I plan an early start in the morning. You are welcome to take the horse back and pick one of your choosing."

She thought for a moment.

"No. I am sure you are a good judge," She softened. "I am grateful for your preparations. But in the future I might remind you to consider that I acquired your services as a guide - not as an outfitter. And speaking of that, there is the matter of what fee you will require for this adventure. I was just heading to the desk to order food for the room when you arrived. Can you imagine it Mr. Montana, such a grand new hotel? They offer something they call room service?"

He looked puzzled. He had no idea what that meant.

Molly was busy taking in Jonah's 'new look'. No longer the dark stranger in the business suit, he had taken on the look of hardened trailsman, half frontiersman and half Cherokee warrior. She decided she liked it.

"I must say Mr. Montana, what a transformation. *Aquaduliha.*"

Jonah snickered.

33

"You mean *Na- s-gi-ya*-i. You like it. *Aquaduliha* translates to you want it."

"Yes. I like it too, but what I mean is I want a shirt like that one. And I prefer moccasins to boots. Don't suppose you have a spare?"

"I'm afraid not."

"I was going to order food for the room. May I suggest I order for both of us? We can take dinner in your room and discuss our plans."
Without waiting for an answer, she was off. A few steps out, she turned and tossed him a key.

"You're in room 232. I'll meet you there shortly," she turned and whisked away.

Jonah opened the door to his room and struck a tender to the lamp as the shadows were beginning to fall outside. The room was larger than he expected with a window that faced the street. He was surprised to find a new saddlebag on the bed, and by the looks of it, it was already packed. A map of the Montana territory was spread across the bed. Apparently Molly had not been idle. She had been shopping, and it appeared she was well prepared for the journey.

Jonah was looking over the map when he realized Molly was standing at the open door. It was very unusual that someone could walk up on him without him knowing.

"Before you get the wrong idea, I have my own room down the hall. I was studying the map, which I intended to leave for your inspection, when I saw you ride into the livery across the street," she pointed at the window. "I headed to the lobby to order food and to meet you there, seeing that you took most of the day to take care of your business. Diner will be arriving shortly. May I suggest we get down to the business of what fee you expect for this excursion?"

He was prepared for this.

"It turns out Miss Langtry that my job is taking me north anyway. I wouldn't feel right taking your money for something I was going to do anyway. So unless we are diverted from my duties, then I suggest we waive any fees for the time being."

By the look on her face, it seemed obvious she was curious about his work. He hoped he didn't have to come up with a story and was relieved that she didn't ask.

"Well, then we will proceed on that condition. There is the matter of the horse."

That has been taken care of as well. As a tribal agent, I have used a voucher at the livery. When I bring the horse back, I will settle on a fee with the owner. I was considering an extra horse anyway, in the event I needed a pack animal. But I have news. I'm afraid we're not ready to hit the trail north. Word is Cheyenne renegades control the area due north from here. We're going to have to get back on the train and head west to Ogden before we take the northern line to Montana. I don't like the idea, but it will save a couple of weeks worth of riding through some rough country if we want to get there before winter sets into the mountains."

"Utah? I suppose if it's the quickest route…"

He thought it might be a good time to press her on the nature of her objective.

"Now Miss Langtry, I think it is time that you provide more detail about where you are going and your intentions."

He was sure Molly had heard him. But she sat on the edge of big bed silent, eyes cast down at the map of the northern territories on her lap. He wasn't sure if it was the idea of getting back on the train or because she was reluctant to talk about her mission, but she was slow to answer.

"When I was a young girl my favorite uncle left home to head out west to prospect for gold. Like so many families in Southern Missouri, uncles and cousins had enlisted in the Union Army while others volunteered for the Confederacy. Jim Lumley, my mother's brother, was torn between the two sides and his ultimate solution was to remove himself from it all. He headed to Idaho, what they now refer to as Montana country, and after a couple of years of digging in the mountains and searching in caves he ended up half starving to death looking for the gold he never found. Turning his pick in for a few traps, he started trading furs for a living. While camping out near a river in the Great Falls region he witnessed a very strange thing, a bright light in the night sky that was hurtling to earth. As it got closer it turned out to be a great ball of fire. Passing overhead it crashed into the forested mountains to the east of his camp. The next day he struck out to find where it landed and soon came across a wide swath of forest where huge trees had been broken at ground level, their limbs had been burned and this path of destruction stretched for several miles, ending in a canyon. Reaching the bottom of the canyon he discovered fragments of what he supposed must have been a meteorite, many of the larger fragments still smoldering on the canyon floor. But as he got close he discovered something very odd, there were carved figures, intricate figures, like hieroglyphics etched across the smooth face of some of the fragments, what appeared to be some form of writing. It was like nothing he had ever seen before."

She looked up to gauge Jonah's reaction. He was stoic and expressionless.

"I can only imagine what he must have thought. It was crazy really. He called it a space rock and ended up spending a couple of weeks in that canyon going through the debris and trying to make heads or tails of it. The fragments, which he said were still warm to the touch for days, were too large to pack out, and when he tried to break smaller pieces off as samples, he said that in spite of all his efforts, the rock was too hard to even scratch," she said.

"He said he even fired off a few rounds at some of the bigger pieces but the bullets just bounced off. Eventually he had to settle on collecting a few of the smaller pieces, those without any of the writing on them, and made a record of as many of the strange etchings as he could. Most of the rest of the story is rather personal, but Uncle Jim came back to Missouri after a few stops along the way. He presented his findings to just about anyone that would listen; a professor in Cincinnati, a U.S. Marshal in Kansas City, a few newspaper editors. But before long, armed with his re-creation of the strange writing on the rocks, he withdrew from friends and family and seemed to become more distant with time. He seemed to think about little else but his canyon experience and hinted at hearing voices and seeing strange things – but he would never elaborate. Finally, returning to the ranch, he spent a year of two mumbling in his empty room and rarely came out. Eventually, after father called in a couple of doctors, Uncle Jim was hospitalized and eventually put in an asylum for the mentally insane where he quickly lost all touch with reality. That's where he remains today."

She studied Jonah again, uncomfortable with revealing her family secrets.

"And you think if you can find these rocks, it might help your uncle in some way?" Jonah asked.

"I suppose so. The truth is, I traveled extensively on his behalf. The last year or so I have traveled from city to city, university to university. Armed with copies of his etchings, I have visited anyone that would take the time to listen. And finally I ran into a fellow that worked in Washington for the State Department. He put me in touch with his colleagues, and as hard as this may be to believe, they seemed to take an interest in my uncle's story. And here's the really weird part: I actually was invited to meet with President Garfield in the White House. He and a couple of men, I assume his aides, listened intently to my story. Unlike others before them, they seemed to take an interest in it. She looked at Jonah and took a deep breath before continuing.

"You're going to think I am as crazy as my uncle, but I was told by the President that they were forming a special government unit to investigate things just like this, and they talked about using me to aid in the investigation of my uncle's story. This was just about a week before Garfield was shot, and after that happened everything just fell apart it seemed. The aides simply put everything on hold. I was frustrated of course, and I'm afraid I became a bit of a problem for them. I have been physically removed from the White House grounds twice now Mr. Montana. No one will talk to me there, and the President is locked away in New Jersey recovering from his wounds. So I decided not to wait for them any longer. I am going to investigate this mystery on my own."

Her eyes were a bit misty but she masked it well. Jonah, on the other hand, was struggling with what he had just heard. So this was the mystery of Molly Langtry. He realized she must be the woman Bell was talking about back in New Jersey. It was a strange twist of fate.

"Molly. I hope you don't mind if I drop the formalities between us, but I'm afraid I have something to tell you."

She looked up and brushed away a tear.

"President Garfield is dead. He passed away last evening."

"Well...I shouldn't be surprised. I haven't seen the newspapers since arriving."

"It's not in the newspaper yet. I received a telegram from the White House here in Denver. Does the name Alexander Graham ring a Bell?"

Her expression quickly changed.

Jonah sighed, and regardless the oath he had taken, he opened up and told her everything. Their objective, by fate or fortune, was the same. She thought he was joking at first when he told her about his meeting with President Garfield and how he became involved. She listened intently and asked many questions. At first she accused him of being part of a government plan to interfere with her plans, but she backed away from it when she realized he had fallen into this as innocently as she had. It was an incredible coincidence, but stranger things had happened.

Jonah thought about dissolving their arrangement with a promise he would try to accomplish the objectives of his job while helping her discover more about what fell from the sky. But he knew by now she was strong willed and bullheaded and knew she would forge ahead into unknown territories on her own anyway, and that probably wouldn't end well, and then he would feel a degree of responsibility.

The food arrived and they continued their discussion long afterwards and as the night deepened they agreed that the strange circumstances that had brought them together may yet have a purpose. The meeting on the train, their respective meetings with the President - the odds of it happening were remarkable. For better or worse, it looked like they were going to be partners in this investigation and they agreed they would get started early the next morning.

CHAPTER THREE
WESTWARD HO

Historical Note: Published in the St. Louis Democrat, October 16, 1865: *"Jim Lumley, a fur trader, was camped 175 miles above the Upper Missouri in Great Falls Montana when he saw a 'bright luminous body in the heavens'. It went rapidly into an easterly direction and crashed through the forest. Lumley followed a wide path several rods wide and discovered an object on the side of the mountain smoldering near a canyon. What was unusual was it had strange hieroglyphics written across the larger fragments that remained, made, he theorized, by human hands."* (See Appendix)

T he first train westward didn't leave until the mid afternoon and it turned out to be good fortune for shortly before noon a messenger from the hotel arrived at Union Station in search of Jonah. He carried with him a package, an item that arrived early that morning on the train from Kansas City. He opened it and discovered a small wooden box and a second telegram From Alex. The box was a camera, so the telegram said, and was loaded with a new kind of 'rolled' film, enough for 100 photographs. He was to use the camera to photograph the strange writing on the rocks, provided he could find them, and return the camera to Bell who would see to it the film would be developed in a government lab. Alex also provided instructions on how to use the new invention, but Jonah passed it to Molly and explained it would be her responsibility. The photographs, he said, might help to prove her uncle wasn't insane and could be valuable in securing his release.

As the noon hour approached Jonah supervised the loading of Shadow and the mare onto the train's stock car and shortly after he and Molly boarded and were underway on their westward trek. It was an uneventful ride though the scenery of the mountains, which was inspiring if not rather frightening at times because of the sheer drops to one side.

This time they had no Pullman compartments and the train stopped often to take on water because the trip through the Rockies was laborious and difficult. By morning's light they had reached Glenwood canyon and were soon steaming west to the Idaho border.

In Ogden fortune smiled on them and in less than an hour they had transferred to the Northern line and were heading into Idaho and on to Helena, Montana. By the time they reached Montana two days later, they discovered signs an early winter was setting in. The last day of the train ride was a cold one and they quickly sought shelter at the Gulch Hotel and rented the last room available for the night. Gold mining was the region's biggest industry and everywhere they went was crowded with miners and prospectors. They enjoyed their first warm meal in two days and Molly laid claimed to the room's only bed while Jonah lounged in the chair nearby. The night was restless because of the noise from the saloon across the street. There was also heavy traffic in the hallway outside with mixed sounds of drunken miners and giggling ladies coming in and out of adjacent rooms. Molly pulled the pillow over her head not wanting to think about the activities around her, embarrassed to be in the company of Jonah while the sounds of such activity bled through the walls till sunrise.

At first light they had breakfast down the street at a bakery and soon had retrieved Shadow and the mare from a stable where they had boarded them and were soon riding northwest out of town along a narrow trail that skirted the mountain but quickly climbed to higher elevations. The sun peeked briefly from the clouds but quickly the sky closed in and the temperature began dropping. They had stopped at a store on the edge of town that sold mountain clothing to secure blankets and soon wrapped themselves tightly to fight away the cold. Molly had changed into clothing more fitting for the trail, looking more like a range hand than a lady. She had acquired a pair of soft deerskin boots, more like moccasins that were lined with wool and was pleased with their comfort and protection from the cold. By the noon hour they had passed numerous mining camps and found the trail leading up even higher into Lewis and Clark Pass.

Molly told Jonah her uncle's campsite had been located somewhere in the vicinity of Cadotte Pass, but by the time they crossed Lewis and Clark Pass and headed down into a small valley, twilight was settling in and Jonah looked for a place to camp that would block the north wind. Snow flurries were beginning to fall sporadically but the biggest problem was the horses were struggling with the thin air of the altitude and they needed to rest.

Jonah selected an area protected by three large boulders that more or less formed a horseshoe that served to block most of the wind. A master fire maker, the Cherokee had to work long and hard on setting a proper flame to the dry kindling he had gathered, but finally struck a small blaze as darkness began to close in. Molly lived up to her claims as a skillful trail hand and settled the horses in while he continued to build the fire. Soon the campfire roared in harmony with the wind as they sat cross-legged wrapped tight in their blankets chewing on pieces of the jerky Jonah had acquired in Denver.

Molly surprised Jonah when she pulled a small hand-drawn parchment from her saddlebag.

"This is one of Uncle Jim's maps of the area where he was camped the night the object fell. As you can see," she held it close to the fire with both hands and tilted it slightly too catch the light. "He has marked Cadotte on the map here in the corner, but it really doesn't say whether it is Cadotte Pass or Cadotte river or Cadotte springs or what. And I don't think he meant it was necessarily located exactly where he scribbled the word. I think that was just a general description of the location. I think maybe this line represents a creek or a river, and this maybe a canyon. These marks I can only guess represent a mountain or a range. The "X" here, of course, either marks where he camped or where he found the artifact. I asked him about it on a visit to the asylum, but I am afraid he didn't answer cohesively."

Jonah studied the map, but it meant no more to him than it did to her. This was big country, and he wondered if they would ever be able to find such a small object in such a vast area.

"He provided no other clues that you can remember, either in direct conversation or perhaps in relating the stories to others?"

"Well, I heard the stories enough times. And the thing is, sometimes he would mention something I had never heard him say before. But they were fleeting comments and often it didn't make a great deal of sense, especially in the last months before he was committed."

She looked sad at the moment and Jonah was sorry to have stirred her memories, but there was so little to go on and such a large area to cover. After a period of silence, she looked at the fire's reflection dancing in Jonah's dark eyes.

"At one point I remember he mentioned the name of an Indian that from time to time he apparently hired to help him bundle his furs and move down the mountains to a small town called Little Deer. That's where the fur buyers would come each spring. He said that this Indian, his name was unlike anything I had heard before, knew these mountains better than anyone and had helped him once when he was lost and unable to find a trail out of the area. But that would be a long shot, unless you know where any Indians might be around here."

Jonah smiled.

"Well, it's a long shot, but we passed by at least two an hour or so back."

"Indians? I didn't see anyone. Cheyenne?"

"They saw you, and no, not Cheyenne. We are too far north and the Cheyenne stick to the plains for the most part. Shoshone, maybe Nez Pierce. Both are known to hunt these mountains and have for years since the Blackfoot chased them from the plains."

"They were watching us?"

"Most likely watching Shadow, my horse. Both Shoshone and Nez Pierce are expert horsemen. And a black horse like Shadow is an irresistible sight to a horse lover."

"So we should keep watch tonight?"

"Keep watch on the horses, yes. Our fire will lead them to us if they are interested. I don't want to lose a horse, or horses. But more importantly, I would like to talk to them."

"And I suppose you speak Shoshone?"

Jonah shrugged his shoulders.

"No – and yes. Our languages are different, but Indians have been communicating with their neighbors for thousands of years. I suspect we can understand each other one way or another if the need arises."

"Are they hostile you think?"

"Do you mean are they on the war path? I doubt it. From what I can gather, the Indians have settled down in this mountain area, largely because of the arrival of so many mining camps. Most of the trouble that is brewing is on the Eastern plains. Having said that, we need to remain on guard until we determine their intentions."

The night was cold and Jonah spent most of it feeding the fire and tending the horses, which he moved nearer the camp to provide a windbreak and to keep better watch. When the morning arrived, he was glad to see sun peak over the mountain top. Molly was just stirring beneath her blankets near the glowing embers of the campfire when Jonah felt a familiar tingling on the back of his neck. He scanned the area with searching eyes and slipped the Peacemaker beneath the blanket he had draped over his shoulders. In little more than a whisper, he aroused Molly.

"Don't move too quickly, but we have company headed our way. I am going to walk a few steps to the end of the boulders. There's a Winchester beneath my bed roll. Don't bother with it unless something goes wrong."

Almost immediately a Shoshone brave stepped into view, a rifle draped across his crossed arms. He eyed Jonah and in a moment was joined by a second Shoshone. Jonah stood tall and casually signed with one hand, an Old Indian signal of greeting. Not feeling threatened, the two braves stepped toward Jonah. He moved forward to meet them.

"Osiyo *o'-gi-na'-lis. Tsadulihas tsa-lda-ti*?"

He had no hope they would recognize the Cherokee language, but he wanted them to know he was also an Indian. At the same time, he signed a welcome using his forearm and passed his other hand across it with fingers extended, rubbing the top of the arm with his fingers.

The oldest of the two braves returned the sign and walked within a few feet of Jonah and faced him.

"*Tsadulihas ga-wo-ni-s-gv tsa-la-gi*? Do you speak Cherokee? Do you speak the white tongue?" Jonah asked.

The latter they recognized. The older of them spoke.

"Yes. Speak like the white man. You are scout?" meaning an army scout.

"No. We do not work with the cavalry. We do not look for gold. We seek only knowledge of these mountains," Jonah knew he needed to keep the language simple and phrase it in a way they could easily understand.

"You're English is not good *uligula*," said the elder Shoshone, referring to Jonah as a half breed. "And your other language is old."

Jonah smiled.

"Very old. I am Cherokee from the green hills."

Apparently the elder Shoshone did all the speaking for the two.

"And you travel with a white woman. Is this wise in these mountains?"

Jonah carefully worded his response.

"It is never wise to travel with a woman," the older Indian nodded in amusement. "But it is for her that we look for a man, maybe a Shoshone, that worked with a fur trader many months ago, a trader who takes furs and found a great burning rock that fell from the sky. His name was Lumley."

There was no expression on the Shoshone's face, but he nodded he had understood the question.

"Why do you seek this rock?"

"It has great meaning to the woman. The white trader was of her tribe. She seeks it to find understanding."

The elder Shoshone eyed Molly and looked at Shadow and the mare.

"It is a fine black horse. Is it for sale?"

"He is not for sale."

"And the other horse?"

"No. I paid a great price. Too much. But I have food to share."

"Do you have sacred tobacco?"

"No. I have *ga-nv-na-wa*, a sacred pipe."

It was true, Jonah always carried a small hand-carved cedar pipe. It was common among the Cherokee, in fact most native cultures, to share the pipe at gatherings. The old Shoshone nodded.

"Let us eat your food and smoke my tobacco in the pipe. I will tell you a story of the mountains."

The old Shoshone handed his rifle to Jonah, who took it with both hands, held it at face level and handed it back. It was a sign of peace, an indication of trust, that the meeting was not to be marked with conflict.

Jonah thought how strange it was that two tribesmen were standing in the middle of traditional Indian country communicating in the White man's language. In one way it was saddening. For now, however, it was good fortune. He turned his back on the Shoshone, another indication of trust, and walked back toward the dying fire. Both Shoshone followed.

Molly appeared nervous, but Jonah flashed her a look and motioned with his hand, palm downward, that all was well. He then opened a pocket on his saddlebag lying next to the bed role, and removed the cedar pipe, turning and putting more wood on the fire. He sat cross-legged on the ground facing the fire and the Shoshone followed his example. Molly, not knowing what to do, remained seated in her bed roll and watched.

Jonah presented the pipe to the older Indian who nodded in approval as he examined it, and open a small medicine bag he carried around his neck and pinched a small wad of tobacco into the bowl. Using the end of a stick with a burning ember, he struck smoke to the pipe four times, blowing it each time in opposite directions. The fifth puff of smoke he inhaled and passed the pipe to his companion. This happened in succession until each had smoked from the pipe without any words between them. When Jonah passed the pipe back to the first Indian, the Shoshone lowered it and spoke.

"There is a story about the burning rock that all Shoshone of the mountains know well. I was a younger brave when this happened, when the great wars with the Blackfeet were being waged on the plains. Times were hard for the Shoshone. A hard winter had taken many deer and the smaller animals that fed us. Many of our people worked with traders in this time. My brother was one of them that trapped beaver for a French trader." He paused to re-light the pipe, slowly sucked more smoke into his lungs and passed it around the circle.

"It was spring as the floods came that the great fire fell from the sky. It burned many trees and smelled of *hu-ni-tsa-tlda*, like the springs that are hot. I do not know of the trader from the white woman's tribe, but I have heard many stories about a white man that stayed long in the canyon of the fire. The story is told that he breathed the vapors of the fire too long, and it caused him great pain. This is all I know of that which you speak."

The pipe had come back around to Jonah and the bowl was spent. Setting it on the ground, he then produced several pieces of seasoned jerky and shared it with the Shoshone, who took it without response.

"This canyon of the fire – is it far from this place?"

"A day's distance – it is in the area where Shoshone never walk."

It was an indication the place was both sacred and revered, or a place that was feared.

"Why do the Shoshone not walk there?"

The old Shoshone made a gesture with his fist, striking it to his breast and slamming it into the open palm of the other hand. It was the sign for a place that was cursed. Jonah nodded.

"What haunts this canyon?" Jonah wasn't certain how to word the question.

"Of this thing we do not speak. A wise man would not seek the place," he looked briefly in the direction of Molly again and then back at Jonah. "But if you must go, follow the morning sun and be gone before the shadows fall. You will find this place a day's walk to where the sun is swallowed by the earth. It is not hard to find for when you get near you see still see the scar it caused on the earth. Follow in the direction where the cold wind blows and it will soon drop into the canyon, and there you will find what you seek."

Jonah nodded, and sensed the Shoshone had said more than he was comfortable saying. He seemed uneasy now.

"The horses are not for sale?" he asked.

"No."

"Is the woman for sale?"

Molly nearly gasped.

"No. But I offer you the sacred pipe as a gift for your company. I have not met a Shoshone before this day. Now it gladdens me that I have."

The old man was satisfied.

"And I do not know why a Cherokee would walk through the mountains with a white woman or seek the canyon of fire, but I am glad also – for the pipe is good one."

At that he collected himself and the two Shoshone walked away as quietly as they came. Jonah watched them go, once the old man turned and waved, and then they were gone.

Molly looked at Jonah, obviously entranced by what had transpired.

"Well that went well. For a moment I thought you might sell me," she managed to smile. "I thought for sure they had come to steal our horses."

"They did. But we are lucky to have made friends instead. The pipe, Molly, is a powerful peace offering."

She smiled again.

"So, if I heard right, we now know where the artifact is located?"

It seemed incredible to her. Fortune was smiling on their journey. Jonah wasn't so jubilant.

"I fear we might find more than we bargained for." She cast him a look of question. "I have heard Shoshone are brave people. To admit his fear of this canyon says a lot about the danger he believes lurks there."

"Superstition you think?"

"Perhaps. But even superstitions are founded in fact. We must proceed with caution and remain vigilant the closer we get."

They quickly broke camp. Molly struggled chewing the jerky Jonah passed to her, but she was glad to get it. She did her part to saddle and bridle the horses and soon they headed east backtracking much of the same ground they covered the day before. When given a choice, Jonah veered to the north and before long they found themselves riding across the side of a huge mountain peak. The sun was still shining and the wind was just a breeze now, so it felt warmer. They spent half a day riding in open country when finally they saw a tree line ahead in the distance. Soon they would be back in the forest and it would feel much cooler again. The sun was beginning to set beneath the high peaks and not far beyond they descended to the tree line again. A few miles later they came across a clearing where it was obvious a fire had burned many of the trees and there were stumps that appeared to be broken as if the trees had been snapped away. Jonah soaked in the scene realizing the only living trees were younger and not as tall or dense as the rest of the forest. He dismounted and bent down to examine the soil beneath the short grasses.

"What is it," Molly asked.

He ran his fingers through the soil.

"There are signs of a big fire here – a long time ago. But I think this is what the Shoshone were telling us. I believe this is the path of the falling object Molly."

The wide path ran to the northwest and southeast straight as an arrow as far as Jonah could tell. Remounting, he turned Shadow northwest into the winter wind. He didn't know how far away the canyon might be from where they were, but he was certain he wanted to reach it before dark or wait until first light. Riding after dark was a dangerous prospect in the mountains, and whatever had spooked the Shoshone demanded respect. They weren't frightened easily.

They had not traveled far when Jonah noticed a change in Shadow. He had become increasingly nervous after walking through the forest. The mare was breathing heavy as well, the cold causing both horses to blow smoke as they labored in the thin air. Their eyes were wide and they would look to the tree line to the right and alternately to the left, and Jonah became more watchful. They had fallen into a silence as they rode in the dim light. The clouds were dropping from the skies again and the fog was obscuring the way. If their path had not been so straight and unwavering, they might have gotten lost. It was cold again, but bearable, and the clouds made the air thick and wet. Jonah was beginning to feel the familiar tingling on the back of his neck when both horses suddenly planted their feet, nearly sending Molly off her saddle and over the mare's head. There was a scream, or a screech, a combination of the two perhaps, and in the distance Jonah thought he could hear limbs cracking. Whatever it was, it was a ways ahead of them in the mist. He calmed Shadow and Molly patted the mare's neck.

"What do you think that was?" Molly was shaken. The mountains, she decided, were an eerie place.

Jonah shook his head. Dismounting he pulled the Winchester from its cradle and listened intently to the quietness of the forest. He thought it strange there was no sound at all, no scurrying of small animals, no birds in the sky; even the wind was silent.

Molly pulled the hand-drawn map from her pocket and studied it. The path of the meteor was clearly marked, and she tried to determine how long it ran before ending in the canyon crash site.

"There's really no point of reference. I don't know how far away we are."

"I don't think we're that far away. I would have stopped earlier to make camp, but I felt we were near. This path of new growth should end at the canyon."

With that, still standing in front of his horse, he walked forward as Shadow followed. Molly dismounted as well and led the mare, her senses alert. They didn't have far to walk. A few minutes later the path began to drop, first subtly then the grade led steeply down. Jonah could tell they were dropping down into a canyon for he could faintly hear the gentle sound of water gurgling below, a stream, perhaps, at the bottom. Carefully, methodically, they worked their way through ferns and low brush which had become thick now as they neared the water source. Shadow stumbled, and when Jonah strained his eyes he could see the ground was scattered with rocks. Soon they reached the bottom of the grade and as Jonah thought, a small trickle of water, hardly a stream, crossed their path just a few inches wide and very shallow. It twisted this way and that as it skirted a field of blackened hand-size boulders that diverted its path and caused the water to bubble.

Across the stream the rocks looked black and there were more of them, there were fewer grasses growing as well. Just beyond they spotted what looked like a large dark hole in the side of the slope on the far embankment. Getting nearer Jonah could tell it must have been an impact crater, but it wasn't that deep. Several large fragments of what looked like metallic rocks, nearly the size of a man, lay half buried in the bank.

"Looks like we found it Molly," he dropped the reins and stepped across the running water with Molly on his heels.

A few yards beyond he knelt by one of the larger fragments and ran his fingers across a surprisingly smooth surface, and like Molly's uncle's description, there were hieroglyphics etched across it. Examining some of the smaller fragments he couldn't see any of the odd looking letters, only on three of the larger fragments, about the size of a horse.

Molly knelt beside him and carefully examined the writing, for that's what it appeared to be, strange looking letters that were similar to what she had seen in her uncle's notes. She turned to Jonah and ran her hand through her damp hair. Darkness was setting in.

"We're going to need to build a fire."

A NEW BOSS

Alex Bell scurried across the polished marble floor of the Library of Congress building. Congressional Librarian Ainsworth Spofford may have been the leading authority on the Library's vast and growing content, but he wasn't an easy man to convince that Alex was authorized to view former President Jefferson's private collection. Alex presented the written authorization bearing late President James Garfield signature, but Spofford argued that Alex's document was invalid because Chester Arthur was now President. It took the best part of a day and the assistance of Secretary of State James Blaine, one of Garfield's trusted friends and, Bell suspected, a Culper Ring operative, to convince him the authorization was still valid.

Once he gained access to the material it paid off. Two days of intense research later he stumbled across the document he had hoped to find. It was a handwritten entry in one of the journals of Thomas Paine, who had consulted with the Iroquois Confederacy to study their culture, language and their democratic form of government, which largely influenced founding fathers like Jefferson to incorporate many of those same principles into the inaugural U.S. Constitution.

But this journal entry concerned and supported Paine's personal philosophy of 'freethinking', and was related to his little-known belief, or suspicion, that prior to the founding of the Republic – indeed dating back several centuries - there was a great, silent and powerful consortium of powerful individuals, a group the document referred to as a secret society, that had been at work "beneath public awareness and scrutiny" that had been directing much of history down through the generations, and that at least some of these powerful individuals may not have been human at all but extraterrestrial entities from another world. It was a startling suggestion and a startling discovery, and Alex shook his head in disbelief.

But Jefferson's personal library, which became the seed of the Library of Congress' vast collection after the English sacked the Library's original content during the War of 1812, had never, to Alex's knowledge, been completely researched in its entirety, much of it believed to be too complex and controversial and dealing with either mundane ramblings of philosophers and freethinkers unworthy of academic scrutiny or simply irrelevant to the conventions of government. As far as he knew, his eyes may have been the first to read Jefferson's collection of Paine documents since they were put in storage at the library, especially considering this rare collection was reserved for only those authorized by the White House.

Apparently Garfield had been aware of Paine's dissertations and directed Alex to research and retrieve the document and surrender it to Cleveland with all haste. That was the day before his death, and Bell was now headed to the Washington hotel room where Cleveland was staying to deliver it and to file his first report to the new "man in charge".

Upon arrival, he was ushered in to Cleveland's room, the door was shut and two men, Bell assumed Ring agents, were stationed outside in the hallway to insure their security and privacy.

Cleveland motioned for Bell to take the chair directly in front of the large oak bed and sat across in the only other chair in the lofty suite.

"So Mr. Bell, in addition to what I read about you in the newspapers, I am discovering Jim prized you as bright new Lieutenant in the service of our country," he didn't wait for a reply. "Very well. I have trusted Garfield's judgment since the War, and I am prepared to honor it now. I assume you have been appropriately briefed on the need for extreme confidentiality in all matters related to the duties of your office?"
Cleveland's eyes were deep, his most distinguishing characteristic, and his gaze was penetrating. Alex felt like his soul was being scrutinized.

Alex nodded.

"I also understand you're the man chosen to serve as liaison with our newly appointed agent Jonah Montana. Tell me about the man. Do you deem him the right one for the job? We're not going to have trouble with him are we? I understand he's educated, and has a good record of service in just about everything he's done. But can we trust him? It's an unusual and highly sensitive role he will be playing in the history of this Nation. He must be trustworthy and beyond reproach."

"I believe he is the right man for the job sir, mind you, I have no history with the man outside of our meeting at President Garfield's home and a briefing that followed. But he comes highly recommended by Professor Willard, and he certainly has the academic credentials as well as the Native bloodline that connects him directly with Grey Wolf, the Cherokee oracle. He is Gray Wolf's grandson in fact."

"Yes, Gray Wolf. The powerful and elite of Washington have been communicating with that old prophet for years. They say President Jefferson, shortly before he died, actually met the man, is that right? But, yes, I know he has been advisor and consultant for more than one president down through the years. They say the old man is a sage, a sort of seer."

"I have only recently heard the stories sir. But I have also heard Montana was groomed by him to one day take his place as a friend of the government."

"Well, we shall see if Montana is worthy. I understand he's out West on his first assignment."

"Yes sir. I am to meet him in Denver in a few days."

"Good, good. Now, what have you brought me?"

Alex handed over the folder along with a stack of notes he had transcribed based on Paine's journal. Cleveland slipped on his spectacles and opened the folder, briefly scanning the contents. Removing the glasses he leaned back in the big chair and studied Alex again.

"Give me the short of it Bell. What do we have here?"

Alex sat forward.

"Well Governor, as strange as it may seem, Paine is suggesting that the society in question may be comprised of some officers that are...well, not of this world."

He waited for Cleveland to laugh, or throw him out of the room at such a suggestion.

"Yes, that's what we thought. Paine was suggesting. And he did?"

"He did sir."

"And details, did he provide details, the who, and where we might find these rascals?"

"Yes sir he did, though I suggest we can't be certain the information is as valid today as it was in 1774."

"And?"

"According to Paine's Journal, that would be somewhere on the Gulf coast."

Again Bell half expected the Governor to be startled – or outraged by the suggestion.

"That makes sense, in territory that was held by the Spanish or the French I suspect," Cleveland stroked his moustache. "Well let's get Montana on it when he wraps up his current mission. I don't need to tell you this organization must be stopped from meddling into the affairs of our Republic. I don't care if Moses or the Martians are advising this group, this is America Bell, and we decide our own destiny. Is that clear?"

Understanding it was a dismissal as much as an order, Alex rose from the chair and grabbed his hat.

"It is Governor."

"And one more thing, Willard is heading to France on a related matter. I am elevating this as a priority now that this meddlesome Society has interfered. They are, you know, potentially responsible for the death of an American president. I want this worked from both ends, every angle. So in the interim you and Montana will be reporting directly to me. I'll be establishing offices in Washington and Louisville in the weeks ahead. Be careful how you use the wire, we must maintain a high level of security in these matters."

Alex nodded again and headed for the door, wondering what he had gotten himself into.

A MEETING BY CHANCE

The fire Jonah started wasn't burning very well. The thick, damp atmosphere made everything wet and the canyon was particularly high in moisture content. Darkness had fallen and Molly had unrolled the blankets again to fight back the cold. Jonah was visibly uneasy, stroking the sputtering fire and breaking smaller twigs and adding them to the low flames. They struggled to take hold.

"That scream earlier…"

"Mountain lion."

"That was a mountain lion?"

"A distressed mountain lion."

"And that's what's worrying you?"

"Why the cat was distressed has me concerned. It sounded like the cat was frightened, and not many things frighten a mountain lion.."

"That's not encouraging. How do you know?"

"I could read it in the eyes of the horses," he turned to look at her, standing near and wrapping her blanket tighter around her shoulders. "More than that, I think we need to do what we came to do and leave this canyon as soon as possible."

"You're worried about what those Indians were worried about aren't you?"

"I'm just worried about getting out of this canyon."

Jonah gave up on the fire. It was burning, barely, but proving little heat and casting very little light on their surroundings, the real reason he wanted it in the first place. He rose and strolled over to the largest fragment with hieroglyphs on it. He ran his fingers over its surface again. If Jim Lumley had tried to break pieces from it without success, he knew they weren't going to have any better luck. He was certain Lumley had searched for smaller etched pieces without success, so he had no reason to believe they would be any more successful finding any either. He looked at Molly.

"It's time to pull out that camera I think."

As she fumbled with her saddlebag Jonah was looking up the slope where he thought he heard a noise, like a twig breaking. Molly caught his gaze, and he motioned her to silence. Pulling the Peacemaker from where he had stuffed it in his belt, he strained to see beyond the dim light of the fire, listening more intently for the tell-tale sounds of movement. A moment passed and there it was again, subtle, like a small animal foraging in the underbrush, but this time it was nearer. Shadow snorted; the mare whinnied. Molly set the camera on the ground and rose slowly, and crossed to where the horses were standing, rubbing Shadow's neck reassuringly. She slowly removed the Winchester from Jonah's saddle and turned back to face the slope.

Jonah was tingling again – fiercely.

From somewhere in the shadows a deep but clear voice spoke, causing Jonah to unholster his peacemaker and point the tip of the revolver at the slope where he judged the noise had come from. He heard Molly chamber a round in the Winchester behind him.

"It has been written long ago a prophet would come from the Valley, whose bloodline extends to the elders. His name would be *asuyeta. hi-tsa-la-gi-s?*"

The entire message was delivered in a language Molly thought was Cherokee, but a dialect she could not understand. Jonah was unable to speak or move, as if what he had just heard was beyond belief. Roughly translated, he thought the voice had said the name would be "the chosen, or selected Cherokee". The dialect was slightly different, perhaps older than Jonah's native language, but he more or less understood what was being said. He scanned the slope carefully but could see nothing in the darkness.

"*Kagagawonisgv?* Who is talking?" Jonah shouted.

"*Tsi-wo-ni-hu. a-h-la-wi-t-di-s-gi.*"

Molly looked at Jonah, his eyes were wide, but he maintained a steady grip on the Peacemaker.

"Jonah, he's speaking Cherokee. What is he saying?"

He ran the words through his head again and translated for Molly.

"He's looking for someone – the chosen one. He wants to know if I am Cherokee – or the chosen one – I think."

"And you told him?

"No. I asked who was talking."

"And?"

Jonah swallowed hard.

"He said he was speaking – he said the one who flies."

To the unseen speaker, Jonah asked in Cherokee, "What do you want?"

There was a moment of silence and the big voice spoke again.

"*Wa-di-go* – I have come to deliver a message to the Chosen one."

"*Do-i-s-di-hi-na*. What is this message?"

"*Wa-di ka-ne-tsv ooh-sss-go Go-knee-gay Wa-ya.*"

To Molly he said "To my grandfather?" Then to the unseen voice, "Why?"

"For understanding," the voice answered in Cherokee.

Jonah soaked in the meaning of those words. The tingling continued fiercely.

"Show yourself!"

No answer came at first, but suddenly, so fast that Jonah and Molly hardly had time to react, the unexpected happened. Jonah had suspected another mountain-dwelling Indian had followed them to the canyon and was using the cover of the slope to hide, but what they saw was a small, non-human creature – for they hardly knew what to call it – that appeared in the weak firelight, not more than a few feet in front of Jonah. It was human-like, standing upright for all its shortness, with thin legs and arms and torso and a head larger than it should have been for such a small creature. It appeared to be absent of clothing with no distinguishing indication of gender, it's large eyes bulbous and dark.

As fast as it had appeared, it darted between them across the fire, scattering the embers, and back up the slope the way it had come. Molly gasped loudly; Jonah felt his heart skip a beat and he nearly discharged a round by accident, but the tingling was beginning to subside. After a long pause Jonah looked at Molly, still very shaken.

"It is gone."

"What was that?" Molly sounded as if she were on the edge of hysteria.

Jonah slipped the revolver back in his belt and turned to her, pulling on her shoulders and drawing her near to reassure her, for she was trembling. After a moment she calmed a little and he released her.

"I think it might have been the *Us-ti yu-wi*, or who some call the *Yunwi Tsundi* " Jonah said.

Molly looked him in the eyes.

"The little people?" She collected her wits. "What did he want?"

"Well," Jonah went over the conversation in his head again. "Apparently he wants us to take a message to Gray Wolf, my grandfather. I think"

Molly just looked at him blankly.

"Your grandfather? A little…person – wants you to take a message to your grandfather? What message?"

"I think he was saying the drawings on the rock are a message, and I believe he was saying Gray Wolf, my grandfather, could tell us what they mean. But to be honest Molly, I'm not sure. The dialect was very old, perhaps not even Cherokee. I understood most of the words I think, but I can't be certain."

He looked around the canyon again to make certain there was no lingering danger, but his senses told him there wasn't. He looked back at Molly.

"My Grandfather is considered a… a seer among our people – one of the last as far as we know. He is greatly respected for his…his unique abilities. Don't ask me why or how – I don't understand this any more than you. But the little…creature…apparently says Gray Wolf, not me as I first thought, is the Chosen One – whatever that means."

Molly stared at him, unable to formulate a response.

"Look Molly – this is as crazy to me as it must be to you. But," it was his turn to search for the right words. "Somehow this makes a little sense to me. I mean, I understand what he was saying more or less, and in an Indian sort of way, I get it."

He expected her to argue, to voice an objection, to ask more questions. Instead, she set the rifle down next to the fire, which was now barely a flame.

"Well, if the Little Creature says take it to your grandfather, then that's what we have to do. Jonah, I don't know that I really care what all this means. I'm in this thing to prove my Uncle isn't crazy. And what I have so far is enough information to either prove he isn't, or to be locked up in the hospital with him because I am as crazy as he is," She struggled to understand, to reason out what just happened, what she was hearing. "No one is going to believe this. So if taking the rocks to your grandfather is the only way we can make sense of this, then by all means let's go see your grandfather."

She had her back to him now, but suddenly turned with a smile across her face.

"He was a very little creature wasn't he? And fast too!" she actually laughed out loud. "You don't think that he was...I mean, he wasn't human, right?"

"I honestly can't say Molly."

Jonah crouched by the fire and blew into the few coals that remained, Adding dry grass and a few more twigs, it sparked and ignited. It wasn't much of a fire, but perhaps it had potential.

"We're not staying here tonight are we?" Molly didn't like the idea.

"First – no, he - it - wasn't human I don't think. Among the Cherokee there is talk of the Little People. There are many legends about them, the *usti a-ni-yv-wu-yu* they are called. They are said to be most mischievous, and much misunderstood. If you are asking me if this creature is related to the fallen rock, if he is from another world – then my answer is perhaps, I do not know. There are many legends among the *a-ni-tsa-la-gi* – the Cherokee people – about such things. It is also well known among my people that when such a little one is encountered, it is wise not to speak of it for seven years. And don't ask me why, I'm just a half breed, remember. As far as staying here tonight, yes. I think, now, this is the safest place we could be till morning light. This canyon...this rock...I believe it belongs to the Little One. And apparently – believe it or not – we are considered his messengers. I don't think we have anything to fear, and I doubt he will be back."

He didn't bother to tell her he felt certain the creature was still watching them.

The fire finally began to catch on as a light breeze began to blow and silence fell between them, each lost in their thoughts.

"Well," Molly said finally. "I picked a hell of strange partner didn't I."

He looked at her, perhaps a little offended. Molly laughed – a real laugh this time.

"Considering you seem to know what's going on here, I wouldn't trade you Jonah for a Comanche War Chief at the moment. Now, I'm hungry."

Jonah rose and walked over to the where Shadow was still tied, amazed at her resilience. He was also surprised at how calm the horses had been through the ordeal. Reaching inside his saddlebag he grabbed the sack of jerky and tossed it to Molly and began unsaddling Shadow and the mare. He began to wonder if Gray Wolf had known all along that Jonah was to have this encounter with the Little One. After all, it was at his urging that Jonah traveled to Washington and ended up landing this job. Come to think about it, he remembered how he was surprised to learn that President Garfield knew his grandfather, or at least knew who he was. Apparently the Old Man was more widely known than he thought. He knew he was well known among the Cherokee of course, and he knew he was a well known healer and an advisor who some even called the Wise One. And important people would come and go to meet with him from time to time, even white men. But what did an American President and a Little One in the Mountains know about his grandfather that he did not know? It was a lot to consider.

He was glad to be leaving the mountains the next morning. Suddenly it felt very cold again. He added more wood to the fire and sat down across from Molly, who in spite of being visibly shaken, had a strange grin across her face - and didn't bother to tell him why. He wondered at her mood change.

He slept surprisingly well that night, waking just before first light edged over the canyon peaks. Looking through his saddlebag he retrieved a small wooden flute Gray Wolf had given him on his tenth birthday. He carried it with him just about everywhere he went, but he rarely played it. He raised it to his mouth, wet his lips and started to play. It was a rather haunting but peaceful melody, one he had never played before, perhaps inspired by the strange incident of the night.

Molly stirred from under her blankets to watch him play. The melody wafted through the air and reverberated off the canyon walls. It made him feel better, and surprisingly, her as well. She waited for it to end then stretched, yawned and sat up. After a moment she started packing up her bed role.

"I'm still hungry," she said as she busied herself with packing. "Think they have a decent diner in Helena?"

"Let's go find out."

Before departing, Molly learned to use the little camera that Alex sent. They photographed the larger pieces from several different angles. As he suspected, there were no fragments with writing on them small enough to pack out of the mountains. In addition to using the camera, Jonah spent another hour doing his best to record as many of the inscriptions as possible on parchment he carried in his saddlebag, discovering in the process there seemed to be a recurring theme to them. Apparently the same message was etched on the stones over and over again. Within the hour they were back on the trail and headed to Helena.

CHAPTER FOUR
THE CREOLE CONNECTION

<u>**Vieux Carré, The Grima House, New Orleans**</u>

F anchon Harleaux, a meticulous man of influence and power, was an upstanding resident of New Orleans' elite Vieux Carré, and was, on the surface, a political supporter of France's Orleanist movement. It was little more than a social front however. His real passion was his unknown involvement in a society known as the Brothers of the Rose Croix, or Order of the Rose Cross, and a member of the Council of Seven.

No one, except for its elite membership, knew the purpose of the fraternal organization or the philosophies behind its founding because it was, by and large, a secret organization with a hidden political agenda. History indicated prominent members of the group were influential in the promotion of the French and American revolutions among other international developments, and were paramount in promoting an alternative system of global policy around the world.

But Harleaux wasn't just a member of the society. Much darker than this, he was also a ruling member of a more secretive circle within the Brotherhood of the Rose, a secret organization within a secret organization, one that was well hidden even from the Brotherhood. While it could be argued the Brotherhood was altruistic, even benevolent in their beliefs that their 'One World' policies were for the better good of humankind, Harleaux's Secret Circle had designs of its own, and their methods for achieving their goals were far more nefarious and dark.

Harleaux's New Orleans compound served as central command for this 'inner circle' of the Brotherhood, operating independent and unknown to the larger group and with a well conceived and most treacherous plan for world domination. Paramount to that plan was a mission that involved the capture, detention and interrogation of a number of key indigenous figures ranging from tribal leaders to so called Holy Men, medicine men, elder council leaders and sages, in an effort to discover the 'Lost Arts of Ancient America', a mandate decreed by its supreme leader Annanubia Thet who commanded the global operations of the group from secret headquarters located somewhere in the heart of Eastern Europe.

Harleaux was designated "governor" of the circle's New World contingent, the American branch, and to him the task of collecting this influential and knowledged group had fallen. It didn't matter that those on the list were unaware or unwilling. By the Circle's decree they were to be collected and impaneled "at all cost" for the purpose of discovering secret knowledge they possessed, specifically the hidden location of seven powerful crystals that had long been lost.

These tektite crystals had been developed by off world science long ago using resources mined from earth and were invaluable in condensing and directing energy to power advanced technologies. These specially designed crystals were the key for certain technology developed in non-planetesimal systems if they were to operate in systems where the laws of physics were different than on their home world – like on earth.

Harleaux scanned the list. There were seven names on it. Two were already in custody. But the recent capture and imprisonment of one other on the list by the U.S. government would make acquiring that individual more difficult without using a show of force, which might cause certain members within the government to become aware of his covert operation – a last resort. It was becoming apparent that a handful of this government's top officials had become aware – he did not know how – that he was conducting an operation involving key figures among the native cultures. While they did not understand its purpose, or that matter knew nothing about his covert organization, they were beginning to suspect something odd was going on. The Chihenne-Chiricahua Apache War Chief and prophet Geronimo had been taken prisoner for crimes against the U.S. government and was currently being held by a regiment of the 7th Calvary in a tower prison in Texas. One of Harleaux's operatives had sacrificed his life in the attempt to bring him to New Orleans, and that's when the government began to suspect an organized plot was involved by this unknown force – one they were beginning to suspect may be a threat to their national security.

A Presidential order had been issued naming Geronimo a ward of the State until an investigation could be launched to determine if their suspicions were well founded. Harleaux was taking steps to address that issue, but more importantly now was the acquisition of the remaining initiates. They included the surviving Sioux chieftain Touch the Clouds, Paiute shaman Wovaka, Shawnee Chieftain Tenskwatawa, Aztec prophet Chapultamec, Q'ero the Inca historian, and the Cherokee spiritual leader Gray Wolf, advisor to the hated Wolf Clan.

To aid in the effort, Supreme Commander Thet dispatched a dozen of his best operatives, specially trained "Kriegers" who would be arriving by steamship later that day. They were well trained, ruthless and terribly efficient in their methods and renowned for their deadly determination.

Time was of the essence if plans were to be fruitful, and within the Inner Circle there was no tolerance for failure. Harleaux must move quickly and decisively if he hoped to accomplish the mission before his adversaries made the task impossible. Commander Thet would accept nothing less.

CHAPTER FIVE
KANSAS CITY BOUND

Back in Helena Jonah checked them into the same hotel where they had stayed their first night after arriving on the train from Ogden. Molly had insisted on cleaning up so he took the time to visit the local Telegraph office to wire Alex a message that they had found the artifact in the mountains. The message was intentionally vague, however, and he didn't mention the strange encounter. He didn't want the telegraph operator spreading that news across the wire. Instead the message indicated they would meet Alex in Kansas City on Sept. 29 instead of Denver on Oct. 20 as planned, or would at least check for an incoming telegraph once they arrived there. He explained that "developments warrant a change in plans".

After the telegraph office Jonah stopped at the depot to purchase tickets, learning the next train south wasn't scheduled to depart for two days. Stopping at the local essay office, he produced a very small sample of the artifact he had collected, one without any inscriptions, in hopes they might be able to identify the black ore-like substance.

They couldn't, but he learned before leaving the office there was a new bath house on the edge of town that only recently had opened at the bequest of Helena's influential citizens and that catered to the few upper class residents and their visitors to the area. Raised near the natural hot springs in Arkansas and ritually traveling there at least once a year to soak in their mineral-rich waters, he decided taking a few hours to "cleanse the spirit" would be a good distraction to help the hours pass while they waited for their departure on Thursday. Arriving at the hotel he gently knocked on

Molly's door. When it opened, he informed her of the delay and of his discovery of the local hot springs.

"My Mr. Montana," she faked a blush. "Are you inviting me to bathe with you?"

He didn't intend for it to sound that way and turned a shade of red, unable to answer right away. Molly giggled.

"I haven't been to a hot spring in a very long time. And don't be so serious Jonah. But I am afraid I am ill equipped. I would have no idea what I might wear."

" Well, I assumed they would have separate baths for men and ladies," he lied.

"Well I would hope so! But I do think it's a wonderful idea. But first I insist we find a place where they know how to cook a good steak. I'm famished."

September 26, Washington, D.C.

Alex Bell read the telegram from Jonah and was pleased things had gone so well and so quickly. He had expected it to take much longer. Apparently Montana was as good as Garfield said he would be.

Jonah wanted to meet in Kansas City and that sounded better to Jonah. It was closer than Denver and as it turned out, there was another case in KC that Bell had been instructed to assign to Jonah. Alex had other obligations, namely a trip to New York, but the new assignment should keep Jonah busy until he could arrive a few days later. He scribbled a reply telegram to inform Jonah of the new assignment and to tell him he would meet him there at the end of the week. The telegram read:

UNABLE TO MEET IN KC ON 29th STOP WILL MEET YOU AT UNION HOTEL KC ON OCT 3 STOP COLLECT NEW ASSIGNMENT FROM DEPUTY MARSHAL JOHN WEBB IN KC STOP REFERENCE: MAN WHO REFUSES TO DIE STOP

He read it back to himself. Yes, that should give Jonah something to do until he arrived. Marshal Web had submitted the case to Garfield's office just hours after Jonah took the west bound train from New Jersey, and it had a ring of real mystery to it. To Bell it sounded like just the kind of case that Jonah was hired to investigate, plus it would give him a second investigation under his belt before being dispatched to New Orleans. He folded the telegram and handed it to the operator.

"Send this to Union Station Kansas City. Addressed to Jonah Montana, arriving from Denver on Sept. 29 – and make sure they get it to him before he leaves the station."

September 29, Union Station, Kansas City

Jonah read the telegram and handed it to Molly.

"Looks like we're going to be delayed a couple of days until Bell arrives," Jonah said.

"Wait till he finds out I'm here as well. The last time he and I parted, I am afraid I had choice words for the poor man."

Jonah had almost forgotten Molly had met Alex. Yes, Alex was going to be surprised.

"So what do we do, grab a hotel room again?"

"Yes, and afterwards I am to see a deputy marshal here by the name of Webb. Apparently there's something Alex wants me to check out before he arrives."

"Well I hope its interesting enough to make the time pass a little faster. I was never good at waiting myself. As long as it doesn't involve riding trains or talking to little people, it will work for me," Molly smiled.

Molly indicated she would secure the rooms using one of Jonah's vouchers while he collected Shadow and the mare and moved them to the hotel livery. Afterwards he would head to the Marshal's office to meet with Deputy John Webb.

Shortly Jonah arrived at the Marshal's office and introduced himself, indicating he had been instructed to find out about "the man who refused to die".

"So they sent you to figure out what's wrong with our priestly prisoner?"

"I guess that's the case. They didn't fill me in with any details. The telegram I received simply instructed me to contact you about a new assignment... So you're saying he's a priest?"

Wood was a tall man with a handlebar moustache he kept twisting on one side. He twirled the end of it and looked Jonah over before responding.

"Well that figures. I guess they thought the less you knew about it the better chance there would be for you actually showin' up," Webb had a deep and gravely voice and when he laughed it rolled out from deep in his throat. "Yep, he's a priest alright, brand new, just arrived last week.. Tell me, are you a religious man Montana?"

"What do you mean?"

"It's a simple question."

"How is that relevant deputy?"

"Well, like I said, the prisoner is a priest, and regardless how hard we try, we can't seem to make him dead."

Jonah looked at him blankly, uncertain where he was going with this.

"Look Montana, we're dealing with a priest gone bad here. Some folks says he possessed by the devil, others say he's just got a black heart. But I say he's just a cold blooded murderer. Now some seem to have a problem with the fact that he's a priest, and if you ask me, that's part of the problem."

"Deputy, I'm not sure how any of this would require my involvement and I really have no idea what you're trying to tell me. I just assumed that a man who refuses to die means you got one that's tough as horseshoe nails. I don't see where that's even a federal problem to be honest. How'd you come to be involved?"

Webb laughed again, a deep rolling laugh.

"I keep askin' myself that same question. Look, here's the short of it, this priest, middle aged, average size, shows up at the church last week and tells the old Father there he's been assigned. He gets himself in trouble when out of the blue he shoves a Rosary cross straight into the eye of one of his parishioners. No motive we can find. Weird huh? So the local Sheriff arrests him but when they get to the jail house he wraps his fingers around the deputy's neck and squeezes the life out him – strangles him to death. That was last week. So they bind his hands and lock him up tight and that should have been the end of it, right? Well, that night the Sheriff checks in on him and he's not in his cell...jail door's still locked, no windows out, no tunnels...nothin'. They find him in an alley out back bending over one of the workin' girl's from the Lone Horse Saloon. He's ripped her neck out with somethin'...never could find what it was, and they take him back to jail. Two days later he's missin' again, same thing, door is locked...no way out. And there was a guard sittin' right outside the cell. This time he kills a young girl in her bedroom a couple a streets over…caught in the act…and they bring over to my jail sayin' he's possessed by the devil."

He laughed that deep guttural laugh again and looked at Jonah.

"I tell you Montana, I'm not a superstitious man, but I am a careful one. We put him in shackles and chains…he's not gonna get out of my jail…or so I thought."

"But he did…?"

"Oh yeah, door still locked, chains are broken and shackles torn open like what only a bear might do. Killed a drunk right out there in the street. This time we catch him and I plug him between the eyes with a bullet," Webb patted his Colt. "Took him over to the undertaker, but I'll be damned if an hour later he's roaming the streets again. I'm not makin' this up Montana. It took three of us to pull him down and chain him up again and take him straight to Judge Maxwell's, but while we're explainin' to the Judge what we got here, a mob shows up outside the door, the girl who was killed in her bedroom, it was her father and several of his hired ranch hands and a couple of town folk. They drug him out, marched him down the street being pulled by a big buckskin stallion and lynched him from a tree on the edge of town. But Montana, the guy doesn't die. They hung him again and this time stood around and watched him squirm until his breath was gone and his limbs were limp. Well, in case you're guessin', he didn't stay dead."

"He didn't stay dead?"

"I'm not lyin'. And that's all there is to it. Oh, we got him again, but we can't hold him, and apparently can't kill him either. He's been shot twice since then, has killed another man, and the truth is, he just flat refuses to die. Whatever else he might be, I'm beginning to believe what the old padre is sayin', the man is possessed. What else could it be? So we sent a telegram to Washington…and here you are. So I hope you'll be takin' him off my hands, right?"

Jonah was astonished. He had heard a lot of strange stories in his time, but not like this.

"I'm afraid not. I was asked to check out the story, not to take custody. But there's another man headed this way from Washington in a few days. We'll let him worry what to do with him. But I'm curious, what does this priest have to say for himself?"

"Say? He hasn't said a thing – not a single word. He's inside there," Webb pointed to a door that led to the back. "Locked up in a box with enough chains around it that a grizzly couldn't break out. You're welcome to go back there and have a talk with him if you like, but not without Chester and his long gun. But don't expect an answer. Like I said, he's not sayin' a single word. You ask me, I don't think he's human."

Chester, Jonah assumed, was the man sitting in the chair beside the closed door with a double barrel shotgun lying across his lap. Jonah looked back at Webb.

"I'm curious…when this priest kills his victims, what kind of weapon does he use?"

"Well…I can answer that," said Deputy Chester, with a longer drawl than Webb. "He don't use no weapon that we can tell. Kills everybody with his hands I reckon. That and he has actually bitten a couple of them."

"Bitten them?" Jonah asked.

"Or ripped 'em open with his fingernails…blood all over the place."

"How do you know he bit them?"

"Blood on his face, in his mouth. I'll tell you Montana, we got a real nut case here, and folks around town are rattled, some are sayin' he's supernatural," added Webb.

"Tell you what Deputy, I'll come back shortly and we'll take a look at your prisoner. There's a couple of things I need to do first."
Webb seemed a little uneasy.

"You are coming back, right? You're not riding out of town and not lookin' back are you?"

Jonah reassured him.

"And miss an opportunity to see this for myself? No, I'll be back Deputy Marshal."

"Well, I'll be here. The more guns we have when we go back there the better. And if you can think of way to kill this blackheart, then we'll dance at your wedding son."

Jonah nodded.

"I think I might know of a way," he said as he opened the door and stepped out on to the wooden porch. "Where's the nearest Catholic Church? And the local saw mill?"

Getting directions in spite of the strange looks they gave him, Jonah headed to the saw mill first. The mill was closing down for the day and the miller wasn't pleased about staying late to sharpen a point on the oak timber Jonah had selected.

His next stop was the general store, and finally the big Cathedral at the end of the street. The doors were unlocked so he slide inside and found what he was looking for right away, an aspersorium, or marble bowl that sat on a pedestal near the entrance. Jonah removed a small water skin he had purchased at the store and set about filling it with the Holy Water from the bowl. As quickly and as quietly as he had come in he departed the church and headed back to the Marshal's office.

He had no experience with this sort of thing; had never heard of a vampyre until he read Sheridan Le Fanu's novel, "Carmilla" while a student at the Seminary. It was the tale of a female vampyre that had an insatiable taste for the affections – and the blood – of young women. Le Fanu, an Irish novelist, was an expert at horror and mystery, and while Jonah didn't care for the novel that much, he appreciated the writing style. But he had to admit that down through the years he had more than one nightmare about the ghoulish descriptions of blood lust penned by the author.

Jonah felt a little foolish collecting Holy Water and a wooden stake. But Bell had warned him to be prepared for the "unusual" and "impossible" during the course of his new job and Jonah was taking it seriously. The truth be told, he never entertained the idea that stories about vampyres could be true. But after the story Webb had just related, he wanted to be ready, and according to the novel, Holy Water and a sharp hard wooden stake were the best defense against vampyres, mythical or not. He hoped, of course, he was acting irrationally, that his imagination was being too active. But he had seen enough strange things in his life and had heard of enough strange tales from Gray Wolf that he didn't want to take any chances. He wanted to be prepared for whatever might happen. Webb said the priest couldn't be killed, so he was doing the only thing he knew to do. Irrational? Yes, but better safe than sorry.

Arriving back at the office, he found Webb, as promised, still waiting. The Deputy named Chester hadn't moved from the chair. Spying the pointed, oak timber and the flask strapped on his shoulder, Webb shot him a strange look but decided it was better not to ask. Grabbing an oil lamp, the deputy signaled for Chester to move and faced the big door leading to the cell area and the slide the bolt open .

"You sure about this Montana. This is, I don't mind saying, pretty scary stuff. I never put a bullet through a man's head before only to watch him walk away from it later like nothing ever happened. Did I tell you most of us here think we're dealin' with the devil? Are you sure about this?"

"If we want this man dead and gone Deputy, I think we had better try something before he gets out and kills again."

Jonah suddenly felt utterly ridiculous. Maybe he had spent too many years reading stories from Verne, Wells and Poe. He wondered if he had lost touch with reality, standing there as he was armed with a wooden stake, a skin of Holy Water, and a prayer that his suspicions were unjustly founded.

But as soon as the bolt slid back and the door swung back on heavy hinges, a terrible stench filled his nostrils and a chill crawled up his spine as the familiar tingling warned of whatever lay inside.

Jonah passed through the door first and stepped into a small hallway that stretched straight ahead for about thirty feet terminating at a rock wall. To either side were two heavy doors, each with a small open window barred with heavy iron. Chester followed Jonah and Webb brought up the rear.

"Which door?" Jonah asked, carefully scanning the dark hallway.

"The one on the right. There's nobody in the other cell," Webb's voice reverberated off the stone walls.

Jonah stepped forward and his eyes rested on the door in question. He took a couple of steps and peered through the barred window. It was too dark to see much of anything inside the cell. Webb crossed in front of the shotgun-wielding deputy and pulled a ring of keys from his belt, fumbling for the right one. Finding it, he slipped it into the lock and turned it, the bolt easily freed the big iron door with a clank. Webb pulled it open slowly.

Jonah looked into the room and his eyes fell on the elongated box in the center of the small cell wrapped tightly with heavy chains and secured on the top by a massive iron lock. It wasn't just a wooden box, but a coffin and he knew the priest lay inside. How fitting, he thought.

Walking slowly, methodically into the room, Jonah and the two deputies encircled the heavy coffin. Webb found the key to the lock and nervously fumbled with it, apprehensive and sweaty despite the chill in the room.

Chester cocked the hammer on both of the barrels of his shotgun and Jonah grasped the oak stake with both hands and planted his feet solidly on the floor as the chain slipped from the coffin with a clank. Slowly, carefully, Webb lifted the edge of the coffin lid and there was a hiss as if the contents of the box were under pressure. Looking at Jonah and the deputy in turn, he heaved on the lid and it lifted easier than expected. In the dim light and shadow of the room it was difficult to see inside the box at first, but as his eyes adjusted Jonah could make out a dark figure lying inside. He could see the pallid, corpse-like face of a man, a ghostly figure in the shadows. He could see the figure was clothed in the typical black cassock and white collar of a man of the cloth. The corpse looked lifeless, peaceful. Jonah was tingling stronger than ever though, a chill climbed up his neck and spread down the length of his arms. He raised the stake above the body and prepared to plunge it deep into the chest of the corpse, but he was too slow, had lingered too long, for suddenly the priest's eyes opened wide and the creature inside stirred and opened its mouth wide revealing two long fangs. If there was ever any doubt in Jonah's mind that he was foolish for preparing for the worst, those thoughts disappeared in a flash. He thrust downward with all his might just as the monster sat up, The stake buried into its throat and there was horrible scream. Blood dripped down across the white collar.

Jonah had missed his mark. He intended to stick the monster in the chest, piercing the heart and sending the undead creature into oblivion – like they did in the books. Instead he had awakened it. It gurgled and hissed and bolted out of the coffin, landing squarely on its feet next to Jonah. The stake had been wrested from his grip and dangled now from the wound, but with one hand the vampyre grabbed it, pulled it free and tossed it with such force that it shattered against the stone wall. Webb was standing at the foot of the coffin frozen and unable to move, but Jonah had been knocked back against the cell wall. The shotgun toting deputy stood between the creature and the open cell door, an unfortunate place to be. There was smoke rising from where the stake had pierced the vampyre's neck. Turning to face Chester, the deputy let loose with both barrels and a deafening boom reverberated throughout the cell, pellets struck the creature square in the chest. Enraged and shrieking louder the vampyre raised a hand and raked it across the deputy's chest with blinding speed, opening a wide and lethal wound that splattered blood across the room. Chester dropped the shotgun and slowly fell to his knees as the creature bolted past him and through the open door.

Jonah fumbled with the skin of Holy Water managing to get the top off and slung it in the direction of the fleeing creature. A stream of it splashed across its back, but it seemed it had no affect. The vampyre looked back over its shoulder at Jonah and flashed an evil smile as it disappeared through the outer door, a gaze Jonah would never forget. As quickly as it had started, it was over. One deputy lay dead on the floor, Webb was still trying to pull his revolver from its holster and Jonah tried to give chase, but before he could reach the outer office, the dark figure was gone, disappearing into the night.

Shaken, startled, and with the taste of fear still in his throat, Jonah collected himself and turned to see Webb emerging from the hallway door, pistol in hand now and eyes wide with fear, cursing at the top of his lungs.

"What…what is that thing?"

"That is a vampyre."

"A what?"

"A vampyre, a member of the undead, a creature neither living nor dead."

"It killed my deputy. It took two shotgun shells to the chest and it ran out of there like nothing happened."

"Yes, and I have a feeling we haven't seen the last of it. Deputy Webb, we need to get the local sheriff involved. This creature drinks the blood of innocent victims. It's injured now and will need to feed. But we need to let them know that bullets alone aren't going to bring it down. They need to pierce its heart with a wooden stake, burn it in fire, or take its head off – I think that's the only thing that will kill it. We need a lot of people on this Webb, and we need to have them move around in no less than groups of two. This thing is a powerful creature," he shot Webb a glance. "Don't ask me to explain it."

"How do you know so much about this?"

"Let's just say that's what they pay me for. Now – do you know the owner of that General Store at the end of the block?"

"You mean the Trading Post, yeah. That's Earl Strummer's place. Why?"

"You need to rouse him, have him meet me at the store. There's something in there we're going to need."

"Well that's easy, he lives behind the store. Just rap on the door hard enough and he'll come out with a rifle in his hand."

Jonah nodded and headed down the street at a brisk walk searching the shadows carefully along the way. He knew the vampyre had taken a good look at him, knew that it knew he was the one that had wounded it. He suspected it wouldn't be the only time he would see the creature before the sun came up.

CHAPTER SIX
INTO THE NIGHT

"How blessed are some people, whose lives have no fears, no dreads; to whom sleep is a blessing that comes nightly, and brings nothing but sweet dreams."   –Bram Stoker

When he reached the Trading Post he did as Webb had suggested and roused Strummer from his bed. For the first time he used the badge Alex had provided to convince the shop owner to open up. He remembered seeing a nicely crafted bow inside, probably traded for seed or flour, and a quiver of arrows that looked to be true and straight. He purchased the items with cash and headed back to the hotel. He needed to fill Molly in on the latest developments. She wasn't going to like it. From little people to vampyres, it was a lot to swallow.

Arriving at the hotel, he found her waiting and anxious.

"Mr. Montana you're simply going to have to work on your social skills. This time I didn't wait for you. I found the hot springs on my own thank you. But I did think you might have joined me after arranging the entire ordeal. I left a message at the desk."

Jonah explained the recent developments and her mood quickly changed, first to one of interest, like a child hearing a riveting story of adventure, but as told her about the incident at the Marshal's office, she became dark and moody.

As she listened intently, Jonah could see the fear welling up inside of her.

"So you're telling me you think this...vampyre...is out to get you now? Jonah, how do you know about such things? I must say, everyday I'm with you the most unbelievable becomes the most probable it seems."

"I don't really know about these things Molly. I have read about them in fiction novels during my Seminary years. But I had no idea that one day I would discover such things actually existed in the world."

He had been told about a lot of strange things as a youth, especially from his grandfather; fantastic stories of myth and legend, things that most children would never hear.

"Molly, in my world...the world of my ancestors...there are many strange tales. I have heard stories about shape changers or skinwalkers as they are called among many indigenous people. Skinwalkers are people that assume animal form at will. I grew up hearing stories about witches – not like the fairy tales you may have heard about as a child - but very frightening stories of real witchcraft. I was raised to believe there are many things in the world that others would call pure fantasy but are rooted in truth older than the hills. So perhaps I am more open to the possibilities. Maybe that's why I was attracted to those strange fiction novels in the first place. What to some may be the invention of fiction, legends of the supernatural, were to me very similar to the stories I heard as a child. They didn't frighten me as much as they excited me. That may be hard for people of different cultures and backgrounds to understand. But I am realizing now that must have influenced many things in my life, including the types of books I read. I enjoyed them, the pure speculation of the unknown. But I didn't truly think at the time that such terrible characters of fiction were real - at least not until tonight. I can't explain it. I can't explain how an undead creature walks the night feeding on the blood of innocent victims. I can only tell you what I saw tonight with my own eyes, and I tell you this...reading them may have been a great past time, but living it isn't so great. I hope you never experience what I went through. And that is why I came here straight away, realizing that I am now compromised, in real danger, and that means you are in danger as well, as long as I am around you and this creature, whatever it is, is out there. Now, I want you to lock this door and close the window tightly. Stay low and out of sight until I return. I fear this night could be a long one."

"And you're going after this creature, this vampyre? But Jonah…"

"Molly. As I said, I fear now fate is in my own hands. It's not I that am the hunter, but the hunted. I think it will come for me. I injured it and I think it won't forget that. And besides, this is my job now. I was warned if I accepted the job there would be strange encounters. In fact, I realize now that was probably the reason I was selected, because it is easier for me to accept such things compared to most – to take them more seriously. My culture, those Indian legends, my interest in speculative fiction, they have prepared me for this job I think. My only advantage is that while it frightened me to see this monster face-to-face, I wasn't stunned beyond belief. It caught me off guard, that's for certain, but I see how it feeds off of the fear of others. And I can not give it that advantage again. I must confront my own fear, and overcome the power it holds over its victims. If I don't find this creature, I am certain he will find us, so lock the door and wait for me here. I do what I must do and nothing more."

It did make some sense to Molly, but she didn't like it.

"Jonah, I should stay close to you. We are a team, are we not? Look, maybe I didn't get hired for this job…maybe I wasn't as qualified as you. I get that. But I was being considered for it, and that means something. I think there is strength in numbers. You taught me in the mountains to face fear down. We did pretty well in the mountains together didn't we? I say we should stick together and track this thing down. I don't like it, but if that's what you have to do, then I'll do it with you."

"Molly, no. I know you are capable. And I think we work well together. But for now, this creature doesn't know you even exist, and I would like to keep it that way. Anyway, Webb is rounding up every lawmen in town at the moment. I won't be alone in this hunt. There's no point in dragging you into this and paint a target on your back. We still have a mission ahead of us. Let me do my job Molly. Stay locked up, and I will return when it's over."

He stood to leave and Molly held her tongue. He was obstinate and she wasn't going to change his mind. Once he was gone, she would do as she pleased anyway.

"Lock it Molly. I'll be back, I promise."

Molly never cared much for strong willed men. And she didn't like arguing. She locked the door behind him, but he was less than a step down the hallway when she turned and began rummaging through her bags for something more appropriate to wear. No one was going to tell her she couldn't join the hunt. Moments later, armed with the Winchester and dressed in her riding clothes, she crossed the brightly lighted lobby and headed north up the boardwalk. Jonah was already out of sight.

September 27, The Docks of New Orleans

Bacchus Lacosta stood on the New Orleans docks in the midnight mist and watched the Nord-deutscher Lloyd Lines steamer, the Adler, secure its berth. Within moments her passengers began disembarking and he watched carefully as a dozen tall and rather regal-looking *Kriegers* stepped on the dock carrying large and heavy bags. He crossed to meet them, speaking in a strange language, and collected their bags and placed them in an awaiting wagon. Within a few minutes the party arrived at Hermann-Grima House and he showed them to the parlor where Fanchon Harleaux awaited.

Arrangements had been made for their next leg of travel, and after the briefing, the warriors of the Circle were divided evenly into three teams and given their assignments. One team would travel to Texas to retrieve the Apache Warrior Geronimo. From there they would head to Mexico City to acquire the Aztec prophet. A second team was dispatched first to the Badlands in the Dakotas to collect the giant known as Touch the Clouds, then to capture the Shawnee Chieftain and the Paiute prophet. The third team was charged with the most important task, collecting Gray Wolf from Indian territory in Oklahoma and bringing him to Harleaux in New Orleans. A fourth team would travel to South America to search for the elusive Inca Holy Man.

The plan was coming together. With the acquisition of these special agents from Europe, soon the Circle would have the resources needed to put the pieces together, the final clues they needed to uncover the lost secrets of the New World. Harleaux inwardly laughed at that misconception. While the densely populated world of Europe and the Orient considered the Americas to be the New World, the Brotherhood knew that life in the Americas actually predated even the earliest civilizations of Northern Africa. There was more lost knowledge in the Americas than the sum total of all discoveries elsewhere across the planet.

Supreme Master Thet would be pleased with the developments and Harleaux envisioned the day he would be awarded the highest degree of the New Order. A new day was dawning in earth history, and Harleaux was riding at the top of the wave of change. He smiled to himself, Grand Master of the Americas, second only to Thet. The long awaited objective would soon become a reality.

Kansas City, Kansas, September 27, 1 a.m.

Jonah collected the bow and arrows he had hidden in the livery stable. Stringing them over his shoulder he checked the Peacemaker strapped to his side. He reasoned the firearm would have little or no affect on the vampyre, but he couldn't be certain. It seemed the creature had been injured by both the stake to its neck and the shotgun blasts to the chest. While it failed to stop it completely, it did frighten it away, slow it down.

He headed back out to the street and considered where he should start the hunt. Where would a vampyre go to nurse its wounds? It would feed of course, but where?

On a hunch he headed towards the Cathedral where he had collected the Holy Water. He assumed it might be hallowed ground, at least according to the novels he read as a youth, but the church might serve as a place of comfort as well, perhaps a base of operations. It seemed like a good place to start. Years of tracking down elusive Indian criminals had taught him to first look at the last place you would expect to find.

Arriving at the front door of the big cathedral his senses began to warn him. Something was not right. Slipping through the door he was immediately confronted with a grizzly site. Father Bernard, the chief rector of the church, had apparently become the latest victim. He was laying face down in a pool of blood on the floor, his throat had been torn open and his body had been drained by the looks of his pallid skin. Apparently bloodsuckers were not restricted from entering consecrated buildings after all.

He scanned the rectory quickly, but when the tingling sensation began to ease he left the way he had come in and headed down the street again, giving wide berth to the shadows and the intersecting alleyways. He hoped his heightened senses would alert him to danger long before he stumbled upon it. He tried to focus on those senses, but as in times past, he was unable to trigger them at will. They seemed to only happen randomly, something grandfather said would change as he aged and learned how to tune them in.

The streets were empty this late at night, the exception being near the saloons and brothels he passed as he patrolled down Union Street. This area of town, he figured, would be an attractive place for a vampyre to hunt. He wondered if the slain church rector would be enough to satisfy the creature's blood thirst, or would it require more before the night was over? Armed only with knowledge he had acquired from fiction tales, he had no way of knowing how it really worked. Until tonight, he thought vampyres were something limited to fairy tales and horror novels.

He considered saddling up Shadow. The horses keen senses might alert him to the danger sooner than his own. It would be faster as well, but he decided against it. Better to be on the ready in the event he did cross paths with the monster, and chances are Shadow wouldn't be too happy or predictable if it sensed the predator didn't discriminate between humans and animals when it came to blood sucking. Kansas City wasn't that large anyway. He covered most of the commercial district on foot in less than an hour, except for the moorings on the banks of the Missouri. This area he discounted because it would be an unlikely place the creature would find potential victims at this hour.

He had walked from one street to the next several times, once stumbling across a trio of local lawmen who were patrolling the back streets. He was required to show his badge to satisfy their suspicions. But Jonah wondered how effective the deputies were going to be - except to become victims themselves. They apparently didn't understand how powerful and dangerous the vampyre might be, or perhaps they didn't even know or believe they were hunting a monster.

Jonah had just rounded the corner and was headed up Union Street again when he thought he spied a shadowy figure a half block ahead. His night vision was better than most, but he could barely make out that whoever or whatever it was, it was wearing dark colored clothing like the priest was wearing. He forced his mind to focus, like grandfather had taught him. He knew he could think like a warrior when required, a throw back to his Cherokee roots perhaps. Greatly feared and terribly brutal in battle when required, the Cherokee warrior was feared by his enemies because of his intensity, focus and stealth. Grandfather had made him memorize the warrior's chant, and he invoked it silently in his head now to slow his heartbeat and calm his nerves. Careful to walk soundlessly, he picked up the pace and closed the distance, but the shadows were still too thick for his careful gaze to penetrate. He moved ahead using the shadows himself, pausing long enough to scan the street carefully up one side and down the other. He strained to find the figure in the shadows again, and once thought he saw a slight movement. If it was the creature, it was playing a deadly game of cat and mouse - and Jonah knew he was the mouse. Putting his back to a building, he listened intently from the shadows, letting his ears do the searching.

It paid off. There was movement just ahead near the alley by the general store. The sound he heard was slight, carefully masked perhaps by a skillful and stealthy hunter, but he discerned it none-the-less, ever so slight like a whisper, possibly the sounds of a boot scrubbing across the hard packed dirt of the wagon-trod street.

Now the tingling was getting stronger, and his keen senses told him he had found what he was looking for. Standing quietly for a moment he made out a dark figure that emerged from the alley. It took a moment for his eyes to adjust, but he thought he recognized the face in the poor light. In seconds he was certain it was Deputy Marshal John Webb. But something seemed wrong. The tingling on his neck intensified. He could see that there was blood on the collar of Webb's shirt, and it trailed down his sleeve. The figure staggered into the light of the open street as it fell. Jonah was about thirty feet away when he could make out the big moustache and hard lines of the deputy's face.

"You've been attacked," he said, relaxing the grip on the bow and arrow he carried. He stepped forward into the street, but suddenly Webb lunged forward. Jonah thought for a moment he was collapsing, but the strong hands of the lanky lawmen clasped his shoulders with surprising strength and he was being pushed backwards. It was then that Webb opened his mouth and , revealed a pair of elongated fangs and cold black eyes. He lurched at Jonah's neck. Fighting with all his might he avoided the initial attack by twisting away from the powerful grip. The tall deputy was strong, more than he should be it seemed, and Jonah realized Webb was no longer human at all. Webb lunged again but Jonah was ready this time. Pulling the same wooden stake from his belt in blinding speed, Webb impaled himself on it by rushing forward, oblivious to the danger. It pierced his flesh into the soft skin of Webb's breast.

It may have been a lucky strike, but the stake pierced the heart and immediately the deputy's face began to smoke and flames began to lick at his collar. Jonah withdrew quickly, leaving the stake impaled in his heart. The creature screamed and burst into flames, falling to the street face first and rolling in agony. For an instant the flames bathed Jonah in light blinding his night vision. All he could see were spots before his eyes. But when his vision returned he realized he was now standing face to face with the real vampyre, the priest. He didn't know how it was possible, but somehow the vampyre had attacked the deputy and turned him into a vile slave. He may not have been as powerful, perhaps no more than an animated dead man that had been used as a decoy, an ambush that allowed the priestly monster an advantage.

Jonah realized his predicament but there was nothing he could do to stop it. Having dropped the bow at the beginning of Webb's attack, he instinctively pulled the Colt from his holster and squeezed off several rounds. The bullets hit the creature in the chest but seemed to have little effect.

But suddenly a flash erupted from behind the vampyre and Jonah watched as blood and meat splattered from the creature's forehead and struck him in the chest. There was another flash and another resounding boom, and a hole opened up on the creature's neck, just below the windpipe. It screamed in pain, but instead of falling dead like a man it turned with amazing speed and agility, and as it did so, Jonah caught site of Molly standing in the street behind the creature holding the Winchester tightly to her shoulder. She fired again and it struck the creature a third time. Still it did not stop him.

It was advancing on Molly, abandoning the attack on Jonah for the moment. It may have been instinct, but Jonah quickly thrust his foot forward, catching the toe of the creature in mid step. It was enough to cause it to lose its balance and fall to the street face first, but quickly, inhumanly, it stood again and continued toward Molly who was chambering another round.

Jonah moved faster, stooping and recovering the fallen bow, notching an arrow from his quiver. He didn't have time to take careful aim, he simply pulled back the deer-gut string and let the arrow fly. Almost before it met its mark he was notching a second arrow. As the first hit the vampyre in the back between the shoulders, he let the second fly and it struck the target near to the spine, penetrating the heart. The creature spun around and glared at Jonah with fear and brooding in its wild gaze, but smoke began rising from its arms and torso and slowly it began to burn, and soon it was completely engulfed in flames, staggering in the street and finally falling hard to the ground. It burned so quickly that within seconds it was reduced to a molten, simmering mass of ooze and burning cloth.

It was over. Molly was gasping for breath and standing wild-eyed and shaken. There were the sounds of men rushing up the street from behind her and he knew help was arriving. But all he could focus on at the moment was Molly. He wanted to scold her, but he realized she had saved his life, distracting the creature long enough for him to get away the lucky shots with the bow. She was a strong woman, and a great shot, but he sensed her heart was beating fast and she was rattled. He stepped over the puddle of burning ooze and embraced her, holding her tight as she trembled. There were tears running down her cheek, from both fear and relief. He gently took the Winchester from her and with an arm around her shoulders led her a few steps up the street when the first of the men arrived.

"The body on the ground," Jonah pointed with the Winchester, "is the priest. The other one is Deputy John Webb, who somehow was attacked by the creature and murdered." Jonah thought it best to leave out the part about Webb being turned into a blood sucker. He felt it better to let the man die a hero rather than a vampyre slave. It seemed the Christian thing to do. He didn't know if Webb had a family or not, but no point in casting a negative light on a fellow lawman.

"I have nothing more for you except a very strange tale that is going to make your reports difficult to write. But for now I'm taking the lady here back to the hotel and will brief you in the morning. But I suggest you continue your patrols tonight and be on watch. There could be other creatures like this out there."

Others arrived quickly and flashing his badge to them he gave them instructions about the nature of the creature and how to deal with others they might encounter, then informed them of the dead rector at the church.

"Agent Montana," it was the local Sheriff who spoke up. "They say you're an investigator assigned to the President's office in Washington.

Maybe you know what these creatures are, but this is something us Kansas boys have never seen before. Is there something special we need to know about this?"

"Vampyres feed off of human blood. I can't say I've had much experience with them either. This one here it's my first. But a man from Washington will be here in a few days and maybe he can tell you more. For now, I'd say be on the watch for more of them and realize the best way to kill them, believe it or not, is a wooden stake through the heart." They looked at him and thought he was joking. "Seriously. As for now, I'll meet you in the morning at Webb's office and we will sort through this thing a little more. In a pinch, you can reach me at the hotel."

Keeping his arm around Molly's shoulder he turned and headed toward the hotel. After a few steps, she politely pulled away and seemed to recover a little composure. She reached down and took back the Winchester and continued to walk beside him, watching the shadows carefully, not trusting the night. She was glad they were headed back to the hotel. She would welcome the morning light.

Truth be told, so would Jonah.

CHAPTER SEVEN
WAITING ON A TRAIN

The sun had just risen when Jonah and Molly saddled up their horses and headed out of Kansas City. They decided getting to Indian Territory and catching up with Gray Wolf was more important than waiting for Alex. The plan was to catch the train south out of Kansas City, but the ticket master had informed them the tracks were under construction south at Palmer, and even if they weren't, there were no cars to transport their horses, so they were forced to ride south to Jefferson City where they could catch the Katy south to Indian Territory and eventually to where Gray Wolf's council fire burned. There was a new telegraph office in *Tahlequah*, and Jonah figured he could check for messages in the event Alex arrived in Kansas City before they arrived in Tahlequah.

Molly was anxious to leave Kansas City, still riddled by the events of the previous night. Jonah thought she handled the strange meeting in the mountains better than she did the confrontation with the vampyre, but he didn't blame her for that. In spite of displaying a surprising amount of courage in the face of impossible danger, he felt it might bring her some comfort if he slept on the floor of her room for the remainder of the short night. He was glad he did. Judging by her troubled sleep, marked by twists and turns throughout the night, she was having a hard time letting go of the ordeal. But they had risen early and she wasn't objecting to an early start to leave town.

Soon they were working their way toward Jefferson City and Jonah breathed in the early morning air, glad for the sunlight and the fresh smells of the morning. They road steadily throughout without a great deal of conversation and none about the events of the night before. By late afternoon they had covered a good distance and Molly seemed to relax with each mile she put between her and the city. She was more herself by the time they stopped for the evening. It was getting dark and Jonah built a roaring fire. She now seemed eager to talk about their experiences.

"You know, I wasn't very happy when I heard someone else had gotten the job I was after and they passed me over. I mean, I was a little blinded by my determination to get to Montana in search of answers that would help my Uncle. I guess I didn't consider what would happen after that," she glanced over at Jonah. "If I would have considered for even a moment that I might end up chasing...vampyres...I certainly wouldn't have taken the job even if offered. What I'm trying to say is, I'm glad you came along. I mean, I'm glad the President selected the right man for the job."

Jonah took pause, not knowing how to respond.

"Well, my grandfather," he looked up and noticed her smile, the first he had seen for a day or more. "...Gray Wolf often said things work out for the best when we expect it the least, or something like that. What I am trying to say is, I am not sure that I am the right man for this job either. And if it wasn't for you Molly, that job would probably have ended for me last night. So that makes us a team."

The reflection of the fire danced across her face and she smiled again.

"Are you saying we're partners?"

"Partners? Well, yeah, I guess. Is that what you want to be, partners?"

"Depends on how much they're paying you," she chuckled. "You think Alex could use another...what do they call you anyway, Deputy Marshal?"

"I think they call me a special agent."

The smile broadened. Jonah was glad to see her spirits rise.

"Special agent of what, you mean for the president?"

"I guess so."

"Well now isn't that something. Special agent Jonah Montana, it's got a ring to it."

The evening was clear and cool and the stars were unusually bright. They feasted on jerky and a stale loaf of bread Jonah had grabbed before leaving Kansas City, and they drank deeply from spring water they had gathered not far from camp.

A comfortable silence came over them during the meal, and having finished, Jonah tended to the horses and set them free to graze on the lush grasslands near the stream. He piled the saddles near the fire and padded them with saddle bags and blankets and settled down near Molly, who flashed him a genuine smile as the flames of the campfire danced across her rosy cheeks.

She had been glancing up into the darkness of the night and pointed to a particularly bright star moving slowly across the sky.

"What do you suppose that might be…see it, the moving star?"

Jonah allowed his eyes to adjust and settle on the tiny speck moving in the sky. He was slow to answer.

"I know what you're thinking," he glanced into her blue eyes and saw the reflection of the fire. He laid back into the blanket he had arranged as a pillow for his head. "There are many tales among my people about the stars that move in the night sky. Some say they are the spirits of the star beings, the creators of the seven tribes. Others say they are the canoes that transport the star people between the rivers of the stars."

Jonah paused to remember the many tales grandfather had told him as a boy. He didn't often speak of them for, as Gray Wolf often said, they were beyond understanding for many, meaning he thought, that white men could not grasp things which they could not touch with their hands. Molly, however, seemed different.

"Molly. Many of the stories I learned in my youth are, well, rather difficult to grasp. To the Cherokee mind, many things we can not understand are accepted as truth without proof."

"You mean like what the preacher tells you about accepting God without having proof," it was more a statement than a question, and Jonah was pleased that she grasped the essence of what he was trying to explain.

"Yes, like what the preacher preaches. The Cherokee, and many Indian cultures believe the Great Spirit made the earth and the stars, and that when he placed the tribes on the earth, it wasn't the only place he put them. To the Cherokee mind, many of those stars above are places not unlike the earth, and on them are many others…perhaps looking down this very moment at our world as we are looking up at them. They may be different than we are, but in many ways very similar."

Molly thought about it for a moment as she watched the tiny light in the sky continue it's journey.

"You mean some of those stars are worlds like ours, and that those that live there are similar to us, but perhaps not all Cherokee?"

"Yes, not all Cherokee. Perhaps some are white like your ancestors, or black like those from across the ocean, or perhaps not as much like us as we might wish to think."

"You mean like the little creature in the mountains."

He glanced at her again. He realized at that moment that her eyes were as mysterious and deep as the heavens above.

"You're a quick study Molly Langtry. I knew you were thinking about the *usdiyuwi…*"

"The little people."

"Yes, the little people. Among many of the clans, the *usdiyuwi* are kind of like magical creatures. They are credited with being industrious, highly intelligent, and perhaps, not of this world. There are many tales and fables, but I believe they may be people from another place sent here for specific reasons, perhaps to help the clans in different ways. Gray Wolf says they were the teachers of fire, meaning they taught the early clans how to build and sustain our sacred fires. Some say the lights we see in the sky at night are like the wagons of the white men, they take the star people from one world to the next. Some say the Cherokee were once star people, and that when they came to earth they discovered their wagon was broken, and since then we have made a home here and are content to remain," he watched the star pass before a brighter star and for a while it's light was lost in the greater brightness.

Molly stared into the fire a moment.

"Then you believe these stories to be true?"

He was slow in answering.

"I believe many things, and sometimes doubt many more. The truth, I have found, is often elusive, and I am discovering the older I get and the more I experience, the greater the mystery of life."

"Like the vampyre."

"Yes. That was a hard one for me to accept, even as a Cherokee."

"So Cherokee don't believe in Vampyres?"

"I wouldn't go that far. The Cherokee are rarely surprised by new discovery. There are old tales of animal shape changers and men who are possessed by the spirits of the dead. Witches, for example, are very real to the people. Not witches like those in fairy tales…or like the women burned in Salem…but real witches who spin spells of dark magic. In this I believe because I knew of one as a young boy. He, for it was a man, was a very frightening creature that many Cherokee young and old feared…very powerful…and no one wished to confront him and his magic though many wished they could kill him, for his evil caused great suffering."

"Witches? Shape changers? Star people? It's no wonder the President chose you for this job instead of me."

Jonah at her blankly.

"I'm not kidding Jonah. I get it. With your background, you're openness to strange tales, I can see where someone of your background, and especially because of your education, would be the perfect candidate. It was silly of me to think that my belief in the possibility of a rock inscribed with words and pictures originated from somewhere out there," she waved a hand at the blackness above "would qualify me for the job. I mean, just look at the things we have encountered in the last few days…a little creature that speaks an ancient Cherokee dialect that sends us to talk with your grandfather - a Cherokee medicine man, and a killer vampyre that feeds off the blood of others and gets his kicks turning others into deadly assassins…honestly, I never would have been prepared for such things. If they had chosen me instead of you I would already be high-tailing it back to the ranch and probably a long stint in the same asylum as Uncle Jim."

She laughed out loud, a hearty laugh, and flashed a smile at him as big as Texas.

"Jonah Montana, you have expanded my horizons, and I have known you less than a week."

It was an awkward moment, not knowing how to respond.

"Well…Molly Langtry…I have learned a great deal from you as well."

"Really," she chuckled. "Like what?"

"Like I had no idea there was a woman in this world that could face down a monster and shoot it with a Winchester through the heart, most probably saving my hide, and still stand afterwards to talk about it."

It caught her by surprise.

"Well…that was accidently brave and terribly stupid, I guess."

"What it was, Molly, was terribly brave and the very thing that bought me the time, by luck or fate, to save my skin. And for what it's worth, I greatly appreciate it."

"What a team we make Jonah Montana."

Exhausted from the trail and their recent experiences, Molly slumped down on the blanket and closed her eyes. He looked at her then in a different way, no longer the frilly woman in the lacy dress he had met on the train; she was high spirited and extremely adventurous, different than any woman he had ever met. Yes, he reasoned, they were a pretty good team.

It was the last thing on his mind as he settled into his own makeshift bed roll and drifted into a light sleep, feeling better now that the miles separated them from the horrors of the preceding night.

CHAPTER EIGHT
CATCH A FALLING STAR

Historical Note: Newspaper accounts from the Nebraska Nugget, the nearest newspaper to the frontier town of Max, reported John W. Ellis and his 'herdsmen' were engaged in a summer roundup when they spied an object high in the sky hurtling down toward the Nebraska plain. One of the cowboys, identified as Alf Williamson, received burns to his hands when he attempted to touch wreckage from (what was obviously) the 'airship'. He was taken back to the ranch house and treated. What wreckage remained of the craft was "unusual" according to the Nebraska Journal. The largest piece remaining was metallic - like brass - about 16 inches wide, three inches thick and three-and-a-half feet long, but weighing "very little". (See appendix)

As the first rays of sun cut across the plain flooding the camp with golden hues of morning light Jonah rose feeling anxious to reach Jefferson City and start the journey south. Gray Wolf, he thought, played a greater role than imagined in directing his young adult life, from enrollment in the Seminary to his time spent with the Lighthorse Brigade. It seemed clear to him now that he was being groomed to take this job as special agent to the President for a very long time.

The night had been filled with dreams about his grandfather and how he had orchestrated elements of his life culminating in the present. He wondered, did grandfather know the day would come when he would encounter the *usdiyuwi* in the distant Montana mountains? And just how much about his future did Gray Wolf know? He understood now, he thought, why family and neighbors considered the old man to be such an accomplished seer. To Jonah he had simply been an aging man who was his paternal grandfather. Like his Mother was fond of saying though, sometimes we are too close to the forest to see the trees.

In retrospect, grandfather had always entertained visitors in large numbers. Some were neighbors and clansmen and others were from distant tribes and who grandfather often led away to council or his sweat lodge where vision quests were staged. It was the Cherokee way. He understood also that the old man was gifted with herbal medicines and was considered wise among the people who would often seek his advice. Some had said he practiced supernatural arts, but this was a rumor the family would quickly deny and take quick action to keep them from spreading rumors that he practiced witchcraft, a serious charge among the Clans. Jonah knew his grandfather wasn't a witch, but he did wonder about his unique abilities and far reaching they might be.

Grandfather had told him often as a boy that he too was gifted with 'the Sight', whatever that meant. Jonah never thought of it as anything more than intuition or an empathetic sense about a person or event that might come to pass. None of his studies at the Seminary had addressed such a thing, and he assumed it must be something indigenous to the people of his clan, as much a legend or myth as it was something scientific. But he also realized that his own ability to sense things before they happened was unique – a gift as Gray Wolf called it.

He was determined more than ever now, especially after the events of recent days, to have a frank discussion with his grandfather when the chance arrived.

He heard Molly rise and wander into the nearby brush. He finished saddling Shadow and turned his attention to bridling the mare. Soon she strolled back into camp and started packing the saddle bags. After exchanging a few morning pleasantries, they hit the trail again as quick as possible and didn't slow the pace for several hours, conversing occasionally along the way but covering a great deal of ground at a quick trot.

Mid day had come and gone and they were still several hours away from Jefferson City when they crested a rolling hill that looked down on a broad rolling plain. There they spied a most unusual scene. In an open field a few hundred yards below were a half dozen men on foot and two mounted riders. There were two dozen or so head of cattle as well, and central to the scene were a number of smoldering fires scattered more or less in a straight line about 300 feet long. There were few flames, mostly just small spirals of smoke wafting in a light breeze.

There was movement everywhere they looked. The cows were running in groups, a few straying on their own, all working their way around the sources of the smoke, some fleeing away from the smoke and fires and others running around in circles. The cowhands, for surely that's who they must have been, were in no less a state of confusion. Two of them were circling one of the larger sources of the billowing smoke, several others running across the field, pausing occasionally where other plumes of smoke filtered up from the ground. The two horsemen, obviously the rancher and perhaps a foreman, seemed to be directing the men, but the distance was too great to hear what was being shouted. One man, attended by another, stood near the riders and seemed to be injured.

They galloped down the hillside and as they approached they could see that the smoldering piles were actually pieces of what appeared to be large fragments of something, like parts of a wagon or rail car that had broken apart and scattered across the plain and were burning.

Spotting them, one of the horsemen turned to meet them. Jonah heralded the rider who approached.

"Special Federal agent Jonah Montana," he quickly produced his badge identifying himself to avoid any questions. "What happened here?"

The old cowboy looked around at the field and back at Jonah.

"Well, as incredible as it sounds, something came streaming out of the sky and crashed, throwing fragments all around. Looked like a meteor from what I hear about such things, but these chunks," he pointed to several smoldering pieces nearby "well, they aren't exactly rocks."

Jonah dismounted and let Shadow's reins hang free as he walked over to the nearest pile. The old man was right. These were no smoldering rocks. It looked to be burnt chunks of metal, like twisted wreckage from a train. The cowboy, who turned out to be the ranch owner, walked up beside him.

"I wouldn't touch it." He pointed in the direction of a man who was getting his hand wrapped by one of the other ranch hands. "Old Alf there made that mistake and he's got serious burns on his hands and arms as a result."

"And you say this just fell out of the sky?"

"As sure as I'm John William Ellis, that's what happened. It was just one big piece before it hit, maybe the size of a small barn, and on fire," William pushed his hat back on his forehead and rubbed the smoke from his eyes. "I once saw a steamboat engulfed in flames on the Mississippi, a fire so big you couldn't make out it was a boat. That's what this looked like, except it was fallin' from the sky. There was a roar to it too, sounded like nothin' I ever heard before, and then it hit the ground like a bundle of dynamite. We were just over the knoll there roundin' up the herd and couldn't see where it hit till we topped the hill, and this is what we found. What do you make of it? Ever seen anythin' like this before?"
Jonah shook his head from side to side.

"Well – a little bit like this," Jonah didn't want to tell him details about the debris-strewn canyon in Montana. "I'd like to get a better look at this when it cools down."

"Well take a look at this," Ellis dismounted and led his horse by the reigns, blurting out instructions to a pair of nearby cowboys chasing down cows. He walked a ways across the field coming to a stop beside one of the steers that was laying on its side, the smell of burnt flesh rising from the carcass. "This one must have been hit by a fragment. She was dead before we got here."

Jonah looked down and could see a gaping hole in the side of the steer's neck. One of the fragments laying nearby and still smoking had apparently passed right through her. Ellis walked a few yards further and came to a stop in front of a pile of twisted metal, kicking it with his boot.

"Here's your cooled down version Marshal. The boys dumped half a barrel of water on it. What do you make of that?"

Jonah kneeled down beside the chunk of debris about the size of a saddle. Testing it with a finger to make certain it wasn't still too hot to handle, he turned it over several times and examined it carefully. He expected to find the same strange runes on the side of it as those in the Montana canyon, but there were none, or else they had melted off from the heat. But the piece of burned debris was certainly some type of metal. He carefully picked it up from one edge and was surprised at how little it weighed.

"Well Mr. Ellis, I don't know what to make of it. And you say it just fell from the sky?"

"Like a rock hurtled down from heaven. One of the boys was the first to see it when it was still pretty high up in the sky, trailing a tail of smoke. Like I said, at first we thought it was one of those falling stars – meteors – but lookin' at here on the ground, I'd say it was somethin' a little more than that."

"What do you mean?"

"Well, it ain't no rock. And what's weird is there ain't no crater, like it blew up just before it hit the ground. That seems pretty strange to me. No, this ain't no meteor. I'll admit I don't exactly got a lot of schoolin', but even I can tell you this looks like somethin' right out of a book."

Molly walked up to Jonah carrying a small fragment partially wrapped in cloth that Jonah recognized as part of the dress she was wearing the day he had met her.

"I wasted a canteen on this to cool it down enough for us to take with us Jonah."

He nodded and looked back at the rancher.

"Is your ranch hand going to be alright Mr. Ellis?"

Ellis turned and looked at the burn victim who was getting help climbing up on the foreman's horse.

"Well, I think so. We're taking him back to the ranch so the Mrs. can put some fat back on that burn. We'll take him into Jefferson City if she thinks it looks bad enough. Say, I don't suppose the government would want to pay me for that cow?"

Jonah smiled.

"I doubt it Mr. Ellis, but I think I would at least butcher it up and save whatever meat you can salvage."

"Yup, no point in wastin' it I suppose."

"We're trying to make it to Jefferson City ourselves to catch a train south Mr. Ellis, so need to hit the trail again if you've got this under control. But I'd like to suggest that you not dispose of this…this wreckage just yet. A man I work with, a scientist might want to call on you to examine these pieces a little closer if that would be alright. And you might ask him if the government would pay for that cow." Jonah smiled.

"That'd be worth gatherin' up and keeping this junk I suppose."
They shook hands and Jonah said he would like to talk to a couple of the hands before leaving. Ellis agreed and went back to work ordering the ranch hands to collect the cows. Jonah spoke with a couple of the cowboys and realizing he wasn't going to get anything more than what Ellis had related about the incident, he and Molly were soon back on the trail. They hadn't gone far before Molly asked what he thought about the debris. Jonah paused before answering.

"I think this is going to be the strangest job I've ever had."
When they reached Jefferson City a couple of hours later Jonah headed straight to the telegraph office. He wanted to send Alex a note as quickly as possible and hoped he could delay their departure south long enough to get a reply. He didn't know what to make of the incident at the Ellis ranch, but thought it important enough to let Alex know.

Leaving the telegraph office they stopped at a diner for a meal of chicken and dumplings and biscuits. After seeing the cow with a hole through its neck and the smell of burnt hide and hair in his nostrils, Jonah wasn't in the mood for a steak. Afterward they headed to the rail station and discovered they were too late to catch a southbound train until the morning and opted for a room at a boarding house across from the telegraph office. There was only one room available and they registered in the book as Jonah and Molly Montana to avoid having to offer explanations. Soon they were settling into the room and Jonah was quick to bridge the subject of the one bed.

"I'll bunk on the floor again Molly. I just wanted to stay near the telegraph office so they could fetch me if Alex sends a reply."

"Mr. Montana, I never thought of your intentions as anything but honorable. I'm a grown girl. I can handle you sleeping on the floor."
Jonah shot her a look and smile, getting accustomed to her brand of humor.
"Well, thanks."

Molly grinned.

Taking the metal fragment collected from Williams Ranch from his saddle bag, still wrapped in cloth, Jonah examined it more closely, turning it over several times. Surprisingly it was still warm to the touch. It was light and metallic, but there was nothing else unusual about it that he could tell.

As he rolled the object and over and over between his fingers he drifted into thought again. He wondered about this new job and what he had gotten himself into. Sure, he had an open mind and enjoyed reading a good work of fiction, but doing this for a living was proving to be a strange experience. It was certainly more interesting than riding across Indian Territory and writing reports about domestic and tribal disputes or arresting a drunk Indian that somehow had broken tribal law. There had been more serious cases of course, and those were challenging. But he had to admit, his adventures with Molly put a positive spin on the current experience, though he wasn't sure exactly what that meant or where it might be heading.

WASHINGTON, D.C.

Alex Bell scanned the latest telegraph from Jonah a second time. Montana wasn't wasting anytime executing the orders of his new position. Vampyres, alien runes and crashed airships were a pretty good haul for such a short time on the job - remarkable in fact. He began to wonder if Garfield was just that good at picking the right man for a job or if Jonah was some Cherokee super hero with a knack for being in the right place at the right time.

When Alex accepted his new position from President Garfield he had hoped it would empower him to develop new inventions and new technologies at the government's expense, but so far he had been little more than an errand boy running reports back and forth between field agents and politicians. But he couldn't deny the fringe science involved in these investigations was stimulating. He was anxious to examine the evidence Jonah had collected, and it looked like he was going to get the chance to do that soon.

He scribbled a response to Jonah. It seemed reasonable to change his plans and head to Indian Territory with all haste. In Tahlequah he could examine the artifacts Jonah had collected, and he thought it might prove an advantage to finally meet this Gray Wolf, Jonah's grandfather, to hear his take on it. President Garfield and Secretary Cleveland seemed to hold the tribal oracle in high esteem and finding out why could prove valuable as he continued with these extraordinary investigations. From there he and Jonah could head to the Gulf coast as ordered, and perhaps be better prepared for what awaited them there.

He worded the telegraph to Jonah accordingly, directing him to proceed to Vinita in Indian Territory, just north of Tahlequah where he would meet him forthright. He then sent another telegram to Cleveland summarizing his plan. As he handed the messages to the telegraph operator he was already thinking about a new invention that would allow for more secure communication between field agents and the men they reported to in Washington. Yes, it was time he thought to exercise his skills of invention. Passing messages over an unsecured telegraph line was a procedure that needed to be changed immediately, and he already had an idea how that could be accomplished utilizing the same telegraph infrastructure by hiding a signal in such a way as to avoid public awareness.

Giving thought to the details, he headed to the depot to acquire tickets for the first train south.

CHAPTER NINE
GRANDFATHER'S HOUSE

Early to bed and early to rise, Jonah and Molly caught the morning
'Katy' train south to Vinita. They would have taken the train to
Muskogee if it were up to Jonah, but he had told Alex they would
check for a telegraph in Vinita, not realizing the train didn't have a
scheduled stop there. By flashing his badge he had convinced the engineer
it was necessary 'for government business purposes' to make the stop, but
trying to get him to hold the train until he could retrieve a telegram from
Alex was out of the question the conductor said.

Upon arriving, the train barely rolled to a stop long enough for Jonah
and Molly to step off and unload their horses before it pulled out and
headed south. Jonah wasn't upset when he retrieved a telegraph from Alex
in Vinita informing him he wouldn't be arriving until the following day.
He left a note for Alex at the telegraph station and a ticket for the
stagecoach to Tahlequah and told Molly they should saddle up and head
south right away. Alex, he said, could join them the following day. Jonah
was pleased at the chance to show Molly a little bit of Cherokee country by
horseback.

Vinita was a hard day's ride to Tahlequah and Jonah was anxious to
get started. By nightfall they were deep into Cherokee territory and Jonah
selected a rather picturesque location along the Illinois River to camp.
They spent the evening chowing down on flatbread and kanuchi, which

Jonah prepared over the fire using nut balls and hominy he acquired in Vinita.

Following the meal they talked long and Jonah told Molly many Cherokee stories. It was a peaceful evening and the perfect cure for the stress of the journey and the remarkable events of recent days. They both fell asleep watching the stars as Jonah identified many of the systems and clusters in the night sky and told their stories to an attentive Molly while the trickling of the stream and the singing of the whippoorwills serenaded them into pleasant dreams of harmony and peace.

By morning's light they were back on the forest trail again and Jonah was feeling more comfortable with the surroundings. Molly, too, seemed cheerful and welcomed the change in the geography. By mid-day they were near Tahlequah when Jonah lead them east in the direction of Gray Wolf's cabin and the place of his sacred fire. When they arrived, the old man was standing by the fire pit in front of his modest log cabin watching them approach.

"I knew you would be coming today," he said when they were near enough to hear him. They dismounted. "And I knew you were bringing the Cherokee girl."

He looked at Molly and nodded a welcome.

"Grandfather, it is good to see you, and you always know when I am coming, often before I know," Jonah smiled and grasped the Old Man by the wrist in Cherokee fashion. "But the girl, she's not Cherokee."
Gray Wolf looked at Molly with little expression on his face, but in his eyes there was a twinkle.

"*Osiyo* Molly," he said and turned to Jonah. "She is Cherokee and does not know it. And neither do you it seems."

Molly smiled and was amazed he knew her name, and more surprised that he would say that she was Cherokee. As if understanding her thoughts, Gray Wolf took her hand in both of his and spoke to her.

"It is from your grandmother, your mother's mother I believe, that the *tsalagi* blood runs in your veins. But you are welcome here regardless. *Ulihelisdi uwetsiageyv* -- welcome to the Tenkiller fire."

She blushed though she did not know why. Gray Wolf, she decided, was a striking example of a Cherokee statesman. There was an air about him she admired immediately – like he was Cherokee royalty; wise and confident, gentle but authoritative. She liked him and could see the resemblance between him and Jonah.

"Thank you," she said.

"You can call me grandfather. The a*nikituhwag*i name is far too long for most tongues."

"Thank you then, grandfather."

"*U l isi a tsu tsa. Da do no O ni yi yu*?" Grandfather asked. "I expected you last night. Did you stop along the river as you did when you were young? I kept the fire burning late, but you did not come."
Jonah instinctively knew Gray Wolf would be awaiting their arrival. He always had, even when Jonah was a boy. As his father said, there was no sneaking up on him or dropping in for an unexpected visit.

"We came as quickly as possible Grandfather. But you always have the fires burning late, and if you were expecting me last night then how did you know I would be here today?"

They both laughed.

"Grandfather, we have much to speak with you about…but I guess you know this already also," Jonah smiled.

"I do not know all things. Come into the *Ga-li-tso-de* and we will speak where the birds can not hear us."

He turned and headed to the house. Molly cast a questioning look and Jonah pointed to the cabin, built of timbers and mud, a blanket hanging where a door should be.

"The Wolf Den," he whispered.

Inside Gray Wolf was pouring stemming tea into three crude ceramic cups and handed one to each of them.

"This is tea made from the *Ani Unasdetlv*, strawberry root. It will soothe the spirit and clear the mind if made the right way, if not it will kill you. But I made this myself, so drink," Grandfather smiled with his eyes again.

Molly shot Jonah a look, not certain whether Gray Wolf was serious or not. When he raised his cup to drink, she followed suit. The tea was bitter at first taste, but the more she sipped, the more she warmed to the taste.

They settled into crude looking low stools that looked like they were covered with thick blankets and some type of stuffing underneath. Four of them circled a small clay fireplace in the center of the one room cabin and were comfortable in spite of their appearance. Twin logs were burning and a thin spiral of smoke rose to an opening in the roof. The smell inside the cabin was slightly smoky with earthen overtones. Gray Wolf fiddled with the fire with an iron rod made for that purpose and added a handful of bark. "This is real piñon bark. I trade an Apache my special tobacco for it because I like the smell. It reminds me of my time near Santa Fe."

Jonah and Molly sipped the bitter tea while Gray Wolf played with the fire, a ritual he had performed since Jonah was just a boy. Molly thought perhaps the aging Cherokee was collecting his thoughts, or performing a blessing in honor of their meeting as long minutes passed without words between them. Soon the old Indian leaned back from the fire and turned to face them.

"The tea should be working by now. How do you feel?" Jonah simply nodded but Molly was trying to say she was feeling very comfortable, perhaps a little sleepy, but she was having a hard time formulating the words. She wasn't quite certain where her body ended and where the soft blanket she was sitting on began.

"This is your first strawberry tea?" Gray Wolf was asking. "The effect will settle in a few moments and your mind will clear and you can focus better on the telling of your story, for I think you have much to tell. Jonah, you have something to show me?"

Jonah was already fidgeting with his saddle bag he had carried in and pulled out the artifacts stowed inside. He handed two of the pieces to Gray Wolf. The old man picked up the fragment they had collected in Montana and turned it over in his hands. Using the palms of his hands and fingers he felt across the objects smooth surface.

"This is very ancient," said Gray Wolf as he held it close to the fire for light. "Did you say there are figures carved across the surface?"

"No, not on these smaller pieces, but there were several large fragments that had figures much like these," he handed him the parchment he used to sketch the figures.

"These are also ancient symbols, and the language is even older though your drawings are terrible. Did you not study drawing at the Seminary?"

"You know I didn't," chuckled Jonah. "What do you think they mean?"

"It appears to be an ancient form of the Old Language. I can not read every word, but I can tell you the meaning."

Molly was becoming more alert now as Gray Wolf had said, and she was intently watching and listening to the alluring voice of the old Cherokee sage. She began to appreciate his wisdom, felt as though she could feel it. He was a powerful figure, reflections of the small fire dancing across his face and his long gray hair that reached below his shoulders.

"But first I must hear the story that goes with this," he said as he leaned further back into his seat and became silent.

Jonah related the story and Molly would join in on occasion to offer more detail. Gray Wolf listened silently as they talked of the creature in the canyon and the message he sent with them. The story lasted some time and when they finished, Gray Wolf nodded and examined the artifact again.

"So the Little One, he tells you I am the Chosen One. Did he say for what?"

"Yes Grandfather. He said you were the one to know the writing. Or I think that is what he said. He spoke in a dialect I could not easily understand. At first I thought he was speaking about me – me being the one. But as I think about it, I think he said it was you that are the one. He said you would know what it meant and what should be done," Jonah answered.

Gray Wolf nodded his head.

"There is a story, very old, that was told around the council fire long before the eastern Cherokee came to the place White Men call the Carolinas. Long before this time there were seven council fires, in the days when Cherokee and Iroquois and Illiniwek and Lakotan and others formed a coalition and burned their sacred fires together and lived in a great city by the big river. The city was Kohaekea, and there were great mounds the people called pyramids, and life was ordered by a central council divided among many clans and many tribes, the growers and hunters, warriors and storytellers. But it was not always so, for the many tribes were once faced with death because the Uk'tena, the water serpent, or the dragon of the stars, who hated the tribes, caused a harsh winter that lasted many times longer than it should, three plus three spring seasons in all. The coalition was formed because the people needed to petition the Great Thunderbird to intercede for they were exhausted as were their resources. The Thunderbird heard their prayers and commanded the Little Ones to build this great city and placed inside the pyramids powerful engines that provided warmth, and once complete it was here that the tribes took refuge from the cold and grew crops beneath the mounds, powered by energy like the sun. This energy came from seven sacred crystals that powered the powerful engines to make them work and for nearly thirty years the people survived the winter, grew their crops and raised deer and smaller animals to feed their people," Gray Wolf sipped his tea and played with the fire before continuing.

"But when the winter finally faded to a long spring, the Little Ones departed, but before going they took the sacred crystals that powered the machines and they hid them in secret locations, for they were no longer needed. The cold winter had ended, and the Little People knew the engines could destroy the tribes, for they would soon dissolve their coalition as they bickered and argued about traditions and history and who among them was the strongest and the bravest. But the little people left with the Kohaekea coalition the knowledge of where the sacred crystals were hidden, one for each tribe to keep watch, a different crystal for each tribe. No tribe knew all of the hiding places, but they agreed to designate Keepers among them, wise men who would harbor the knowledge of where the tribe's crystal were hidden, so that if winter should ever fall again, the tribes could come together and reveal where all seven crystals were hidden so that the engines could be powered again to save the people as they were once when the great city was built. The Cherokee had possession of a master crystal for they were the principle people, the *Ani-Yunwiya*. Each tribe received their own crystal according to their talents and their power. The Lakota guard the white crystal and the Cheyenne and Shawnee the blue crystal and so forth. So it was that the tribes went in different directions, each carrying with him knowledge to the location of one sacred crystal."

Gray Wolf paused to sip from his cup again and to toss more piñon on the fire.

"It came to pass that the tribes of the coalition grew on their own and forgot much down through time, but one – the wise one of the tribe – or Keeper of each tribe never forgot for it was his charge to keep the secret hiding place of the crystal and to pass it to no one but his apprentice, the one who would replace him when the Great Spirit called his soul to the skies. Years later the old enemy, the Uk'tena, entered the city after it was abandoned and took the powerful engines, but they could not use them without the hidden crystals."

He glanced across the fire at them, reading their emotions, gauging their ability to understand. He knew the tea would open their inner eye, and he gave them time to absorb his tale before he continued.

"This is where the story begins. There is much more, but it takes time to tell the story, and time for you to understand it."
Molly had been listening intently, focusing on each word because she felt so personally involved because of her shared experiences with Jonah. Or perhaps it was the influence of the tea. But either way, she had questions she wanted to ask.

"Grandfather, how could the Little People...how could they have such great power like the energy of the sun? And the Thunderbird, isn't that a creature of myth? And I don't mean to be disrespectful, but how could the water creature, the dragon, have waged war on the people if it could not leave the water?"

Gray Wolf looked at her and answered politely.

"*So-ga-i-ni-si*, grandchild, your question does not offend me. Even among the Cherokee there is much misconception." He glanced into the fire again as if looking for the right words. "What I will say about the old ways I tell you because of your experience with the Little People. Such words would fall on deaf ears to many, but you have earned them."

He studied her and could see her confusion. But she would understand he reasoned, if he told her more.

"There are many among the Cherokee who have forgotten the truths of our beginnings," he said. "Even chiefs among us have forgotten the oldest of our stories. That is why among the Cherokee there are *v-ga-nu-we-u-we*, or the Keepers, and then there are conjurers, the *da-du-ne-s-gi*, and the *a-dv-ne-li-s-gi*, or wizards. There are many titles, many jobs. To my family passes the task of *ka-no-he-s-gi*, history tellers and the keepers of the crystal knowledge. Each clan must have a history teller, and each clan is responsible for certain parts of our history. There is the history of our wars and our migrations, of our blood line and history of our hunters and growers. Each history is magic, and to me falls the magic of our Gods. To me has passed the knowledge – the history – of our relationship with our Gods. This is my magic."

Molly hesitated, but she was following his words carefully and thought she understood.

"You are the Cherokee storyteller, the keeper of the crystal knowledge," she nodded.

"Yes, and now you must understand the story of the Great Thunderbird. In our hearts, the Cherokee heart – and to many of our brothers of the other tribes - the Thunderbird is a powerful messenger of the Great Spirit clothed in magnificence - a frightful beauty. We symbolize him with pictures on stones, a great bird with strong wings and eyes that cast lightning. Its flight causes the thunder to roar and the winds to blow across the land. This is what we see in our minds, but in our hearts the Thunderbird is the great messenger. Molly of Missouri, our ancestors did not come from this place we call Earth, but from places we see in the night sky, from stars beyond, in the most ancient of times. The Great Spirit still dwells in the skies, and when we look to the stars at night we are praying to the Him that brought us here. The Great Spirit rules most of the star people, but not all of them."

He finished his tea and continued his story.

"Some of the star people are at odds with the Thunderbird race of the star cluster we call the Seven Sisters – Pleiades. They are the people the Lakota call Wankan Tanka, the Cherokee call him *U-ne-qua*. The Thunderbird and the Uk'tena are not monsters of the earth or creatures of myth and legends, they represent two races from distant stars systems. The Thunderbird comes from the Seven Sisters in the southern sky. Here resides a race of people, not unlike the Cherokee, but more ancient and much more powerful; different power, different magic, and different science."

"The Uk'tena originate from a place we call the Little Bear, a different star system with a different race of people. They also control the star system known as Sirius. The Uk'tena and the people of Pleiades have warred for longer than time can remember, and both have had an interest in other star systems, different suns, and many of the planets strewn across the universe. Earth is just one of those places. Down through the generations the people of the Little Bear and the people of Pleiades have interacted with the people of Earth. And this is the story of how the energy beneath the Pyramids comes from the stars, from Pleiades, and how the people of the Uk'tena covet this energy, they want to posses the power of the Pleiadeans as they once did, before it was taken from them."

He was tiring it seemed, and paused a long moment.

"As far as the Little People, they too are alien to this world, but like the Thunderbird, they have come to bring their science and magic to the people. They serve the Pleiadians - are their allies. It was their engineers who constructed the great pyramids and similar structures across the Earth. Their science is beyond our understanding, but they have given us help many times down through the ages."

"What you experienced in that mountain canyon Molly, Jonah, was one of the Little People. They have always been close, but they hide from us until they are ready to reveal themselves. Their language is the very root of our own language, the *tsalagi*, or Cherokee. We call ourselves the primary people for our history tells us we were the first to come to this planet earth. We share many of the same words with the Little People, and the People of the Thunderbird, but slightly different. This is why you were told to bring me your story."

Gray Wolf rose slowly but suddenly.

"And now I must go beneath the stars and remember much that I have forgotten – to understand the meaning of this message. Tomorrow Jonah's friend the inventor will arrive by stage, and by then I need to have to answers."

With nothing further to say he turned and walked through the blanket covering the door and into the night air to stir his sacred fire and ponder the story that told him about their encounter with the little one. Night had fallen and Molly and Jonah were left in the cabin as the fire slowly began to die.

"You grandfather is an amazing man, and his stories are even more amazing."

Jonah nodded.

"For the moment, this is out of our hands," Jonah told her. "In the morning he will counsel us. But for now the magic of the tea bids me to sleep deeply. Do not be surprised if your dreams are vivid tonight."

With that Jonah leaned back in his blankets and rested his eyes. In a short moment, Molly was dreaming too.

Long before the morning sun peaked over the horizon Jonah stirred from a restful sleep, threads of dreams still fresh on his mind. Molly was still sleeping soundly and he ventured from the cabin careful not to disturb her. He wanted to speak to Gray Wolf alone and knew he would find him by the sacred fire outside. As expected, the aging sage sat cross-legged in front of the fire, his back to Jonah and the cabin.

"Grandfather?"

"Come and sit with me *u-ni-si*. I can feel you have questions."

Sitting down next to Gray Wolf, Jonah was slow to start.

"Grandfather, when you spoke of the old story last night, there were many things I had heard before, but many things I had not. You have instructed me much about the Thunderbird and the star stories. But the tales of the Uk'tena I do not remember."

Gray Wolf was long in thought before replying, which was often his way.

"Of the Uk'tena little is spoken Jonah. The very word can strike fear into a man's heart, and not just the Cherokee heart, but Chickasaw and Lakota, Creek and Apache. The name is not always the same among the nations, but the concept is. It is a name and a topic which we do not speak about easily. Your own clan especially Jonah, the Wolf Clan, know of the Uk'tena, though it has been a generation since an encounter with the vile creatures has happened, at least among the Western Band."

"You speak now of the Uk'tena as a creature, and last night you spoke of them as star people, the enemy?"

"Yes. They are both grandson. But these star people, the people of the Uk'tena, are unlike the others, they are vile creatures, not animals that walk on four legs but two legs like a man. To the unknowing eye some of them may seem as any other man. But inside they are wicked beyond our ways, hateful creatures that feed on the misery of men. In the old days their numbers were great, but then there was a war, bigger than you have ever heard Jonah, and they were thrown down. But a few remained and went into hiding, for the Cherokee hunted them, even your own family, the Wolf Clan, and they were also hunted by other tribes. They feared our warriors for their power was diminished, for the *Wakaja*, warriors of the Thunderbird destroyed most of their war machines and took from them the crystals that powered them, and later gave them to the tribes as you will learn. These crystals are made from a material not unlike what we call mica, and they are critical in making their airships fly and their other technologies to work. Without them they can not leave the earth and they must remain here and live like men."

Jonah considered it. Grandfather was talking about star people, beings from another world. He spoke of their airships, what Jonah took to mean a reference to the star wagons of legend. It seemed to Jonah that through his many years growing up he would have heard of such a thing.

"You have never told me of these star people that walk among us grandfather. There are the people of Pleiades, the Thunderbird race you called them, and then there are the enemy star beings, the Uk'tena. If the enemy walks among us, then where are the Pleiadians? Do they not walk among us as well?"

"Jonah there is much I have yet to teach you. The Pleiadians have long since left the earth to wage their war and protect their interests far out among the stars. But many of the Uk'tena are stranded in this star system, the Milky Way as the Greeks called it. They're only hope to leave our primitive planet and rejoin the war is to recover the sacred crystals."

"Then why grandfather have I not seen these star beings, the Uk'tena, if they walk among us and are trying to recover the crystals?"
The old man cast him a glance and stared at him a long moment.

"Jonah, you have encountered them, and this is why I told the story last evening. Your encounter is a disturbing sign, and I think it was not by chance alone."

Jonah returned the stare.

"In your travels grandson, you crossed paths with a vicious killer,." Grandfather added.

"You mean the vampyre? How did you know, and are you saying the Uk'tena are vampyres, one and the same?"

"Vampyre is one name by which they are called by many people of earth Jonah. Our people call them by their real name, the Uk'tena. Many clans have their own word but it is the same Uk'tena. In many cultures, not just the seven tribes, the creature has been known - and now a part of legend. A few have immortalized them in books...the kind you liked to read when you should have been studying the old ways."

"Books? Wait - the vampyre tales of fiction are really the actually the Uk'tena?"

"This I think you already knew, but your white man's education has numbed your senses." Jonah looked at Gray Wolf, but the old man was laughing with his eyes. "But the vampyres, as you call them, are not the only kind of Uk'tena – simply one form they take, for their science has given them the ability to alter their physical state. Through coding of their bodies memory, some have taken the form of a man, others are very large and have skin like that of a snake. They are giants. This, I think, is their natural form."

"You're talking about the science of genes. I have heard of this, but it is little more than a theory grandfather."

"No, it is a science from the far reaches of the stars. I do not understand it, but the knowledge of it has been passed down by our own people, the star people can do this – and they have."

Jonah stared into the fire. He had other questions to ask, but as morning's early light crawled over the hills, Molly stirred from the cabin just then, walked through the blanket covering the cabin door and stretched.

"What was it again that was in that tea?" She asked.

CHAPTER TEN
A MIDNIGHT SNACK

Vieux Carré, The Grima House, New Orleans

Fanchon Harleaux eased into the provincial settee in his Chateaux parlor just as the sun disappeared beneath the horizon. He was gloating over the perfection of his plans. The *Krieger*s had been dispatched and were well into their assigned missions by now – and they never failed at their tasks.

As important as they were to his plans, the truth is, he was glad to see them go. They were soldiers of the Circle, the best warriors on the planet, and so well trained that nothing could stop them, no one could keep them from their tasks. But they were greatly feared. Even he feared them. They were killers, Thet's personal guard, his assassins, and whether you were friend or foe you could not escape the oppression of their presence.

Hosting them in Hermann-Grima House was an exhausting experience and now he was famished, empty, and ready to dine.

Bacchus Lacosta entered the parlor with two young women in tow. Harleaux looked them over, young and beautiful Creole girls, professionals by the look of it, dressed boldly in festive if not cheap street fashion like so many of the girls in 'the city that never sleeps'. He liked what he saw and did not care how much coin Lacosta was required to pay to have them deliver their services to his parlor. He was in need of the both of them, and he would have them if they cost him hundreds or thousands. Money was no object.

"Leave us," he commanded the servant.

The girls lost their smiles and quieted their giggles as their eyes fell on Harleaux's huge dark figure lounging on the settee in the dimly lit room. It wasn't that he was unpleasant to their eyes, but his looming size and unforgiving glare made them feel immediately uncomfortable. But he patted the sofa seat next to him, an invitation for them to sit, and they succumbed to the gesture, sitting one on each side. He smiled at them, first one then the other, running a finger down the exposed thigh of one, and turning to the other and placing an open hand on her chin, cradling it, before gently turning her head away from him exposing the soft flesh of her neck. He shuffled in his seat to reposition himself to face her and bent low to softly run his tongue across the warm black skin below her ear, pulling her gently nearer.

It was a passionate caress, and a deadly one, for as his lips parted, two razor sharp fangs emerged from his upper lip and he buried them into her flesh. With his free hand he reached behind and grasped the wrist of the other girl who was attempting to stand and flee, and with a strength beyond reason clasped on to her with an unbreakable grip as he fed deep on the first victim, her screams muffled and gargled as the life was drained from her.

Finishing with the first he turned to the other, still grasping tight to her wrist, and consumed her in like fashion, drinking her blood until none remained to covet.

When at last he released her, she, like the first, slide from the settee to the floor, already the warm and luscious dark tone of her skin turning pallid, drained of its life. For a moment, tempered by his ecstasy, he softened from the rage required to feed uncontrollably, and his eyes, once dark like the shadows of night, flashed green and yellow, the pupils taking the oval shape of a serpent's eye, revealing his true nature, for Fanchon Harleaux's bloodline, like all the members of the secret inner circle, was Uk'tena in origin, a creature not of this earth but far from a water-covered rock in the distant Sirius system.

A trickle of blood still ran from one corner of his mouth when the servant Lacosta returned, as if knowing his master had completed the feeding.

"Prepare the control room and dump the corpses in the channel," Harleaux looked down at the lifeless forms of his victims with disgust on his face. "Miserable creatures, Bacchus. Even you would be a king among them."

He laughed then, not as a man might laugh, but in guttural, gargling tone, the sound of the beast within.

CHAPTER ELEVEN
ALEXANDER BELL CALLING

The rains were bad enough, but stagecoaches were worse. They were hot and dusty and uncomfortable, and Alex began to wonder if the stagecoach driver was a sadist, for it seemed he purposely hit every bump, every rock and every depression in the road. Ten miles into the fifty mile trip from Vinita to Tahlequah and Alex found himself exhausted. By the time the stage rolled to a stop at its destination, he was uncertain if he could even stand to exit the carriage door.

Outside in the fresh air he felt better though, and while waiting for his carpet bag to be untied from atop the coach a familiar voice called his name from behind. Turning, he was glad to see Jonah and a smile broke across his face – until he spotted the red haired woman standing behind him. The smile on his face disappeared.

"You! What...I mean why are you here?"

"Hello Mr. Bell, welcome to Indian Territory," Molly was grinning. Jonah looked at her and then at Alex.

"I see you know each other," Jonah was grinning too.

"Know each other! This woman assaulted me the last time we met. What are you doing here anyway Miss Langtry?"

"You can call me Molly."

"You assaulted him?" Jonah was surprised.

"Molly? Miss Langtry…Jonah. Yes she did. Do you know this woman?"

"It wasn't a roundhouse punch, just a slap in the face," Molly offered, blushing slightly.

"Yep. I know her well Alex. She's been helping me every step of the way," Jonah looked at Molly and then at Alex again. "I guess we need to talk. Can you ride a horse?"

"It wasn't a little slap Miss Langtry. And what, ride a horse? Well yes, more or less."

Alex's carpetbag thudded on the ground next to him, thrown from the stage above.

"Well, grab your bag and let's take a ride. We need to cover a few miles to reach Gray Wolf's fire."

"There's been a fire? What horse?"

Jonah picked up the bag himself suppressing a smile as big as Texas. Walking toward where the horses were tied he called back to Alex.

"These horses over here Alex," he said nodding at Shadow, the mare and a old Gray tied to a rail in front of the new telegraph office.

Struggling with placing his foot in the stirrup, Alex finally managed to swing himself into the saddle, almost overshooting the horse. Jonah slide effortlessly up on Shadow's back and Molly followed suit. Reaching across with Alex's bag, he hung it on the inventor's saddle horn and motioned the way with his head.

"Just try to keep up."

Alex was cumbersome in the saddle having little riding experience, but after a mile or so he began to get control of his nerves and the gray and settled into the horse's rough gate.

They were riding three wide now along a shaded trail that the trees reached across to form a green canopy overhead, birds harmoniously serenading them as they passed beneath the thick boughs of the rose bud, cypress and birch. Jonah filled Alex in on the details of how he met Molly on the train, their experiences in Montana, Kansas City and on the ranch outside Jefferson City.

"Good heavens! That's some adventure!" Alex exclaimed, swallowing hard and trying to wrap his head around what was being said while trying to remain in the saddle at the same time. Leaning forward and looking across Jonah's horse addressed Molly.

"My apology Miss...uh, Molly. You do understand my surprise. I understand you wanted the job that we awarded to Jonah. But he was the better qualified, and your reaction at the President's decision was, well, not only unexpected, but forgive me, rather rude and I must say inappropriate. I wasn't the one making the decision you know, it was strictly President Garfield's decision."

"And I apologize Alex – you don't mind me calling you that do you?. But I was under great pressure at the time. I didn't know there was a more qualified candidate," she looked at Jonah. "But I'm glad there was."

"You are?" Alex didn't understand the change of heart. Jonah seized the opportunity to riddle her.

"So you admit facing the Little Creature alone would have been overwhelming?" he asked.

"I admit I don't speak an ancient dialect of Cherokee. I would have no idea what the little creature was saying if not for you," she retorted. Grinning again and looking back at him, "And I'm glad I wasn't alone when he popped out of nowhere."

Jonah smiled back. Alex looked first at one of them then the other.

"Well, all things are well that end well they say."

They had rounded the last turn in the wagon trail and Jonah spotted Gray Wolf sitting on the doorstep of his cabin, anticipating their arrival - as usual.

Dismounting, the riders tied their horses to the rail by the water trough.

"Did you get lost again, or perhaps stopped to watch the leaves fall into the river?"

It was Gray Wolf's way of a greeting.

"Grandfather, this is..."

"Alex Bell," Grandfather said. "Bell is a Cherokee name you know. My Mother's family was Bell, from the Bell's of Echota. But I don't suppose you're from around here are you?"

"Well no...Gray Wolf...I'm sorry, I don't know the proper way to address you, but I certainly have heard about you, and am honored to meet you sir." Alex reached into his jacket pocket and produced a sealed envelope bearing the seal of the White House. He handed it to the Cherokee elder.

"This is a communiqué from President Garfield. He handed this to me the day before he succumbed to his injuries and asked that I pass it along to you. I understand you knew the President."

Grey Wolf took the envelope.

"I have known a few of the White Fathers in Washington, but none too closely. Most of them thought me crazy by the things I told them. Garfield, he was different, as was Jefferson. But that was many long years ago."

"You knew others," asked Alex.

"I have met some. Jackson…I especially did not like him. Much talk and full of promises. He was no friend of the Cherokee, though he pretended to be. But this is for another time. You did not travel from Washington to hear my take on your presidents. Tell me, what have you invented lately?"

The question caught Alex by surprise.

"I, eh, spent the last two years working on a talking device…"

"Ah yes, I have heard of this. Did you bring one with you? I could call the president."

"It still needs a bit of work," Alex was surprised at Gray Wolf's command of the English language - and his wit.

"I have an idea for an invention, a rifle with many barrels, and a turning device that pushes bullets into one barrel while another is being used, giving great fire power to the one who operates it. What do you think?"

"Well…there is already an invention like that I'm afraid. They call it a Gatling Gun."

Gray Wolf stared at Alex a long moment.

"Ah, Richard Gatling, the white doctor. I knew he was going to steal my idea when I told him about it many years ago. He stole the propeller idea for steamships too you know."

"You knew Dr. Gatling?"

"Yes. Didn't think too much of him either. Why would a doctor invent a gun that could kill many men at one time. Do you think he was short on patients?"

"I don't think he actually ever practiced medicine," Alex offered.

116

"I speak of the doctor unkindly. He was a good inventor I suppose. But be glad you did not meet him or he might have invented the talking machine."

Alex wasn't sure if Gray Wolf was serious or not.

"Don't listen to grandfather. He'll talk you in circles all day. He's a champion at it," offered Jonah.

Gray Wolf collected a shovel that was leaning against the cabin wall and walked over to Alex.

"Are you hungry Mr. Inventor?"

"Why, yes, I suppose I am."

Handing the shovel to Alex he pointed at the ground just beyond the fire pit.

"Then dig over there. There's a pig in the ground, and I am tired of waiting for my grandson who is always late."

Alex looked at Jonah, who shook his head slightly and relieved him of the shovel.

"You're actually in for a treat Alex, if you like roasted pig."

Digging where Grandfather had directed, Jonah pulled a heavy wrapped potato sack out of the ground that was charred on one side from the heat of the coals buried beneath the dirt. Cutting the bindings with his knife, he unwrapped the cloth sack revealing a perfectly cooked piglet inside. Cutting a section apart with his knife, he offered Alex a taste. Taking it reluctantly, he sniffed it quickly and popped in his mouth, and his eyes opened wide.

"My goodness. I haven't tasted anything like this before."

"Molly," called grandfather. "There are several cups in the cabin, and a jar of fresh tea. Would you bring them that we may feast?"

And feast they did, sitting on low rock benches around the fire pit. After carefully taking a sip of her tea, Molly was sorry to discover it wasn't made from strawberry root.

They ate heartily and drank their tea and talked about Garfield's untimely death, about Cherokee politics and how Grandfather had once met Napoleon.

"I didn't like him either," he said.

Finally Jonah and Molly caught Alex up on the story of their recent travels, as they had Gray Wolf the night before. They also showed him the artifact they collected, and the light weight metal they picked up on the

Missouri plain. Alex was visibly shaken when hearing the grizzly tale of the vampyre incident.

Finally, Gray Wolf's turn arrived again, and he told them how he had examined the artifact by his sacred fire, and explained that Jonah must have misunderstood the old language. It was not the message on the rocks that Jonah was to deliver, but the message from the Little One. The writing on the rock was the handiwork of the Little People and no one knew how to read that language for it was not of this world. What the Little One wanted was for Gray Wolf to call a council of the Seven tribes together, a meeting where the history keepers of each tribe could gather, for the winds of war were blowing. The secret crystals were in danger. The Uk'tena were rising again and they sought the crystals, and he told them soon they will come for those in the tribe, the story tellers, the keepers of history, who hold the secret to their hidden locations. In the wrong hands, he said, the crystals could cause the power of the engines to work once again and a terrible energy could be unleashed against the world as in the days of old.

"In the vision, while I slept, I saw others who covet this lost knowledge and they also seek it." He glanced at Alex, "There are those who would hope to use the power for what they think are worthy causes. But either way the power would be greater than the wielders."

He paused and fell deep in thought. When he started again, his voice was lower, his demeanor had changed, and there was sweat on his brow.

"In my vision I saw that several of the crystals have already been uncovered and are in the hands of the ancient enemy. Even now he actively seeks the history keepers of the remaining tribes to obtain the other crystals. This we must not be allow to happen."

"Does this mean these star people, the Uk'tena, they will come for you Gray Wolf?" Alex asked.

The old man nodded.

Silence fell among them. They had talked for many hours and now the shadows were long and the day was beginning to pass with the setting sun. They had become sullen and quiet, considering all that had been said.

After a long while, as twilight at last arrived, Gray Wolf rose from his bench and collected sticks and a pair of logs from the nearby wood pile. He stacked the wood carefully in the pit and struck tender to it, and then broke the silence.

"Alex Bell, you are from the place called Scotland across the sea. This may be hard for you to believe, but long ago the Chiroque – the ancient ancestors of the Cherokee today – lived on a great Island, Turtle Island, in the middle of the sea. When a great tragedy came upon them they were sent to the four corners of the earth, to places you call China and India and Israel and Scotland."

He studied Alex's face a moment.

"Your name is Bell, and that is a Cherokee name. You should remember this, for all you have heard today was intended for Cherokee ears and for the Cherokee heart."

Alex nodded as if he understood, but in the truth the best he could make of it was that the Old Cherokee wise man was telling him that he was to keep his mouth shut and his mind open. Alex, for some reason, thought he understood.

"So grandfather," Jonah asked. "You are being instructed to gather a council of the seven tribes, not the principle chiefs, but the wise ones, the Keepers who possess the knowledge, the secrets of where the crystals can be found. This is the message of the Little One?"

Gray Wolf watched the flames rise in the pit and selected his words carefully.

"We must gather the a-na-s-ka-yi, the members of the high council of the seven tribes, yes. This council has not met for many generations now, but each of the member tribes will still have a representative appointed to this secret council. But we can not be certain they will respond to a call, it has been long."

"Who are these history tellers grandfather? Do you know them?" asked Jonah.

"No one knows them all. Not anymore. As the oldest and wisest of them ages and withers, a replacement is appointed. This replacement has received oral instruction, he has been prepared for many years, as I was prepared to replace my father Two Feathers before me. To this apprentice the knowledge has been passed in each of the seven tribes. He would know of the council and its purpose before his time to serve arrives, he would know the old stories as I know them for he would be required to learn them all through his years. Each apprentice is chosen at a young age and dedicates his life to the training. But in truth, the council does not meet, has not met but once in my life time...and I fear now many of the seven may not agree to council. But we must try."

Jonah understood Gray Wolf had been training him for many years as his replacement -- though he had never said it directly. He knew there was a council of the seven tribes, but he did not know their purpose

"Which tribes are the seven Gray Wolf?" asked Alex.

"Each of the seven tribes are represented by many clans – more than seven in all. The Cherokee of the east and the west, and those in Texas, they are represented by one u-la-gu - one council member, who also represents the Choctaw, Creek, Chickasaw and Seminole. Among the many Lakota tribes and the Cheyenne there is but one u-la-gu, one council member. But there is only seven in all. There is one far south in southern Mexico that represents the Maya and Zapotec and their brothers the Toltec, and one farther south," Grandfather answered. "Bringing them to council will be no easy task."

"And if you can gather these Keepers together, then what?" Molly asked.

"Then we must decide how to protect the secret knowledge, and determine if the location of the *e-ti-ka-i-e-le ny-va* has been compromised, and what to do with them if that is so."

"Gray Wolf, these crystals, are they large, small. Can they be moved?" Alex wanted to know.

"Yes. They can be held in one hand. How they work we do not know, but they are small." He sighed. "But I am weary now, and you also I sense. When the sun rises perhaps we will have answers to the question of how best to proceed."

As if on cue, Molly and Jonah stirred from the bench and Alex followed blindly.

"Alex, there is a warm place by the fire inside where you can catch some sleep. Morning's start early here," Jonah advised him

"Yes, thank you, but I have a few more questions for you...inside. Goodnight Gray Wolf and...well...thank you for speaking so freely. I can imagine such conversation is not meant for a stranger's ear such as mine."

"Um, Gray Wolf grunted. "You are a representative of President Garfield, or so it says in his letter to me. I will treat you as his replacement. You are welcome at my fire. And I think you are not so strange."

Turning back to his fire, it became obvious that Gray Wolf had said his last words for the night. He needed to consult with the spirits.

"Right…" Alex mumbled as he followed Molly and Jonah to the cabin.

Once inside, Alex found a comfortable spot to sit near the fire and looked around the cramped cabin at the collection of artifacts and memorabilia strewn across the room. There was a large and well used wooden pipe on the circular hearth that he assumed was for smoking, tanned hides bearing unfamiliar words written in the Cherokee syllabary hanging on the walls, a number of ceramic pots illuminated with geometric designs, and other Native American paraphernalia scattered randomly throughout the crowded room. It was almost surreal to Alex, an easterner as he was, sitting in the cabin of an Indian holy man in the heart of Indian Territory.

Molly had settled down by the fire Jonah was building and wrapped herself tightly in a blanket for there was a chill to the air.

"Jonah," Alex needed to bring Montana up to date. "I'm still trying to comprehend all this – these old stories are so foreign to me, of course. But I need to fill you in on some changes in Washington, there have been a few changes in the hierarchy of your, rather our service. With the death of President Garfield, technically we are working for President Arthur, but in a strange twist, Governor Cleveland of New York is a member of…" he glanced at Molly and decided she was part of this loosely organized team now, "the President's Ring and is now our new contact. There is a movement underway for him to seek nomination for the presidency at convention two years from now…probably our next president if the rumors are to be believed. I have met with Cleveland and have been instructed to report directly to him, meaning that is our boss. Garfield apparently handpicked Cleveland for the job until Arthur is…well, no longer president. I needed to make you aware of this. The Secretary of War is on board with this move, so this apparently will be where our new orders will come from. Cleveland is well aware of the nature of your, I should say our service, and is surprisingly supportive of our operations. He also has new information about a boiling conspiracy. There are powers at work Jonah, dark powers, with designs to bring down our American system, and Cleveland believes this is connected with the work we are involved in."

He waited for Jonah to respond. When he didn't, Alex continued.

"What I am saying is that for the time being it appears as though we are to operate independently of Washington. I will, of course, keep Governor Cleveland apprised of any major developments, but I suggest we remain guarded until we discover exactly who we are working for and have a better idea of the how that will work and what, exactly, is our new charge – if there is one. Washington is in a strange transition I'm afraid."

"So Alex, you're saying we're on our own."

"Well yes, I suppose, more or less. So determining our next move, we must work closely together, you and I."

"And Molly. Alex, I am afraid Molly is an important part of this team now and we need to make this official. You could say I have deputized her." Jonah informed him.

"Oh my, well…" Alex looked at Molly and back at Jonah, uncertain if he had the authority to add another agent.

"We don't have a choice in this Alex. You can tell Cleveland this if you like. We started this thing, and she has proven invaluable in making it work. Without her, in fact, you would be attending my funeral. So we need to put her on the payroll."

"Yes, well…" Alex had little choice. "I suppose I can arrange that. I have been given a budget – they call it a black budget, discretionary funds I understand, to use as required. So yes, Molly, welcome to the team after all, but you must not raise your hand to me again? Clear?"

"I can agree to that Alex, and for what it's worth, I apologize for taking a swing at you before. But as you said, all things are well that end well," she smiled. "Alex, how would you like a cup of strawberry tea?"

"Now that sounds wonderful Molly."

Jonah snickered.

CHAPTER TWELVE
A FOX IN THE HEN HOUSE

Ridley Willard had just returned from France and was meeting with Grover Cleveland for the first time since the Governor had assumed his new position as head of North American Culper Ring operations. The death of President Garfield was a troubling sign, not that it wasn't expected after taking a bullet to the chest. But evidence indicated that the assassination wasn't a random act, rather a planned attack by an organized group whose larger goal was the destruction, or serious crippling, of U.S. executive authority. Now Willard had new information about that conspiracy that he needed to share.

"Though we have never met Professor, your reputation proceeds you. I am well aware of your accomplishments as an educator and as an American. I understand you were the one that tutored young Montana?"

"I can't take the credit for that Governor. It was his grandfather, Gray Wolf, that directed him to me at the Seminary. It's fortunate for us that his grandfather is supportive of our cause," Willard was well aware of Cleveland's reputation as well, and was glad the new director was known for his honesty and straight-shooting style.

"Yes, Gray Wolf. Tell me, would you say the old Indian is loyal to the government?"

Willard was careful in his answer, but honest.

"Gray Wolf wasn't a major supporter of the rapid expansion of settlements into Indian territory over the last fifty years. Is he anti-American? No, I wouldn't say so. He understands times have changed and there's no going back. I believe he also views the U.S. government as the lesser of many evils. He believes there is a far darker force at work that is a common enemy to both the U.S. government and to Native culture."

"I see. What about Montana? Where does he stand on that issue? And tell me, wasn't the Seminary you directed actually a girl's school?"

"On the surface that was its purpose Governor, and it continues to enlist and instruct young women of the five civilized tribes. At the heart of it, it was a recruitment tool for young Indian men who had demonstrated a rare capacity for science and politics, a tool the Ring was using to help identify the best candidates to aid in the search for the answers we long have sought about the mythology, cosmology and secret arts of the local culture. The men's program was added six years ago and Montana was a member of the first graduating class."

"So the boy is educated, he holds a degree?"

"He graduated with honors. In fact, his aptitude goes far beyond the others enrolled in the program. He speaks multiple languages, is a master of modern literature, proficient in science and mathematics – a remarkable student."

"A half breed I understand"

"He is. His mother is mostly Irish, but even her grandmother was a half breed Cherokee."

"Well…let's hope he is more loyal to our cause than most of his kind. But that's not why you're here is it Professor?"

"No sir. I am certain you have been briefed on my recent travels in Europe. I have uncovered much I need to report." Cleveland nodded and leaned forward placing his hands on the desk across from Willard and motioned for him to continue. "I am sure you are aware of the Order of the Rose Cross."

"The Masons?" Cleveland asked.

"Not exactly Governor. The Masons are related, but mostly an auxiliary organization. In fact, the hierarchy of the parent organization is so complicated that it's nearly impossible to understand which was first, which is at the center of the broader network of organizations. Thelemic societies, the Society of the Horseman's Word, the Odin Brotherhood, the

Rosicrucians, the Illuminati, the Thule Society, the Order of the Rose, Freemasons, the Scottish Rite – they may all play a role large or small – or none at all – in what I have discovered to be the most secret organization of them all - operating within many of these same societies but with a much different mandate. "

"I have heard many of those names before. Go on..."

"I believe a nefarious and central organism exists, one that is very old, perhaps pre-dating the Greeks, that has obscure designs and interests to undermine the efforts of social advancement around the world for their own dark and unknown purpose. The other groups, such as the Masons, are not even aware of it. The end objective may be control, a power hungry and insatiable appetite to rule or subjugate. While I have no name for this secret organization, I have discovered they are often referred to as 'The Circle', or the 'Inner Circle', and I believe they have designs on our own government, perhaps because of our interest in the ancient arts and sciences of ancient America. A full report, filed with your office this morning, outlines the evidence I have collected, but let me say I believe that this group, this organization, has interacted in the past with many of the Native cultures of our nation. And I believe Gray Wolf may be able to shed light on this."

"Gray Wolf you say. That names keep coming up. And tell me Professor, do you believe this organization is at work within our own borders?"

"I believe they were here before us sir, and they have never left. I caution that this is an organization so far underground that it's possible many of their members could be our neighbors, our friends or even our ministers."

"Yes well...trust no one then, this is what you are saying. What else?"

"Just this Governor, a man lost his life telling me this, but it would seem that the core of this organization's operation in America is located in the City of New Orleans. I am afraid I don't have a great deal more, such as names and exact locations, but I do know that a ship arrived this week carrying what might be called a group of top operatives, specialists, from Europe, and I now have the name of that ship."

"Then prudence would dictate that you leave immediately, and take whomever and how ever many agents with you as needed. Should we send the Calvary I wonder?"

"I am afraid this will be a game of discovery and infiltration sir. And traveling there would require more time than we may have to discover this organizations operation and the purpose of these agents. An operation of stealth and secrecy is in order, and I believe Montana is our man."

"Of course, Montana. Where is he now?"

"In Indian Territory at last report, not far from the Gulf Coast by rail."

"Then make it so Professor, and supply him with whatever resources are required. But I want you there as well. Take your best man and let's get some answers. This is the first solid clue, perhaps, we have ever uncovered. And your sources can be trusted?"

"The Ring agent who lost his life to pass this information to me was my brother sir. I stake my life on it."

CHAPTER THIRTEEN
CHARIOTS OF FIRE

It is said there is no sin in killing a beast, only in killing a man.
But where does one begin and the other end...
-Gwen Conliffe

We knew the world would not be the same. A few people laughed, a few people cried, most people were silent. I remembered the line from the Hindu scripture, the Bhagavad-Gita. Vishnu is trying to persuade the Prince that he should do his duty and to impress him takes on his multi-armed form and says, "Now, I am become Death, the destroyer of worlds."
-J. Robert Oppenheimer

T he night was a short one. In spite of a few sips of strawberry tea to help them as they slumbered to focus on what they had heard, a great thunder roared in the sky outside and lightning flashed just beyond the blanket hanging over the doorway, rousing them from sleep. Jonah rolled out of bed reaching for the peacemaker in his holster, for this was strange sounding thunder like he had never heard before.

Alex was calling to him but the thunder drowned out his words. Molly was already up and reaching for the Winchester, which she had kept near her since that night in Kansas City.

The wind outside whipped the blanket over the doorway, revealing the shadowed figure of Gray Wolf standing there - and he was shouting.

"Get out of the cabin!" They could barely make out what he said.

Somewhere outside Jonah thought he could hear Shadow whinny, gusts of wind were blowing through the door and he could see only a small patch of night sky past grandfather. But staring at that patch of sky he suddenly stopped cold in his tracks. Then rushing past Gray Wolf he tried to focus on the giant shape that was hovering in the sky a few hundred feet in front of the cabin.

Molly stepped out behind him brandishing the Winchester but came up short when she spied the object as well, what could only be described as a giant metal airship in the night sky, a row of lights flashing around its circular body. Just then Alex ran into the back of her and nearly fell to his knees as he gasped at the sight.

Gray Wolf had darted into the cabin after their hasty exit but no one noticed for their eyes were frozen like their feet. The roar and thundering booms in the sky were nearly deafening, and when they did move, they skirted quickly to the side of the cabin. The boughs of the great Cypress that partially shaded the cabin were rocking and dust had filled the air.

The airship was substantial, at least the size of a large barn. Instinctively Jonah knew it must be the star people grandfather had been talking about – and not the friendly ones either, for as he watched every move of the giant machine, thin blue lines of what looked like lightning were forming on the leading edge of the circular disk. A moment later a bolt of this lightning shot down towards the ground and where it landed there was a small explosion. Dust and dirt and rocks went flying through the air and where the lightning struck there was a crater in the ground a couple of feet deep.

From the corner of her eye Molly saw Gray Wolf dart from the cabin door carrying something, she could not tell what, and he ran to the other side of the cabin and under the shelter of the trees on that side, his tunic blowing in the wind.

Jonah spotted Shadow and the other horses who had broken free of their tethers and were running away down the trail behind the airship. It was then the lightening flashed again and an explosion erupted on the ground not thirty feet in front of them. It was obvious the blast had been aimed at them and it sent them scrambling deeper into the woods. Another flash and another explosion hit the ground where they had been standing. Whoever, whatever was guiding this airship had spotted them and was firing upon them.

Jonah grabbed Molly by her hand and Alex blindly followed half in his boots and half out causing him to fall slightly behind. Stopping just long enough to raise one leg and pull the boot on securely, he jumped forward just in front of another of the blasts, narrowly escaping certain death.

Soon, under cover of the thick trees, they watched the airship spin quickly back toward the cabin, and then with another round of flashes and explosions the log and rock and mud cabin of Gray Wolf disintegrated into pieces, wood chips and chucks of mud and mortar thrown high into the air scattering across the landscape.

Jonah bolted toward where the cabin had once stood, fearing Gray Wolf was still inside. But before he could leave the cover of the trees an arm reached from the shadows of the thicket and Gray Wolf pulled him against the trunk of a large cottonwood. The airship circled over near where the cabin had once stood, hovered a few moments and then moved quickly away, disappearing over the near horizon. Watching it go, Grey Wolf loosened his grip.

"It is over Jonah. The day I have feared has arrived. The enemy has found at least one of the crystals, otherwise their ship would not fly, and they have come in search of the other crystals, of this we can be certain. War is on the horizon and they have cast the first stone. I saw this last night in a vision."

"The flying ship then, it is the Uk'tena?"

"Yes, it is the Uk'tena Jonah, and now our mission becomes urgent."

Alex and Molly stumbled up to them in the dark. Gray Wolf looked at Alex.

"You must get word to your leaders in Washington and tell them about the flying ship. They may know if this is the only one that has been seen or if there is more. The great flying warships have not taken to the skies for many generations. What we have seen bears ill news."

"Of course. I will send a telegram at first light."

"Grandfather," Jonah was realizing the truth. "If the flying warship, the aircraft, came for the purpose of destroying your cabin, this means it was not by accident. They know who you are, where they could find you."

"They know who I am, yes. They know much more than they should. If they are hunting me, then the other Keepers of the tribes are at risk as well."

"Jonah," Molly was piecing together the puzzle. "The creature in the canyon, you said you did not understand all that he said. Could he have been warning you to return here, to Grandfather, because he knew this was going to happen?"

Jonah considered it.

"There was an urgency in his message. Perhaps so. Yes, I suppose. I did not understand every word. But he indicated there was an urgency about bringing the message to Gray Wolf. Grandfather," he turned to his elder. "I did not think his message was a concern for your safety, but it may have been."

Gray Wolf nodded and walked toward the ruins of his cabin. The sky was turning lighter, the predawn had arrived and the old Cherokee began rummaging through the debris, casting aside first one item and then another.

Jonah, Molly and Alex joined him.

"Grandfather, all your belongings are lost," Molly couldn't find the right words to express her sorrow.

Without stopping his search, Gray Wolf glanced at her.

"All things can be replaced except for one."

Jonah looked at him a moment and realized what he meant.

"You're looking for something specific?"

"Here. Beneath the hearth," he squatted at the remains of the clay fireplace that sat in the middle of the cabin. The debris had been blasted in every direction but had caused no fire, nothing was burning expect for where the fire had once smoldered in the fireplace. That was how Gray Wolf found it. Grabbing a flat rock that had once been part of the hearth, the old Indian began to scrape at the last embers in the fireplace. A few inches down he scraped across metal.

"Here."

Jonah joined in clearing away the debris around the area and could see what appeared to be a metal object beneath where the fire had burned. They worked at clearing a larger area of ashes and embers and soon had uncovered the object, an oblong sheet of metal about two foot by three foot in size. The edges of the metal appeared ragged and torn. Alex joined in and carefully they pried first one end then the entire sheet up and slid it to the side exposing a hole in the ground beneath.

"When this cabin was built I dug a whole beneath where I was going to build the fireplace and covered it with this metal. The metal was taken from the field of battle when the Uk'tena attacked the Great City so many years ago. I believe it is part of one of their flying warships that was blown apart on the field of battle. As you see," Gray Wolf tapped on the metal sheet. "It is strong but light and does not burn when fire touches it. My father and teacher, Two Feathers, passed this to me many years ago and I used it to cover this hole in the ground. Inside I hid other things found on that battlefield. They have been kept in our family for many generations."

It had taken some time to uncover the hole and the first rays of the rising sun were stretching across the landscape bathing them in early morning light.

"We have company," Molly said nodding up the trail where several men were approaching. Gray Wolf looked up, sliding the metal back over the hole..

"Neighbors," he said. "They will wonder about the explosions."

He dusted off his hands and waited for the group to arrive, greeting them.

"Osiyo, *U na li he li tse ti.*"

The four visitors were neighbors and, as Gray Wolf said, had heard the explosion. Two of them had seen the airship fly away and all were concerned for Gray Wolf's safety. Looking at the field of debris, there was excited conversation and Jonah joined in. After a few minutes and much head nodding the men turned and headed back up the trail. Jonah turned to Molly and Alex, who had stood idly by watching it all but understanding little, or in the case of Alex, nothing at all.

"The tallest of the men was Principle Chief Bushyhead, and yes Alex, that is his name. Chief Marshal Tom Watie was the man in the blue shirt and two others were close neighbors. There will be a general council before the sun sets to talk about this," Jonah told them. "Gray Wolf explained that an old prophecy has come to pass and spoke of war coming to the nations."

"Oh my, an uprising," Alex said, genuinely concerned.

"This time Alex, I believe we will be fighting on the same side," Jonah responded. "Molly, while Grandfather is at the council, we must prepare to travel."

"And where are we going?"

"To a place near Cookson Bluffs on the river, to my father's home."

"Your father? You have never spoke of your father," Molly said, but Jonah had already turned to Alex, who was again rummaging through the debris of the cabin.

"Alex, You must send a telegram to…Governor Cleveland, and must travel to Fort Gibson and notify a Capt. J.C. Bates of what has happened here. You will need to use that little badge, I suspect, to get him to listen to you. He must be informed that the civilized tribes are preparing for war in response to the attack from the airship. He will probably think you are crazy, but you must make him understand and involve the President's office if necessary. The last thing we need is for the Calvary to think the tribes are preparing for war with them."

"Dear God Jonah, this goes beyond…I mean I have never…well, yes, of course. I see your point. War. That's such a frightful term," Alex looked uncertain.

"Tell him only what he needs to know. He must understand there is a new enemy, not only of the government, but an old enemy of the tribes, and that what is coming will require us all to work together. You can tell him you and I, representatives of the President, are working with the tribes to rally them to this cause."

"Yes…now that sounds good. How do I get there?"

"You can ride into town with me," Gray Wolf offered. "I will send a warrior with you, Chatsu, who the Calvary knows. The ride is not far. You can use the telegraph at Tahlequah."

Alex picked up his carpet bag he uncovered in the debris, still intact surprisingly, and holding up the slightly charred bag, he smiled.

"The telegraph, yes, well, that may not be necessary." He fumbled through the bag and pulled out an odd looking object with wires attached in several places. "I hope this isn't damaged. Yes, I think it's alright. I just need to hook into the telegraph line somewhere."

"Alex – your telephone."

"What? Oh, what a delightful name. I was wondering what to call it. Yes, yes…this is it, or a variation on it actually. And this one works, or it did when I left New York. Governor Cleveland has one in his office, we shall soon see if I can find somewhere to tap into the telegraph line."
Jonah looked at Gray Wolf who was shaking his head from side to side.

"I should have thought of that invention," he said with a twinkle in his eye. "Now, Jonah, help me here."

Jonah walked with Gray Wolf back to the metal plate covering the hole underneath where the fireplace once stood. Kneeling by the hole, he reached down into it and pulled up a cotton sack that appeared to be full of something. Setting it on the plate, he motioned for Jonah to open it.

It was wrapped and tied with leather strips and Jonah had to use his knife to cut the binding. Opening it and looking inside, he carefully, slowly removed an object shaped very much like his Colt peacemaker, but slightly larger and made of the same type of light metal the plate was made of. It was obviously some type of weapon, and suddenly Jonah became anxious and excited at the prospect. He looked at his grandfather in disbelief.

"These items were recovered long ago on the field of battle when the Uk'tena warriors assaulted the Great City. The warriors of both the Thunderbird and of our people fought side by side against them and many lives were lost. The war with the Uk'tena lasted many months and in many different places and the price we paid for it was many times greater than you can imagine."

There was sadness in the old man's eyes as he spoke of those ancient days as if he himself were there to suffer the losses. He cleared his throat and continued.

"Our ancestor Totomosku was the war chief our tribe, chief of the great city's warriors long ago. In those dark days when the war ended the enemy were thrown down, their ships disabled and most of their warriors destroyed. A small band of them fled and survived by hiding in the mountains to the far west. But they still had many of their smaller weapons, like the one you now hold in your hands. And now we know they still had some of their flying ships. Another time I will tell of how we sought them in their hiding places. But now I tell you of the sadness that comes with this last great battle. The Pleiades warriors, the soldiers of the Thunderbird, were small in number compared to the enemy, but they fought bravely beside the Cherokee and the Choctaw and warriors of the other tribes, and they gave up their lives on that battlefield. Only one survived."

Gray Wolf stood.

"Walk with me."

Jonah put the star gun back in the cotton and sack and twisting the top carried it with him as he followed Gray Wolf. Alex and Molly were busy rummaging through the debris again in search of their personal belongings that could be salvaged and they did not hear the conversation between Jonah and his grandfather.

Gray Wolf led him into the woods and down an embankment to the edge of a creek that flowed behind where the cabin once stood. Sitting on a log and motioning for Jonah to sit across from him, he continued his tale.

"The Pleiades survivor of that war, the last Star Man he was called in years that followed - for all the others had died and the larger contingent of Pleiades Star Men had long since left the planet to fight in the wars across the depths of space - but this last warrior wed a Cherokee woman who was a half breed herself. She gave birth to one son, and as he grew in years he married and was father to a single child, for it is inherent to the race of Pleiadians to have but a single child. Afterwards, whether woman or man, their seed dries up and they can bear none other, or can cause no more children to be conceived. It is their way and a part of their body's science, one I do not understand, but it is so. I tell you this because the time has come for you to understand many things about your own heritage my grandson."

Jonah fidgeted on the log because that familiar tingling sensation was crawling up the back of his neck. He was uncertain if he was prepared to hear this story.

"Grandfather, we are descended from this Star Man?"

"Not we. You my son, for your mother is the only descendent that survives in our time that carries the bloodline forward. You are her only child, and now you carry the blood of your star ancestor. It is true you are also Cherokee, born of a Cherokee father, a member of the warrior cult, the Wolf Clan. But it is from your mother that you inherit the blood of the Thunderbird, and this is why you walk a different path than others, why it was important for you to get the white man's education, to work for the white man's government. To you passes a great responsibility. If we survive this war, to you falls the responsibility of producing a son that will insure the blood of the star men does not end. But according to our ancient prophecies, it will be the son of star men that will lead the people in our final battle. I had hoped the war would not come in your lifetime, but I fear the Great Spirit has decided that time is upon us." "

"This is hard to grasp Grandfather, like a dream.".

"Yes my son, but it is not all that I have to tell you. The wolf clan, Jonah, while they are not a bad people, they are the dedicated enemy of the

Uk'tena. They are fierce because they are Cherokee warriors. But there is more to their story. As I told you, the Cherokee are known as the principal people. Long before the great mound city with its pyramids and star engines, our ancestors lived on an Island, Turtle Island, in the middle of the ocean. The Star Men of Pleiades brought us here thousands of years ago, and we lived in this Island kingdom and mined the earth on their behalf, not as slaves but as free people and by choice, for our craftsmen were expert in forming the tektite crystal that was found deep in the earth there. We took the raw material and refined it and crafted it into precious crystals that the Star men used to power their technologies, for our Milky Way, our universe, is but one of thousands where the technology of both the Pleiadians and the Uk'tena can not work without the crystals. If they do not have the crystals, they can not venture into thousands of star systems like ours, and in their war with one another, these star systems are important for there are other resources they need that are found only in these systems – like on the earth."

Jonah hung to every word now because he realized he was hearing history so ancient that few had ever heard it before.

"When the Uk'tena learned of the Island star base on earth they came and launched a great attack from the sea, for they are from a water world and are strongest in that element. There were Pleiades star warriors to protect the Island, and the Wolf Clan who served as the warriors of our own people. But the attack was swift and unexpected and the enemy was powerful and the Island kingdom fell into their hands eventually. They enslaved our people and killed our star guardians and for two generations we were slaves to the Uk'tena, the Dragon people."

"Grandfather, I am not sure I understand. My father, your son, taught me much about war and the warrior's way. The two of you taught me to hunt and to move like a panther in the forest and to walk invisible before men. But what are you not telling me? There is more to our warrior spirit?"

"A warrior must have the warrior's heart, and yes, there is more. Some things come natural for a warrior of the Wolf Clan. You have never been forced to use your warrior instincts, but the power is within you as it is with all Wolf Clan warriors, and I must show you this for speaking of it alone is not enough."

And with that Gray Wolf fell into silence, and for a moment Jonah feared the old man was suffering a heart attack, for he began to breath heavily, his fingers twitched and then his arms begin to flail and Jonah stood suddenly afraid for him. When he grabbed the arm of the old man to attend to what surely was a sickness or a seizure, Gray Wolf stood suddenly with great speed and Jonah jumped back quickly, for his grandfather's figure was no longer stooped but tall, much taller than it should have been. In fact, it was no longer Gray Wolf that stood before him, looming above him, but the figure of a beast. He wanted to run but his feet would not move and he suddenly gasped for breath but could find none. Fear seized Jonah, running up and down his spine, and the beast, who but a moment before had been his aging grandfather, was snarling and gurgling. It was a like a dream, a nightmare, and as if on cue, Jonah felt the tingling along his neck change to something more sinister, for as Gray Wolf transformed before his eyes, he looked down at his own hands and his fingers were extended, getting longer as were his arms. His chest heaved and he could feel his own face crawling with skin and muscle. His neck extended and his shirt began to rip from the transformation his own body was experiencing. His mind raced, and for a moment he felt he had lost all touch with reality.

Taking a step backward, Jonah tripped over the log on which he had been sitting and fell, nearly tumbling into the creek. He was on his feet in a second though and he could feel his heart beating in his chest, rapidly and strongly. He looked at grandfather again with eyes that were no longer his own, and to his surprise, Gray Wolf no longer looked like a beast. He was the aging Cherokee sage whose hair was silver white and long and there was a smile across his face. As suddenly as it had come the moment was passing. His breathing became more steady again, his arms and fingers shortened and in a moment he was the Jonah he had always known as well.

"Jonah," Grandfather was saying. "Relax grandson. It is over."

"It...what...Grandfather..."

"Be still and I will explain. Breath deeply and sit again with me."

Gray Wolf resumed his seat on the log and motioned Jonah to do the same as if nothing had happened.. Reluctantly he complied.

"There was no easy way to show you grandson that the Wolf Clan are shape changers by nature. That includes you, your father, and I. It has been this way since the days of old when the Uk'tena changed us forever with their science. It is our power, our magic, but also a curse, perhaps. The enemy star people experimented on our ancient ancestors centuries ago, modifying what they call our genetic structure to create a slave race of warriors they could command on earth. But the plan failed in time, for those early shape changers grew powerful and turned on their slave masters, the hunter became the hunted. We are their enemies Jonah for we swore vengeance for what they had done. You see, they are shape changers too Jonah, but not like us for we bear the distant blood of the Pleiades star people, and when they altered our genetic structure something went wrong. They wanted to make us more like them. But what they created was something much different. We could change, but only into the shape of the wolf, for that is our heritage. They realized their experiments had failed for we had a mind of our own, and they had intended us to be mindless servants. They feared us for we were stronger than they were in some ways, more powerful when we changed. In years that followed we sought them in their mountain hideaways and we destroyed them whenever we could find them and they grew to fear us even more."

Questions flooded Jonah's mind. Many things he did not understand, and would not for years to come.

"When you were changing, transforming, you did this by will?" he asked.

Gray Wolf nodded.

"But I too began to change and I was not trying…did not will it."

"It is new to you Jonah. One day you would have changed on your own, but you may not have realized that you did. It would seem like a dream when it was over. This magic, this curse, it can be controlled, and this is the real power. You must concentrate on the transformation and doing so you can call it or refuse it. These things you have not learned. But now you must. And because of your mother, you have a pure bloodline connection to the Thunderbird star race, unlike most of us. In you the power is even stronger. This is why I think the creature you call a vampyre was after you. He was a Uk'tena shape changer, and I believe he was waiting for you in Kansas City because the enemy has discovered you are the star child. It was not by accident."

"How could he know I would in Kansas City grandfather?"

"I think the enemy has many spies now. They may have followed you since your meeting with President Garfield. I do not know Jonah"

"And my mother, she can change?"

137

"No. Your mother can not change, for the bloodline comes from your father, from the Cherokee bloodline. But because you are a child of both, you are special among our people, son of Wolf Clan and child of the stars.

Now, your mother and father await you grandson and each will tell you more, that which they have hid from you for many years."
Gray Wolf picked up the cotton sack from the ground and handed it to Jonah.

"Inside are the powerful and ancient instruments of war. When you are alone, examine them and learn to use them. You will need them. Now you must go to your mother and father and learn more," he said.

Gray Wolf stood and headed back up the embankment to rejoin Molly and Alex. Jonah was slow to follow, absorbing all that he had heard, but grabbing the sack he hurried along as a chill crawled up the back of his neck.

CHAPTER FOURTEEN
THE ENEMY'S PLOT

A belligerent state permits itself every such misdeed, every such act of violence, as would disgrace the individual. -*Sigmund Freud*

Fanchon Harleaux stood in the basement of his New Orleans Château in a War Room full of sophisticated electronic devices and strange looking equipment, blinking lights on several panels flashing in time with the drama that was unfolding on the view screens stationed around the room.

At the largest of these screens Ntsuuman Igatruub, Premont of the Uk'tena forces, sat at a control panel listening to reports being offered by the captains of the two Uk War Birds only recently reactivated by the crystals they had recovered. He was clothed in the uniform of a Uk'tena warrior for there was no need to conceal his true nature inside the fortress room where no human dared to walk. The scaled breathing organs behind his ears rose and fell as the reptilian-like creature struggled to breath the poisonous earth atmosphere in and out of his three lungs, assisted by a latex tube that rhythmically provided bursts of oligopeptide-enhanced mist that made earth's harsh environment tolerable and survivable. When not assuming the shape of the human creatures it was difficult to breathe on this world. On his home world the atmosphere was rich in moisture, so dense that the walls would run with condensation and the floor was perpetually wet. Even though the war room environment was controlled and great humidifiers kept the moisture content high, it was wasn't nearly as rich as his natural habitat and it caused his lungs and gills to labor.

He ran a hand over the scaled ridge in the middle of his forehead and his fingers traced it back to the top of his head and down the back of his neck where it connected to his ribbed spine. His unusually large and bulbous eyes darted across the control panel, a device that allowed him to keep track of their assets in the air. His job was to control and command the War Birds, sending them where Harleaux directed. But these War Birds were piloted by *Kriegers*, and he, and everyone else, feared them, and he was careful not to issue commands they might consider contrary to their own designs. It was a difficult position to be in, but he knew he shared that concern with Fanchon, who in spite of being High Governor of the American contingent of the Circle, was none-the-less lower on the pecking order in the eyes of Supreme Commander Thet than was his beloved *Kriegers*. They were his pets, his trusted personal guard, and respected assassins. To fall in their disfavor was paramount to professional suicide – if not worse.

"Fanchon," the commander addressed Harleaux by what was actually his rank and title and not his name. "The Cherokee sage was not found, but his dwelling was destroyed."

Fanchon Harleaux was visibly agitated.

"I want that War Bird back on the scene. This Gray Wolf is key to our operation, and his grandson, this Montana, he is a critical target as well. They are together now and we must capture one and kill the other."

"Yes sir, but the War Bird is currently in pursuit of the ghost dancer Wokava and Krieger Hrlwh Wrhll has decided to pursue the Paiute first. Should I order them off and send them back at your command?"
Harleaux considered it for a moment. The Paiute was also a key element in the plan, but more importantly, he feared to lock horns with the Krieger.

"Have them capture him quickly and then return capture the Cherokee oracle and destroy the young Tenkiller. And what of Commander Khlgg's ship?"

"Khlgg is far south over the place called Teot. He has decimated a village where the Aztec sage was last known to frequent and they are following his trail into the mountains. The ship has landed and the *Krieger* is scouring the area searching for his scent. It has been reported that the trail is fresh."

Harleaux stormed from the war room and headed back to his private chambers. He hated that the *Krieger* were now involved, in spite of them being assigned directly by Supreme Commander Thet. It was a two-edged sword. If they were successful in this campaign, the crystals would be acquired and the power restored to the Uk'tena. But the credit would fall to Thet and his faceless assassins. It could be construed as a failure on his part, a mismanaged campaign that required Thet's involvement, and he could easily fall out of favor in an organization that was as ruthless and heartless as their designs on the planet.

Had he been successful in recovering the crystals without the Krieger's involvement, or if the artificial crystals he attempted to develop would have worked in powering the airships, Thet would have had little choice but to acknowledge his worth and shower him with the rewards that were his due. But his utter failure to reproduce new crystals over the years, ending in the loss of at least two air ships, required him to resort to recovering the ancient crystals from the Keepers.

He secretly hoped to find a way to steal the victory from the Kriegers in the end. He could only hope that many of them, at least a few, would meet an untimely end at the hands of the Wolf Clan people.

At the thought of the Wolf Clan he shuttered, not with fear so much as with hatred for their kind. He absently ran his fingers over the long scar across his neck, a reminder of his last contact with them. Fanchon was old even by Uk'tena standards, and he remembered the battle on the plains of the Great Mound City. It was here the Wolf man called Totomosku had transformed into the form of the beast and ripped through his muscle and tissue and very nearly ended his life. He had not forgotten - would never forget - and vowed vengeance against all the people of Earth, especially the Wolf clan.

Now that chance was becoming a real possibility and he could almost taste the blood of his enemy. There was nothing he wanted more than to persecute these miserable creatures who had spoiled his plans and nearly caused his entire race to disappear from the face of this wretched planet.

His hatred made him hungry again and he called for Lacosta. He would taste the flesh and drink the blood of more humans, and in so doing would find strength and inspiration. It would bring him comfort and pleasure knowing that soon it would be the blood of the Wolf he would taste, and he savored the thought.

The servant Lacosta entered his chambers, somehow knowing the will of his master before the words were ever spoken. He simply nodded at Fanchon and left the chamber to find more earth women for his feeding.

While he waited for Lacosta to secure his next meal, Harleaux began to formulate a plan that would discredit Thet's Kriegers in the end, and perhaps even serve to make Thet himself appear auxiliary to the great victory he was planning. After all, if the crystals were recovered, they would be in his hands first, and what an opportunity that would provide to for him to make his move to the top of the order. Supreme Planetary Commander Harleaux – he liked the sound of it.

CHAPTER FIFTEEN
THE WINDS OF WAR

We've made too many compromises already; too many retreats. They invade our space and we fall back. They assimilate entire worlds and we fall back. Not again. The line must be drawn here! This far, no further! And I will make them pay for what they've done!

Jean-Luc Picard, STNG

Their plan had been put in motion. Alex traveled west to Tahlequah with Gray Wolf and was to be placed in the care of Chatsu, the Wolf Clan warrior. Had he known he would ride with a shape changer that could turn into a beast and devour him at will, he would have died of fear alone. But Chatsu was stoic and had been charged by Gray Wolf to take the inventor safely to Fort Gibson. He would die before abandoning the task.

Along the way to Tahlequah Gray Wolf pointed out to Alex where he could tap into the telegraph wires that stretched across Indian Territory. Demonstrating an amazing agility for his age, Gray Wolf scaled the pole and cut the line, dropping one end so that Alex could hook it into his telephone.

It took some time to raise Cleveland's New York office, and more time for Cleveland to be rustled out of an important meeting. But once the Governor came to the phone and with much electronic interference and many adjustments, Alex was able speak to him. Cleveland was amazed and impressed with the invention, but it was necessary for both of them to shout into the mouthpiece in order to hear each other. None-the-less it worked, and in a reasonably short time Alex conveyed the latest developments in Indian Territory. Cleveland acknowledged the message and they signed off, the first long distance phone call in history, though few would ever know of it.

Gray Wolf scaled the pole again and reconnected the two ends of the telegraph line before they continued their way to Tahlequah.

Soon Alex was on his way to Fort Gibson with Chatsu and Gray Wolf sat with the Cherokee General Council and brought them up to date not only on the recent developments, but took the time to recount their ancient stories, especially the tales involving the Uk'tena. The council lasted long into the afternoon and in the end it was decided a special council of the Five Civilized Tribes was required, and runners were sent to villages across the territory. They would meet that night or the next morning once representatives of the tribes arrived.

Jonah and Molly headed northeast up the Illinois river basin in route to Jonah's childhood home for a reunion with his father and mother. He was uneasy bringing Molly along, but circumstances dictated his action. It was better to have her with him after the encounter with the flying airship. Now that he knew he was being targeted, he was afraid to leave her alone in the event the enemy returned, but he was also concerned about how he was going to have a serious conversation with his parents about the heritage they had kept from him in the presence of Molly. Perhaps, he reasoned, it would be better to tell her what he had learned from Gray Wolf now and avoid surprises later. But he dreaded telling her that she too had become endangered because he had become a target. They talked as they rode gingerly through the a countryside and after an hour or so Molly summed it up and made it all sound simple.

"So let me make certain I am understanding this correctly. Your mother is a descendant of a star being and your father is actually a werewolf, and that makes you a beast who came from another planet, one this enemy wants dead, and me along with you. Why would that be hard to understand?"

She wasn't trying to be funny. She didn't intend to sound cynical. Things were simply the way they were, unbelievable in many ways, hard to accept in fact. But so had most of their shared experiences. She still wondered if it was possible some of what grandfather had told him could have been allegorical, and she said so.

"Okay Jonah. Look. It's not that I am skeptical, but do think some of this you have learned could be part of Cherokee legend or myth? Transforming into a beast - it's incredible. And now you're going to confront your parents with this. I mean, are you sure this is the right thing to do?"

Jonah knew how incredible it sounded. He was still trying to wrap his own head around it and now he was trying to explain it to a person who perhaps could not possibly understand.

"Molly. I admit it's hard to swallow – even for me. It's crazy. But I know what I saw, and it was not an illusion or an hallucination. I know grandfather speaks nothing but the truth. Meeting my parents knowing what I know now, I can't imagine how that might go. Can you imagine your own father and mother keeping something from you your entire life only to discover it later from someone else - then having to face them over the issue?"

She surprised him again. More softly, the disbelief gone from her voice, she leaned over in the saddle and grasped his shoulder in a gesture of reassurance.

"Jonah, life with you has been one big adventure. The things we experienced, what we went through in Montana and Kansas, they were incredible too. And look at it this way, I accomplished what I set out to do. I have proof that my uncle is not crazy. As far as this incredible tale of shape shifting and enemy star people and how they're breathing down our necks and how we might die at any moment – what the heck. With you, the impossible seems to be possible. We've survived so far haven't we? "

She smiled and Jonah tried to smile back. It was a crazy tale alright, more than any story in any book he had ever read. But he was glad in one way that he had Molly with him. To be such a loner, he needed a friend now.

The trail led over a small hill and they looked down at a farm house, not unlike the one in which Molly was raised, smoke streaming from a chimney, sheep standing in next to a red barn, and chickens running around behind the house. It was a tree studded valley and looked like a perfect place to grow up.

"That's it Molly, that's where I was born and where I grew up."

"Well, it's picture perfect. Shall we ride down and meet mom and dad?" She refrained from the wise crack that crossed her mind.

Taking the path down the bluff and fording the river they rode into the farm yard just as Jonah's father, Tillman Tenkiller, came out of the door and stepped on to the porch. Spotting the riders, he called over his shoulder and a moment later Jonah's mother joined him, a smile on her face.

"*U-s-ti wa-ya*. You've come home," Jonah's mother was an attractive woman, and Molly thought she looked more Irish than she did Cherokee, or a star being - whatever they might have looked like.

Sliding off the rear of Shadow he met her on the bottom step and hugged her.

"Hello Mother. Father."

Tillman grasped Jonah by the shoulders with both hands and said something in Cherokee that Molly did not understand. It was a homecoming that so far seemed perfectly normal to Molly.
Jonah turned to her as she was slowly dismounting, and introduced her.

"This is Molly. We work together. She is my partner."

"Work together?" His mother sounded disappointed, but smiled and extended a hand of friendship. With a small grin on his face, Jonah's father simply nodded.

After salutations and small talk they were invited in and Molly was surprised again that the log farm house was cozy and well furnished, not unlike the house where she was raised. It was a great contrast to the simplicity of Gary Wolf's cabin, which she assumed was a typical Cherokee dwelling. This home certainly had the tell-tale touch of a woman behind it and she immediately felt a degree of comfort; she felt at home.
Loraine, Jonah's mother, insisted on tea and Molly was pleased to find it was not made from strawberry root. It tasted sweet in fact, and slightly nutty, and very pleasant.

There was more small talk between them for a while and soon it was time to get to the heart of the reason for their visit. The mood changed as Jonah told them about their encounters across the West. He only touched on their encounter with the so called vampyre, Molly reasoned because he wanted to spare his mother of the gore and violence, but he did go into detail about the flying airship and the emergency council that Gray Wolf had called. And then he dropped the bombshell.

146

"You know that I think the world of both of you. And I would never harbor unjust feelings or resentment for the decisions you have made as it relates to my upbringing. I understand that when I was younger I was not ready to hear many things about our family history. But I need to ask you some questions now, and please don't hold back because Molly is here with us. She has been a part of this unfolding story since the beginning. Grandfather has approved of her being present during his tales about our heritage and I want you to know she can not only be trusted with what may be said now, but it is important that she knows. As I said, she is my partner and she is very much involved in the developments that are facing our people. I know much more about our history now because Gray Wolf has told me about our Wolf Clan, father, and mother about your guarded past and how that relates to me. I have been told about our ancient enemies, the serpent people. And I know of our magic. I watched grandfather transform this morning, and I partially transformed myself."

This Molly did not know, but she remained silent.

"Mother, I know that I am the last of our race on earth other than you. I also know you harbored me from this knowledge for good reason and I do not hold this against you, I understand it was necessary. But a new age has arrived and grandfather says I must step into the future. I have come to learn the old ways of both clans; what I am and how I can use it to protect our people."

It was a day for surprises. He had half expected them to show some degree of guilt over keeping this information from him. He expected them to be reluctant about telling him more, especially with Molly in the room. But it was not so. Grandfather's approval apparently weighed heavy with them, and they were both surprisingly eager to talk and answer his questions. The conversation went on well over an hour and Molly absorbed it all, an incredible story that sounded like the plot of a book unfolding.

Mid afternoon had arrived and Loraine retired to the kitchen to prepare a late noon meal. Molly helped her in the kitchen, and Loraine spoke openly to her, accepting without question that she was a part of this now and a trusted part of her family. Molly admired how trusting the Cherokee could be once they accepted you.

While in the kitchen, Tillman talked with Jonah more about the clan's history and recounted many great battles credited to the clan. He spoke of controlling the beast and how to force the change to happen and how to make it go away when the form of the beast was no longer desired or needed.

It was more information than Jonah should have learned in one day, but he clung to every word and asked many questions. After their meal Tillman took Jonah to the barn and there he transformed for him, not like grandfather had turned, but a complete transition to a wolf that could stand on two legs or run on four, and then he insisted that Jonah make the change as well. Jonah was amazed at how easy it was for him, a matter of will, knowing what would happen, remaining in control, a contrast to his first experience. He had feared he would lose control, like the stories he read of lycanthropes and werewolves. But it wasn't that way at all. And as a wolf he ran from the barn with his father and for a short time they explored the woods down by the river and Jonah was amazed at his enhanced sense of smell and hearing and more so at the strength he possessed; his ability to climb trees using claws and jump large obstacles in a single bound. He then found it easy to transform back to human form and found himself exhilarated by the experience. Afterwards he laughed hard, as did his father.

Eventually they went back into the farm house and as they entered Loraine laughed at them and their tattered clothes. Molly was slightly startled at their ragged appearance but managed to smile as she ruffled Jonah's unkempt hair. This wasn't at all how she expected this meeting to go.

It was getting late into the afternoon and the time had arrived for them to head back to check on the recent developments in Tahlequah, but not until Loraine tried to convince them to stay the night. Jonah expressed the urgency to return to Tahlequah and they headed out where the horses had been stabled. They were rested and the ride back should take less than two hours, putting them back in Tahlequah shortly before dark if they hurried, so off they rode as an early October moon rose above the bluff across the river. It was not a full moon, but Jonah laughed at the thought. The moon, as it turned out, had nothing to do with Wolf lore, contrary to the books he had read.

Tahlequah, Five Civilized Tribes General Council

Cherokee council meetings were rarely short and the one in progress now required a great deal of story telling. Gray Wolf commanded the attention of the tribal elders, who had assembled from across Indian Territory on very short notice. He spent hours talking of the ancient stories and slowly but surely brought them up to date with the most recent developments.

There were a few elders among them that remembered the old stories and had kept them fresh in their minds; a few had heard only parts of the stories or believed the old tales were as much myth as they were truth. But there were large numbers of Cherokee that had seen the Uk'tena War Bird flying and many of them were asked to recount their stories.

Long after midnight the council had made a decision. The tribes would be instructed to prepare for war, and runners and riders were sent to the far reaches of the five civilized tribes. Other riders would carry the word as far west and north as was possible to inform the distant tribes, the Sioux and Cheyenne in the north, the Apache and Navajo and Pueblos in the West. It would require many weeks for the word to reach them all and the Council knew by then it could be too late.

Another problem was a greater challenge, how to gather the Keepers of each of the scattered tribes and bring them to council. The tribes had ventured too far and too wide in recent times and tribal conflicts had alienated them and caused great divisions. There was little communication between them in modern times and Gray Wolf worried they may not be able to determine if the Keepers of each tribe were still active. Most important of all the Council agreed they needed to discover how many of the seven crystals had been uncovered by the enemy and how to best protect the remaining ones.

Gray Wolf knew in his heart their chances of finding out these things was nominal at best, and he was suddenly sad that the tribes had drifted so far apart and were divided by so much dispute and cultural difference. His best hope now rested with the White eyes, their Calvary. If Washington could send telegrams to distant forts, perhaps they could at least provide fresh reports about airship sightings. He would also provide them with the names of the Keepers that he knew in hopes they might be informed of the need for council. He didn't like the thought of relying on the U.S. Government for it had seldom been a friend to their cause. But he also knew the dangers presented by the Uk'tena outweighed his distrust. At least they were human – even if they rarely acted as such.

Fort Gibson, Indian Territory

"Excuse me, but may I see that badge again. I have never heard of a special agent to the President," Captain Bates was all military and protocol. "Of course," Alex attempted to sound confident and authoritative. But the West was for men like Bates and Gray Wolf, not him, and he felt terribly out of place. Bates was being difficult at best, a practical man who was accustomed to all things being black and white. Alex knew to convince him, to spur the Captain to action, he must be firm and convincing.

"But I can't impress on you enough the need for haste. Captain, as far flung as the story may seem to you, I am charged by the President of the United States, your Commander in Chief, to address the threats that pose a risk to our national security, and this threat, a flying airship of advanced technological capabilities, and an alien race of slave traders hell bent on destroying our country, our nation, is far above your rank and your clearance level. Now I invite you to telegraph my superiors, or the President himself if you like, and get whatever clearance you require to get off your backside and call the troops to action, and while you're at it, you might explain to the President why you are dragging your feet when the nation is at danger."

Alex was bluffing of course, making an attempt to sound tough. He secretly hoped the President wouldn't receive a telegraph. President Arthur probably didn't even know who Alex was. He decided he had better add to the story to cover himself just in case.

"Let me be perfectly frank Captain. Since the death of President Garfield, our new President may not be up to par with the procedures in place related to matters of our national security. Let me add that the enemy has planned and plotted for this, and we have reason to believe that is why President Garfield was the victim of a diabolical plot involving his assassination. New York Governor Grover Cleveland, who I might add will be your next president, is in charge of this operation along with senior members of the President's Secret Service," Alex had just made that name up, but it sounded good. "So for God's sake and for sake of country sir, please do what you must to get your confirmation with haste. Don't go down in history as the man who failed to move his feet fast enough to avoid defeat at the hands of an enemy so great and powerful that our government could crumble because of your indecision."

Alex was proud of the speech he made, and it obviously got Bate's attention. He looked visibly taken back, nervously looking first at the other officer in the room, his adjutant, and back at Alex, apparently considering what action to take.

"Mr. Bell, I had the great pleasure of meeting President Garfield last year, just before the election, and I was a supporter of his run for high office. We'll get that confirmation, but first we will answer the call for action as you have convinced me of the urgency of this matter. Provided you are willing to accept the responsibility for it, then we shall proceed as you suggest. We as of yet do not have telegraph service at this Fort, but I will make my troops available to your cause as required, for God and Country sir."

Alex breathed a big sigh of relief. He had been pressed to perform in an area outside his comfort zone. Military operations, anti-government conspiracies, policy making decisions - these were things for which he was not at all qualified. But his bluff had worked, by hook or crook, and that was all that was important.

"Thank you Captain. I will make certain that my report reflects your admirable caution as well as your quick response to the emergency. Perhaps in the near future I will address you as Major Bates."
It was the right trigger to pull by the look on Bates' face.

"Now, let's get envoys moving to the four corners of this territory and let them know that a High Council in Tahlequah is preparing the tribes for war with an enemy that has command of flying warships. If it flies, it's not friendly Captain. Let's make the tribes aware that the U.S. Government is in full support of their preparing for battle, and make certain they understand we are all on the same side in this conflict. Every man woman and child, Indian or white, is at extreme risk from this enemy. You can tell them this enemy is known among the tribes as the Uk'tena. This they should understand, and you must tell them that their Keepers, their chief history tellers, are to travel to Tahlequah with haste for an emergency council with Gray Wolf, the Great Cherokee sage. This is the message we need to deliver to the tribes. Let's make it so."

On the Road to Tahlequah
Jonah and Molly had followed the river south and had ridden for more than an hour when they reached another section of bluff where large

boulders were scattered about. The moon had risen higher though the sun was yet to set. There were no homes or farms nearby that they could see, so Jonah pulled up near the bluff and dismounted, pulling the cotton sack from his saddlebag, the same one he and Gray wolf had pulled from the hole in the ground beneath the fireplace.

"I was beginning to wonder when you were going to tell me what was in that sack," Molly said as she climbed down from her saddle. "I saw grandfather give it to you. I had hoped it was something to eat."

"You really like to eat don't you?" He smiled at her. "I don't really know what all is inside. This was in the hole beneath the fireplace. Grandfather said they were ancient relics collected from the battlefield where the tribes and the Thunderbird warriors fought the Uk'tena many years ago. He said we would need them. One of them, which I have briefly seen, is something you're going to like."

Reaching into the bag Jonah pulled out the star gun. Molly looked it over. It was obviously a weapon for its shape was similar to a revolver but wider in the middle, constructed of the same light metal they found on the Kansas plain. The object sported a longer barrel than a Colt Peacemaker and was wider around, but it appeared to serve the same purpose.

Jonah could see no place to load bullets, but noticed there was what looked like a trigger on the bottom side and three switches on top. Carefully, he moved the first sliding switch with his thumb. Nothing happened. But when he tried the second switch, it clicked into place and there was a slight whining noise that came from inside of the star gun. He tried the third switch and the whining intensified. He toggled the switch back and the noise returned to the way it sounded before.

Molly watched him handle the object carefully and he began to feel a little uneasy.

"You know that is not from this world. I would be very careful."

But it was like handing a new toy to a child and telling him not to play with it. Jonah turned and looked at the river below the bluff and lifted the star gun to arm's distance and slowly squeezed the trigger. In an instant there was a flash, much like those they had seen come from the flying airships but without the lightning, and immediately there was an explosion at the edge of the far bank of the river. Jonah looked at Molly and back at the gun. Molly looked startled, but she smiled.

Moving the second switch back where the whining noise was greatest, Jonah again took aim at the bank, about 50 yards below them, and squeezed the trigger a second time. There was a another flash, but more brilliant this time, and when an impact struck the bank a second time, a huge chunk of earth was obliterated leaving a gaping hole that quickly filled with water from the river.

Jonah yelped with excitement.

"Yeah! Now that's what I'm talking about!"

He tried the remaining switch again and still nothing happened, but when he squeezed the trigger a third time, larger bolts of energy sprang from the barrel, this time the blast divided into five distinct energy charges and peppered the distant bank in a wide array of destruction.

"Now that's what we needed this morning when the airship was hanging in the sky above grandfather's cabin."

Molly nodded in agreement, but the shear power of the weapon, she thought, was frightening. Yet, she immediately wanted one!

"Is there's another one of those in there?"

Jonah toggled the power switch off and could hear the whining noise subside. Handing it to Molly, he reached into the bag again, pulling out a circular object, similar to a pocket watch with two switches below the blank face. Sliding one of the switches a light came on and a checkered grid formed on what turned out to be a small screen. There were small lighted letters that formed on the bottom of the grid but Jonah did not recognize them as any language he had ever seen.

"What is it?" Molly asked.

"I don't know," Jonah slid the second switch and the grid became smaller, but still there was nothing more to see. He placed the object on a boulder and reached into the sack a third time, bringing out the last two items. It was a pair of identical instruments small enough to fit into the palm of his hand. There was a single switch near the top and on the side of each, but when he tried to slide the switch as he did on the other two objects, it would not move.

Setting the star gun on the boulder, Molly took one of the small objects and fiddled with the switch as well.

"I can't make it work."

They both were startled, for not only could her voice be heard as she spoke, but the words were coming from inside the other small object that Jonah held in his hand. Jonah looked puzzled.

"Oh, Alex is going to like this. Do that again."

"Do what?"

"Keep talking and play with the switch again."

"I didn't play with the switch, I pushed down on it."

When she said 'down again' she had pushed in the switch a second time and again Jonah could hear her voice inside the small box in his hand.

"Stay right here," Jonah picked up the gun and with the other device trotted off across the bluff a few hundred feet. As he ran he pressed down on the switch on the box he held.

"Can you hear me now?"

"Oh my God. Your voice is in the box. It's like Alex's talking box," Molly said while pushing down on the switch of her box.

Jonah turned and headed back toward her pressing his switch again.

"I only heard part of what you said. You must press down on the switch and hold it firmly, then talk before I can hear you."

They played with the boxes for a few moments, and then Jonah jumped on Shadow's back and trotted away down the path toward Tahlequah. A good distance later he pressed the switch."

"Can you hear me now?"

There was a slight crackle sound and her voice came ringing through.

"Like you were standing right next to me."

He repeated the process again and again riding further away down the path. After a couple of miles, he called and asked her to ride up and join him.

Catching up Molly was all smiles.

"This must be technology from another world Jonah. I know you know this, but it's so fantastic. But what about that other item?"

They both dismounted and Jonah was already playing with the object again, but this time he noticed something different. There was a small flashing light located in the upper corner of the grid. And it was moving. Toggling the other switch he noticed the flashing light was still visible on the smaller grid but the little light was even smaller and further away from the center. They watched the light move across the grid for a while, switching between the smaller and larger grids. The shadows were beginning to fall now as the sun reached the horizon and soon dusk would arrive, but still they studied the instrument and wondered at its purpose.

"Jonah, I can't make heads or tails of this, but you know, it slightly resembles the grids of a map, a larger map and a smaller map maybe."

"Then how would you explain the little light?"

The 'little light' was still moving in the larger grid, a little faster on the smaller grid and nearing the center of all the grid lines. As if on cue, Molly heard the slightest whir of sound in the air in the distance and looked up across the river to see what she thought might have been an eagle or vulture in the sky. Watching it a few moments, the realization set in. Jonah had come to the same conclusion almost simultaneously.

"Molly, take cover!"

Jonah slapped the mare on the rear and kicked Shadow into action. The mare ran up the trail and Shadow ran down the trail in the opposite direction. The thick trees and the boulders offered good cover for Jonah and Molly and they quickly ducked out of sight in opposite directions. Jonah fumbled at putting the grid device in his only pocket and grabbed the cotton sack that held the gun.

Molly had found a section on the bluff and took cover behind a particularly large boulder, brandishing the Winchester which she always carried with her. Almost immediately the Uk'tena War Bird swooped from the sky and released a barrage of energy blasts in their direction. It looked like the same bird that had destroyed Gray Wolf's cabin early that morning, though they couldn't be certain.

The initial barrage scattered across the trail where they had been standing leaving a line of impact craters some 10 feet apart and three or four feet deep. Because of the bluff behind them, the War Bird had to pull sharply up as it passed overhead. It slowly began to swing around though Jonah knew it was coming in for a second pass. He wondered why the flying ship was targeting them, how could it have found them on the open trail. Little did he know that when he fired the blaster across the river it had registered on a screen inside the airship - in spite of it being hundreds of miles away at the time. It was already on a return run to Cherokee country as ordered by Premont Igatruub when it picked up the energy signature of Jonah's blaster.

While the ship made its wide circle preparing for another strafing run, Jonah seized the opportunity to gain higher ground among the boulders above and behind him. He switched on the Uk blaster as he ran and found an appropriate crag between boulders where he could dig in and await its return. There was a squawk on the communication box in his pocket and as the airship came back into view across the river, he fumbled getting it out once he heard Molly's voice on the other end.

"Are you alright Jonah? Can you hear me?"

He triggered the button and yelled into the box.

"Molly, turn off the box. Put it down and move to another location. I think the airship can hone into these instruments when we use them. Molly!"

It was too late, for indeed, as soon as the War Bird made the wide circle and approached their position, lower in the sky this time, a signal appeared on the control screen inside the ship and the Uk' gunner marked Molly's position first, and then Jonah's second. He let loose another round of blasts at his first target and quickly retargeted to get a round off in Jonah's direction. The first volley fell slightly short of the boulders where Molly was hidden, yet she screamed at the impact. By the time the ship fired on Jonah, he had already moved to higher ground and the blasts fell harmlessly fifty feet behind him.

Jonah was running on the bluff jumping now from the tops of one boulder to the next, fully exposed and in the open. Having heard Molly's screams and thinking she might be injured, he hoped to draw their fire and get into a better position to get a visual on her location. But when another round of blasts erupted in the general direction where he guessed she was hiding, he pulled up long enough to raise the blaster in his hand and took a wild shot at the War Bird in hopes of distracting it. To his surprise, with the switch still set to full array, two of the five energy blasts hit the ship on its leading edge causing it to wobble and then veer from its flight path. Small chunks of metal were thrown out from the ship and a thin stream of smoke billowed from the impact point.

Almost immediately the ship righted itself, but turned suddenly and moved away over the ridge above him. Jonah aimed and fired again but his shots went wide. The War Bird disappeared behind the ridge and Jonah whipped out the grid device from his pocket. Consulting it, he confirmed the ship had crested the bluff and settled down on the ground a short distance beyond.

He fought his way to the top of the bluff and peered over the edge. When the smoking ship landed, three spider-like legs had extended from underneath and a door located on its belly had opened and a ramp extended to the ground. Three occupants had emerged, two appeared to be human but larger and dressed in some form of uniform. The third figure was larger yet, but it was no man. Jonah thought it looked like a giant reptile, a cross between a snake and the alligators he had once seen at a traveling show. It must have been eight feet tall and carried a star gun not unlike his own, except larger and longer.

The two human-looking figures were scanning the hilltop and he knew they were looking for him, or Molly. One of the human figures motioned for the snake creature to head up the incline of the hill. Though it did not see Jonah crouching behind the ridge, it headed up the bluff roughly in his direction. If it continued, it would eventually intersect his position. He was considering sliding back down the bluff and moving north to avoid it when suddenly the familiar sound of the Winchester erupted from a short distance away and he knew instinctively it was Molly shooting off rounds from the top of ridge nearby. He watched as one of her shots rang true and struck one of the human-like figures, apparently in the leg for it doubled over and hobbled a few feet back towards the ramp and re-entered the ship's open door.

As soon as she started firing again both the second human figure and the snake creature turned their attention to where small puffs of smoke were circling above her giving away her position. The tall reptilian creature nearest Jonah moved with alarming speed for his size and was attempting to flank Molly by crossing higher on the ridge and slightly out of her sight. The second human below produced a star gun like the one Jonah carried and started firing at the hill top in Molly's direction. Apparently he had missed for she returned fire with the Winchester striking the figure in the shoulder.

It was Jonah's turn. Molly had grabbed their attention and that allowed him to carefully zero in on the reptile figure who was now moving away from him in her direction. He slide the switch on the blaster to change the rate of fire from an array to a single blast and squeezed the trigger gently. When the blaster erupted Jonah was startled when the blast not only found its target, but immediately the reptilian giant fell backwards on to the ground and one of its legs was blown off with such force that it landed some distance away, severed from the body about mid thigh. Almost immediately the high pitched whizzing sound of the airship became louder. It was powering up again and the remaining human with the star gun turned and ran back up the ramp where the other had disappeared and the ramp started retracting into the belly of the ship. Apparently they decided Jonah's star gun had evened up the odds, and with the ship already damaged, they chose to retreat rather than fight, leaving the reptile creature laying on the ground still where it had fallen.

Grima House, New Orleans

Fanchon Harleaux's war room was abuzz with activity. Premont Igatruub had been joined by the Fanchon and two other lower ranking Uk'tena technicians. Communications between Krieger Hrlwh Wrhll and the Premont were rapidly passing back and forth and Igatruub was trying to keep an impatient Fanchon up to date with developments as they happened.

When the War Bird detected the energy signal of the blaster and called in the report to the Premont, Fanchon ordered the attack thinking it might be the Old Cherokee warrior Gray Wolf on the ground. To his knowledge, he would be the only one to possess a Furris field blaster. But when the ship received damage, Fanchon immediately changed his strategy. He ordered the ship to land at a safe distance and to launch a ground assault instead, for he reasoned this would provide a better chance of success without the possibility of further damage to the ship. But the Krieger in command of the ship was either incapable or had underestimated his opponent and set the ship down within striking distance of the enemy. The entire operation had been put at risk and now a Uk'tena warrior lay dead on the ground, one of the Kriegers had been wounded and his precious War Bird damaged.

He couldn't understand why the Supreme Commander valued these Kriegers. To him they seemed little more than an unwelcome complication. In fear of losing the ship, he ordered the War Bird's hasty retreat. At the moment he only had possession of two crystals, meaning he had two ships in the air, and they were too precious to run the risk of losing, at least until more of the crystals could be recovered and more ships put into action.

"Fanchon," Premont Igatruub had more disparaging news to report. "We have a communiqué from our operative within the White House."

"Read it."

"Report # 371..."

"I don't care about the number Premont, get to the message."

"Yes, Fanchon. Our operative reports Washington has authorized the mobilization of the 22nd Infantry at Fort Gibson. He reports the tribes are mobilizing and believes these developments could be an indication that the two groups are working cooperatively."

Harleaux was struggling to maintain composure. The plan had called for the rapid acquisition of a handful of primitive tribal leaders utilizing two War Birds of Destruction and a handful of fully equipped strike warriors and a dozen specially trained Krieger assassins. How could the mission possibly fail, resulting in damaged War Birds, dead warriors and wounded Kriegers? He knew, in the end, that he would bear the blame if the operation was not successful, and he feared the reaction of the Supreme Commander, who would be far less forgiving than he.

"Premont. See to it the damaged ship is repaired immediately. And find out what progress Krieger Khlgg's ship has made. We need them back here expediently. Once the repairs are made on Wrhll's ship, dispatch it to Indian territory and start with the government Fort there. Destroy it. If it is war these humans want, then war we will give them."

Trouble In Tombstone

HISTORICAL NOTE: Around the Superstition Mountains not far from the town of Nogales, a published story surfaced in the 1970s about an Arizona lawmen who chased a crippled UFO into Mexico before occupants of the craft abducted a member of the posse. The incident allegedly happened in the late 1880s. The incident was reported by an eyewitness, Jorge Hernandez, who told the story to a Catholic priest, Father Joel de Mola, before he died in 1971 at the age of 107. (See Appendix)

Krieger Hrlwh Wrhll piloted his damaged War Bird west across Indian Territory at speed in an attempt to determine the extent of the damage it had received. The best he could tell, a plasma coil had been ruptured, and that in itself did not preclude the cruiser from performing its duties.

He had received the order from the Premont to take the ship down for repairs, but it had been many years by earth reckoning since last he sat at the controls of one of the star cruisers and he wasn't about to relinquish control at the whims of Fanchon Harleaux, who he considered an upstart in the hierarchy of the Uk'tena Federation. Wrhll answered only to Thet, and with open war stretching its glorious hand across the earthen landscape, he was going to throw his resources head long into the glory of battle.

For hundreds of years he had waited for this moment, when the Uk'tena could rebuild and once again exercise domination of this sector. The acquisition of two of the crystals signified the beginning of a long awaited moment. There would be time to repair the coil soon, but now was a time to exact damage, a long awaited chance to strike back, and on a personal note, against the hated Chiricahau, for it was this tribe that had brought down his last cruiser during a battle they call Apache Run. It was a dark spot on his otherwise perfect record, and he hated them above all.

Over the many long years since the Chiricahau had migrated west and now were occupying an area in Arizona Territory near a place called Fort Lowell, an outpost of the U.S. Government. He had no experience with the white-skinned Europeans, but they were human and therefore his enemies. All humans must be subjugated under Uk'tena Law. And now he would begin his prosecution of the American West and destroy the outpost that represented the only organized military presence in the area. Harleaux's Fort Gibson could wait, for this would send a direct message to the Chiricahau that they were next on his list.

Wrhll was a tenacious warrior, but for centuries he had feasted on the blood of helpless humans and had been far away from the rigors and demands of war. It had softened his judgment, taken away his edge, for he grossly underestimated the extent of the damage of his War Bird in favor of exacting his personal revenge. Now, flying across the Arizona landscape, the big War Bird began heaving and coughing and losing its ability to maintain flight. The crystal was overheating and he lacked the resources on-board to make repairs.

Against the judgment of his First Officer, Wrhll targeted the base called Fort Lowell, little more than an outpost really, and with three passes of the airship completely obliterated the site, destroying every building and most every soldier on the base. From here he planned to recon across the mountains in search of the Chiricahau stronghold.

But instead he was forced to set the ship down frequently to restart the plasma inhibitors as a result of the damaged coil that his engineer was unable to by-pass. It was during one of these frequent stops in the desert that a group of horsemen approached the great War Bird. They numbered less than fifteen and posed no actual threat with their primitive weapons. But Wrhll was zealous, and had he the ability, he would have destroyed them. But the overheating coil had become critical and he was running the risk of damaging the crystal more if he fired his weapons, so in a game of cat and mouse, each time the curious horsemen would draw near, Wrhll would order the ship to move several miles away where it would set down once again. In this way he was leading the human party deeper into the desert and preventing the need to unload a ground force to deal with them.

Finally tiring of the game however, and because of the human's persistence, he set the bird down one last time and ordered a full repair crew to exit the War Bird and cauterize the damaged coil. This would limit his on-board weapons ability further and would, against his will, force him back to base for appropriate repairs. But he had little choice.

The task was nearly complete when the operations officers informed him that the horsemen had caught up with them once again, and now one of them was approaching the airship. What he hoped to accomplish Wrhll could not guess, but it maddened him. He ordered a centurion to capture the human and bring him back inside, but by the time this was accomplished the coil had been cauterized and he was ready to lift off again.

"Krieger, what should we do with the human? He is on board now." asked his First Officer.

"Take us up above the clouds and eject him through a refuse chute," turning back to his command module, he entered a series of codes and the War Bird lifted from the desert floor and headed east.

Chatsu's Return

Calvary envoys had been dispatched from Fort Gibson and none to early. By the time Alex and Chatsu were prepared to depart and head back to Tahlequah the first reports of flying machines began filtering into the Fort.

One credible report had come from a Calvary scouting party who had seen an airship up close when it passed directly over their heads, spooking their horses and causing several of the soldiers to be thrown from their horses. An over zealous soldier took a pot shot at the flying machine and managed to hit it apparently, for several of the soldiers reported hearing a *'cling'*, like metal bouncing off of metal, but it had no apparent effect.

News of the sightings coming into the fort were welcome news for Alex for it reinforced his story, and now Bates was actively prosecuting his directive. Alex felt certain he would continue to make good his promise to inform the tribes as he had instructed.

When finally they departed Fort Gibson the sun was beginning to fall toward the western horizon. Alex wasn't accustomed to such long rides on horseback and he was dreading the trip. There were many miles to cover and he longed for the comfort of a train.

Chatsu could speak English well and in spite of remaining silent most of the trip to the fort, Alex had engaged him in conversation now. He discovered he liked the Wolf Clan warrior, a man of few words perhaps, but an interesting and capable companion on the trail. When finally they arrived in Tahlequah just past midnight, he found Gray Wolf still in council, and there was word of another council that had been called, and he wondered how many would be necessary to convince people that the world was facing destruction and that they must act. It seemed their politics were as convoluted as those in Washington.

Tired, road weary and exhausted, Alex rested in a stable where his horse had been put up for the night, selecting a large stack of fresh hay as a substitute for a bed. It didn't matter. Soon he fell away into a dream-filled sleep of alien monsters and gigantic airships, a world like he never imagined before.

CHAPTER SIXTEEN
PROOF IN THE PUDDING

A good plan violently executed now is better than a perfect plan executed next week. - **George S. Patton**

fter the airship hastily departed Jonah rushed toward Molly's position calling her name to be certain she didn't riddle him with bullets. She heard him coming though and rose from a point on the crest some fifty yards away and waved.

"That'll teach them to shoot my horse...Jonah...the mare...she's dead."

Jonah nodded, relieved it wasn't her, and told her as much. Turning their attention to the giant reptilian creature, they ventured down the slope together to take a closer look and to make certain it was no longer a threat. There was blood, or what they guessed was blood, on the ground, enough to indicate the life had drained from it.

Jonah poked it with the tip of his blaster, then rolled it over on its back.

"Now that's one ugly creature," Molly suggested as she kicked it hard with her boot. "Kill my horse will you? We shot your airship! How do you like that?"

Jonah carefully searched the body and collected a second blaster laying on the ground next to the corpse and handed it to Molly who smiled. Then. retrieving Shadow from across the bluff, Jonah draped the big corpse over the saddle and tied it into place. Molly had to help because it weighed at least as much as two men. Shadow was charged with the burden of carrying the reptile creature back to Tahlequah while Jonah and Molly walked ahead of him, moving slowly now that night was falling. They remained alert in the event the airship should return.

"I think you damaged the ship pretty bad from what I could see. It was trailing smoke as it flew away."

Well I certainly like the – what would you call it?"

"Blaster, hands down," she replied as she looked at the one she carried in place of the Winchester. It was more like a rifle than a revolver, but Molly liked it that way. "I can't wait to fire it."

It was a few hours before day break when they finally strolled into Tahlequah to discover there were many more people there than normal. The council fires were ablaze and Jonah could just make out Gray Wolf standing before a circle of tribesman, a few of them he recognized, others he did not.

Without stopping, Jonah, with Molly in tow, proceeded to the large fire and walked into the circle leading Shadow and the dark figure draped across the saddle. A silence fell on the group. Without uttering a word Jonah loosened the ties on the strap that held the reptilian creature, draped face down, and tossed it off of Shadow's back. It fell and landed hard on the ground face up, the flames from the council fire dancing across the green and golden scales on its face.

There was an audible murmur as Jonah walked in a wide circle to face the council members.

"Uk'tena warriors…they have returned. This one we killed by the river an hours ride from here. We also encountered a flying machine." Jonah offered,

There was a murmur again among the elders of the tribes, and someone asked, "Were there more of these…creatures?"

"There were three of them, this one the largest. The two others had human form. But there were others in the airship, we do not know how many."

"And this airship," it was Yellow Bear, a Cherokee Jonah recognized. "It attacked you?"

Molly spoke up.

"Yes, but we damaged it. There was smoke coming from it when it flew away."

Molly lifted the alien's large blaster for all to see. Many eyes had been on it since they walked into the firelight.

"This is their technology. It is many times more powerful than a rifle or a shotgun," she told them. "It can damage their ship, and blow their legs off."

"Their ships have these weapons also…but larger ones…and they can fire them from the sky. We now have two of them and will use them against the enemy. But our people must be warned of the danger. I have encountered this enemy twice now. The one before you is large and strong, but others that look like a man walk among us and are more dangerous perhaps. They feast on the blood of men and are many times more stronger and any one of us.."

"Who is this beloved woman?" asked a Cherokee council member. A 'Beloved Woman' in Cherokee society was one who had earned the right to speak at General Council or who had proven her ability on the battlefield. It was a compliment, which later Jonah would have to explain..
"She is Molly Langtry and a partner with me in the service of the Government. We have been investigating these strange events and these serpent creatures," Jonah replied.

There were nods of understanding among the council.

"Among the Choctaw there are tales of such blood seekers, the *oklafalaya*. They have long been the enemies of the people and are said to sleep in caves," Pushmataha, the Choctaw chief said. "We have not heard from them in many generations. If they are back, then talk of war is wise."
There was a murmur of agreement among the elders.

"Let the Cherokee Keeper speak more of these things," spoke Tenawa, Comanche elder.

Gray Wolf stood again to address the council, and Jonah nodded to Molly to follow him as he walked away from the council leaving the one-legged reptilian on the ground. When they had gone a safe distance away, he placed his hand on her shoulder.

Jonah collected Shadow and walked toward the stable. There was a group of stern looking riders just coming in to town. Jonah spoke to them in a language Molly didn't recognize and pointed them toward the council fire. Nodding, they passed them and headed in that direction.

"Apache." Jonah told her.

"I didn't know you spoke Apache."

"That and about seven other Native dialects," Jonah said as they reached the stable. "But not very well I'm afraid."

As they entered the barn, Jonah spotted Alex sleeping in the hay. There was his strange looking talking box not far from his head and a crackly voice was coming from it. Jonah reached down and grabbed Alex by the shoulder and shook him.

"Alex. Alex. Someone is talking in your box."

Alex opened his eyes and stared at Jonah for a moment and the voice in the box started talking again. With a start, Alex sat up, fumbled with the talking device, placed the conical shaped receiver to his ear and immediately began talking back.

"Yes…I'm here. Alex Bell here. Can you hear me?"

The voice on the other end sounded stern, and spoke rapidly, but now that Alex had the hearing device pressed to his ear, Molly and Jonah couldn't make out what was being said.

"Good God, no Governor…yes….in Tahlequah….yes…Captain Bates…I see….yes….Willard?"

Jonah was unsaddling Shadow now, but at the mention of Willard's name he became more attentive. Alex was still talking.

"In New Orleans…yes, he's here with me…they are meeting in council now…yes sir….yes sir…I see…Governor, I understand…will do…thank you, sir…and good luck in Washington."

Setting the receiver down Alex looked pale. The vivid dreams of slumber were still with him, and worse, news from Governor Cleveland indicated his nightmares were coming true.

"The aliens," it was the first time he had used the word, and it was one that would stick for some time to come. "They have attacked Washington, blew up a number of buildings. The President is missing, the city is burning. Jonah, the war has spread."

War Room, Grima House, New Orleans

Fanchon was furious as he watched the war board and the events that unfolded there in real time. He was the Fanchon, the Governor of the American branch of the Circle, he was in charge! But the Krieger were pets of Annubias Thet – Supreme Planetary Commander of Uk'Tena Forces. Harleaux found them to be undisciplined, ignorant and irreverent to his authority. They disobeyed his command and ignored his orders and operated independent of his desires. Now they had attacked the wrong government fort, prosecuted an attack on the American capital, and they were putting precious hardware at risk.

But there was favorable news as well. Krieger Khlgg had returned from the land of the Inca. The Inca chieftain had been captured and the crystal recovered. Three crystals were in their possession now, but only three. There were four more that needed to be retrieved. If only the Kriegers would follow his orders, if the crystals could be systematically recovered, then Thet would have to recognize his superiority. One day, perhaps, the Uk'tena of Sirius would return to earth and would find him sitting in the ultimate seat of authority. He would be heralded as a hero of the race, and perhaps he could work his way into a more important role in theirs plan for galactic domination. He wanted to be that hero. He wanted the Kriegers to respect his leadership. But his plans were slow to develop and he was saddled by insubordinate Krieger commanders that were prosecuting the war as they saw fit. Attacking Washington was the wrong thing to do at this point. He needed more crystals; needed more War Birds in the air. He knew the coming hours would be the most important of his lifetime.

HISTORICAL NOTES, 1800s NEWSPAPER REPORTS

"When [the mysterious light] first appeared it was seen moving rapidly from the northeast and heading in a southwesterly direction. As it neared the southern boundary of the city [of Sacramento] it turned directly toward the west and after passing the city went south, being distinctly visible for upward of 20 minutes. -From the San Francisco Call -- This light was observed by many prominent individuals including Deputy Secretary of State George A. McCalvy, District Attorney Frank D. Ryan, and E. D. McCabe, the governor's personal secretary.

In Milwaukee, the Sentinel published a report of a sighting: *"It seemed to assume different colors, and moved at a good speed. With a glass it showed up cone shaped with a bright headlight."*

On the Northwest Coast, *"Several fishermen were awakened in the middle of the night by the presence of a strange craft that they described as an "electric monster." Their watches stopped and the craft emitted electricity and light. The craft also made a loud sound. Two men were knocked unconscious in the encounter. The rest of the party fled in terror."*

Olivier House Hotel, New Orleans

Reports were filtering in to Culper Ring headquarters in Maryland just outside Washington, and were passed to Ridley Willard at the Olivier hotel in New Orleans. Most were simple cases of sightings but a few involved actual conflict in the way of brutal attacks on forts, communities and even a west bound train. Others were casual encounters with strange looking creatures or, as in many reports, involved personal attacks with human-like creatures that had left victims dead and drained of blood.

Willard had agents spread across the city in an effort to uncover evidence that might reveal the secret location of the Uk center of operations. Reliable intelligence had indicated there had been a great deal of suspect activity at various places, and he was following all the leads.

Several nights back a ship had arrived at the New Orleans dock and a dozen or so 'strange looking individuals' were taken off of it and transported to a location he now had under surveillance, a promising possibility. While that was all the details he was able to gather before the Ring operative turned up missing, they at least had managed to get the name of the ship involved, and U.S. Naval vessels were scouring the Gulf in search of it.

Willard had a small platoon of specially trained Ring agents holed up at the Naval Yard and ready for an assault on the center once it was identified. But Willard needed help. He had been meeting with local police officials, following unusual crimes and looking over recent cases of homicide and missing person reports in hopes of uncovering clues. He reasoned it would be impossible for such a nefarious organization to operate within the confines of a city without leaving some clues along the way. For one, these UKs were said to be involved in some type of blood ritual, and that shouldn't be too hard to uncover.

Tahlequah, The Home of Tommy Two Bears

Two Bears was an affluent half-blood Cherokee that operated a successful ranching operation surrounding two sides of Tahlequah. He was Jonah's cousin on his father's side; his wife, Marela, was Wolf Clan. Two Bears owned the stable in town and when he caught wind of Jonah and company's plight after Gray Wolf's home was destroyed, he offered them a Sunday House, a type of guest house, as a place to stay.

It was actually larger than Gray Wolf's cabin and adequately furnished with everything they needed. Sitting around a large oak table, they discussed their next move.

"If we've been ordered to New Orleans, Alex, then they must have identified an important target there. Other wise they wouldn't have Professor Willard on the ground there."

"I'm not certain," Alex responded. "But it makes sense. I am hoping Willard will make contact with me, otherwise we – or at least I – may be forced to head to New Orleans alone. Considering what you have going on here, that might be the better choice anyway."

Molly wasn't so certain that dividing the team would be a good idea, and she was about to say so when there was a knock at the door. Being nearest the door, she opened it. Standing there was Chatsu, the guide who had taken Alex to Fort Gibson.

"Osiyo," Molly greeted him,. He nodded but stood there without speaking.

Jonah came to the door and greeted him.

"*Osiyo* Chatsu."

"Jonah *Tohitsu*."

"Osda."

"*Waya Ugaya*. The Clan, are meeting in the big house. *Nvla*."

"*Naquu*, now?"

Chatsu nodded and waited for Jonah to follow. Looking back at Molly and Alex, he explained.

"There is a clan meeting being held in the ranch house and they want me there. I should see what's going on."

"Molly nodded. Alex simply looked at him blankly. Jonah followed Chatsu, closing the door behind.

"I will never understand that language," Alex cried.

Wolf Clan Assembly

When Jonah entered the large living area of the ranch house there were at least twenty clan members assembled. Two Bears was not among them, but his wife Marela was. There were a lot of heads nodding in Cherokee greeting and Jonah found himself constantly nodding back in response. All eyes were on him and he wondered what they were thinking. Many of them he recognized; knew by name. Many more he did not, though there were many familiar faces among them.

Marela was standing in front of the largest fireplace Jonah had ever seen and she had obviously been addressing the group before his arrival. She continued now, first bringing Jonah up to date.

"Tahoni Tenkiller," she called him by the birth name given by his father instead of Jonah, the Christian name assigned by his mother. These are the men that lead the warriors of the Wolf Clan. Each controls a group of no less than twenty warriors. The largest groups belong to Redbird, One Owl and Falling Sky, each has over thirty warriors. This represents the sum of shape changers remaining among the Western clan. Gray Wolf would lead this meeting, but as his *a-de-lo-qua-s-gi* – his apprentice – he has delegated his authority to you."

Jonah was taken back. First and foremost, he didn't know there was a formal organization of shape changers. He didn't even know shape changers existed until yesterday, except in legend, and he didn't know his grandfather was the leader. Secondly, how could he now lead them when he did not know anything about how they worked, how they were organized, or even their purpose. He said so.

"I'm afraid I lack the qualifications for the job. Red Bird there, or Falling Sky – probably many more of you, are better qualified to lead. I have much yet to learn."

Falling Sky stood and the murmur that had started immediately ceased. He was a respected clan member, a senior member, and when Falling Sky spoke the Clan listened.

"You are the sky captain Jonah Montana, as prophesized. Those among us, and those that came before us for many generations, have been waiting for you to come."

Jonah cleared his throat. He didn't understand, and selected his words carefully.

"I am no one to question the word of the wise Falling Sky. But I would yield to your leadership, for you are experienced in such matters while I am not."

"*A-ye-ga-li*," It was a rebuttal, an order to be quiet. "You are the son of the stars. Even you can not abandon what you were born to do. This is my final word."

Falling Sky sat down and the matter was settled, and by the nods moving around the room, the others agreed. Alright, Jonah thought to himself, he knew there was no arguing. The job was his whether he liked it or not. He looked at Marela and nodded for her to continue.

"You should know Tenkiller, it is the job of the *Waya* warriors to protect the tribe in times of danger. The attack on Gray Wolf was no accident, and he must not fall into Uk'tena hands. The people are also in danger, and already the *i-na-ge-hi wa hya* warriors are roaming across our lands from boundary to boundary in search of Uks that may try to infiltrate. We have five times five groups of two who will patrol for half a day each. If Uks find their way to Cherokee land they will perish. *Eliguv?* Is this enough?"

Jonah worked his way to the front of the room and Marela took a seat on the big hearth when she saw he was taking over.

"I think the numbers are sufficient. I would say that the blood seekers, vampyres as they are known among many, are the most dangerous, though they are smaller than the Uk warriors. But they will blend in better – the Uk warriors would be easy to spot. Also I think we should dispatch three *i-na-ge-hi wa hya* to each of the Keepers of the other tribes once Gray Wolf indentifies them. These are the primary targets for the Uks. Our principal chief and high council should also be carefully watched. Do we have sufficient numbers without taxing our warriors?"

"We have sufficient numbers if we send four *i-na-ge-hi wa hya* to the Keepers. This will let them shift in pairs, and we can still provide enough numbers for our own people," it was One Owl who spoke.

"We will also have Chatsu and Jaygokwe serve as your lieutenants. They will be in your personal service and can run between the war chiefs – the captains – with your orders," said One Owl. "And they will help you to understand the way of the *i-na-ge-hi wa hya*, and you can instruct them in the way of the star blood."

Jonah wasn't sure what that meant, but thought it might not be the time to ask. Chatsu and another young Cherokee, he assumed it was Jaygokwe, stood and took a position near the fireplace to the side.

"Concerning the flying airships," Jonah needed them to understand the danger. "We must make the people aware they are to leave their houses, their cabins, and take shelter in the forest if they see one approach. For the *i-na-ge-hi wa hya*, we have only two weapons, star guns, that can bring them down, so if an attack comes from the sky, you must only defend yourself and not attempt to confront them. I will council with Gray Wolf and we will leave one star gun near the village so you might use it if needed. If you encounter a UK warrior with a star gun, we must try to acquire it, using it is much the same as any rifle. Gray Wolf will know more about this if you need to know. What else? Marela?"

"Only that Gray Wolf wants the people to hear the old stories again for many have forgotten, but this we leave to the general council."

"Alright then, tell your warriors we have fought the Uk'tena before and tasted the sweetness of victory. It will be no different this time. Now is the time for courage."

As if on cue most of the *i-na-ge-hi wa hya* captains stood and began filtering out of the room. Chatsu and Jaygokwe remained.

"Jonah," Chatsu addressed him. "It is time for us to show you how the *i-na-ge-hi wa hya* makes war. Let us go to the forest."

He quietly and quickly headed to the door. Jonah nodded to Marela and followed. Outside, near the edge of the woods, Chatsu and Jaygokwe paused.

"Gray Wolf says we should transform to the wolf together. We shall run through the forest and back to your Sunday House. This way you will know how strong you are and how fast you can be. Changing can be fast or slow, but after changing once, you will understand better when you need to release the wolf inside."

Without waiting for an answer, the two lieutenants removed their shirts and quickly transformed in the dim light of the moon, and Jonah welcomed the chance to transform again, but failed to remove his own shirt. The experience with his father had been exhilarating and he found that he was excited about feeling the power of the beast again. Transforming was easy.

It took only a few seconds, and before he realized it, he was looking through the eyes of the wolf, manlike in stature but larger and more powerful. He could feel the heat in his leg muscles, taste the air and smell the scents of the forest like he had never done before. His night vision was greatly improved as well, and he could see insects crawling on the barks of the trees. At a distance he could hear voices and knew instinctively they were far away.

Chatsu and Jaygokwe, in full form, dropped to all fours and scrambled deeper into the forest at blinding speed. It took Jonah a moment to make his feet move, but once he did, he too sped into the underbrush and followed them.

It was an exhilarating experience! Soon he was overjoyed, like a child who had discovered a new game, and he ducked and jumped and swerved through the dense forest at remarkable speed and with grace and agility. At one point his companions leaped up a tall cottonwood and scrambled across its branches, dropping again to the forest floor. He followed but chose to leap first to another tree which put him ahead of them. Dropping to the ground he faced them as they approached, turned and bolted again into the forest, this time leading them in a game of catch-me-if-you-can, but they could not. At best they could keep up with him, but his quick turns caused them to swing wider and they would struggle to catch up again. He was a natural. He was a beast.

He led the chase through the countryside for some time, much longer than they had planned. He was enjoying the freedom he felt and the power that drove him forward. Finally they reached the clearing and Two Bears' Sunday House was visible in the distance. It was a large field used for planting corn in the spring and Jonah seized the chance to test his speed. He put all he had into the effort and in a surprising few seconds he reached the house ahead of the two warriors. Standing on two legs again he willed himself to change, but not until Molly, hearing the sound through the door, opened it and gasped at the horror of the sight. Once again his shirt was torn and he noticed his feet were sore, his moccasin boots he must have lost somewhere in the forest, but before he could calm Molly, Chatsu arrived and a moment later Jaygokwe, and they quickly changed back into

173

human form. They were breathing heavily. So was Molly who was attempting to hide her astonishment and fear.

"Chatsu." Jaygokwe was excited. "You are the fastest among us and he left you behind!"

Chatsu grunted.

"Maybe I was holding back for him to learn."

"And maybe you weren't. Jonah Tenkiller, this was the first time you changed?" Jaygokwe, the younger of the two, was genuinely excited.

"Well, no. And not the last." He didn't say it, but he wanted to turn again and run through the forest more. The experience was amazing. "But now there are things that require my attention. Molly…"

She regained composure and realized she would need to accept this, for whatever it was worth. It was what he was, like it or not.

Jaygokwe looked at her and for a moment and saw, or perhaps sensed, the fear in her eyes. He was like a young boy who had just seen the most beautiful woman of his life.

"The Beloved Woman…it is a pleasure to meet Jonah Tenkiller's partner."

Chatsu simply nodded at her.

"Yes…I mean, nice to meet you…"

"This is Jaygokwe – or Jacob in English Molly, and you have met Chatsu. They are…Wolf Clan brothers," Jonah wasn't sure what to call them.

"So I saw…see," Molly said. "Jacob, nice to meet you, and to see you again Chatsu."

"Well…" Jonah stumbled past the awkwardness of the moment. "Here's where I leave you brothers."

"We are not going anywhere," Chatsu informed him matter-of-factly. "We will be outside and watching for the Uk. In the morning Lame Horse and Tommy Sure Foot will relieve us."

He turned and walked off around the corner of the house. Jaygokwe was slow to follow, a smile still stretching across his face from ear to ear and his eyes still riveted on Molly.

"Jacob has never seen a woman with red hair before," he offered. "I, uh, am sorry you had to see…"

"Jonah Montana…Tenkiller? I am getting accustomed to seeing strange things, and realize there is much more about the Cherokee than I ever knew. Yes it is strange and frightful. But from what I understand, your...ability...well, it will be of great value in the days ahead."

Jonah nodded and followed her inside.

"What was all the ruckus outside?" Asked Alex.

"You want Jonah to show you?"

Grima House, War Room, New Orleans

Fanchon Harleaux was back in the war room and in a slightly better mood. He would never admit it, but perhaps the Krieger's prosecution of the mission – while ambitious to say the least – wasn't as bad an idea as he first thought. In fact, things were going rather well.

Aztec prophet Chapultamec, Q'ero the Inca historian, the Shawnee Keeper Tenskwatawa, were all in captivity and their hidden crystals had been recovered. The Sioux Keeper Touch the Clouds was also imprisoned in the lower dungeons of Grima House, but in spite of extreme torture, he was resisting. But he could not last forever; he would break and his crystal would soon be recovered, leaving only three to find. He had confidence now that the crystals of Wovaka and Geronimo would be forthcoming. Wovaka had been cornered in Utah and it was only a matter of time before they drug him from the canyon lands where he was hiding, and the Apache Geronimo would be his soon as well, caged like a lion in the top of the tower at a fort in San Antonio. A detail of Kriegers and three Uk warriors were on the ground after mass destruction and havoc was unleashed on Fort Sam Houston. The chain of command had been disrupted, the fort largely damaged and only a hand full of ill-equipped Calvary separated his men from gaining access to their target, the Chiracahau Apache war lord. That left only Gray Wolf. The old Cherokee war chief.

Three Krieger and nearly a hundred Uk had been dispatched to the Cherokee lands, and Harleaux was more than confident that no primitive force could stand before them. During and following the First War, large numbers of the hybrids and the modifieds, the hated Wolf Clan, had revolted and were a terror to the surviving Uks for many years, driving them deeper into hiding. But that was centuries ago, and there had been no reports of hybrids or changelings in many long years. At worst, the old sage Gray Wolf may hold the power, and perhaps a few of the elder clansmen, but since the Europeans had conquered the American continent, the old ways were largely lost and forgotten as the Indian spirit had been broken. He reasoned that if changelings existed among them, then they would have slaughtered the settlers from the east, a certain indication the Cherokee had lost that ability.

He had been watching the command screen with interest. Live images of the assault on the tower in Texas were flooding the screen. Bodies of American soldiers were scattered across the ground, and in the distance he could see smoke rising from buildings that either had been decimated or at least partially destroyed. Two Kriegers and three Uk commandos, specially trained warriors, were ascending the stairs of the tower now. The Apache War Chief Geronimo was caged at the top, and soon, in moments, he would be their captive and would be returned to Grima House for interrogation. When his crystal was recovered, there would remain only the Paiute and the Cherokee to capture, and Fanchon knew he could break the Apache, as he would the Shawnee. He always had been the master of interrogation. No one had ever withstood his technique. Even Gray Wolf would reveal the location of his crystal in the end, and Harleaux would possess all seven – the magic number.

On the command screen the Krieger had reached the top of the tower, but when they yanked the bars from the door with brut force, the Apache was not inside. At least that's what Harleaux thought at first. Geronimo must have heard them coming, and somehow had clung to the ceiling of the cell. With blinding speed and the element of surprise, he lunged down upon the first of the Krieger who had entered the cell, overpowering him. He darted for the door and immediately a scuffle began, the second Krieger and now two of the Uk warriors were engaged.

It seemed impossible to Harleaux, but somehow the Apache continually escaped their grasp and fought them off with power and prose that was amazing. He was fierce and he struggled against all odds. He had managed to grasp a knife on the belt of one of the Uk warriors and thrust it to the hilt in the chest of another. The Uk went down. One of the Kriegers, Harleaux did not know which because now both were engaged in the struggle, received a deep wound in the neck. Geronimo brandished the knife like a master. In a few moments, after another Uk was thrown down the stairs, the Apache was subdued when one of the Uk commandos struck him hard across the head with the butt of his weapon.

"Good. Make certain they don't kill him before I discover where his crystal is hidden. Have them bring him back here immediately," he ordered the Premont.

"Yes sir."

Tahlequah, Indian Territory

Nearly a week had passed and slowly representatives from tribes all across the Americas began filtering into Tahlequah. Most of them were elder chiefs or representatives of their councils who had come at Gray Wolf's request, but among them was the Paiute Wovaka, creator of the Ghost Dance movement, a Keeper who was being pursued by the enemy.

Word spread quickly among the Native people in spite of the great distances, and there were some among them that remembered the old stories and legends, or at least parts of them, and they were not surprised with the recent developments. Strongest among the believers were the delegation of Hopi who understood their star origins. And there were Navajo that had their own stories to tell about the days that blood seekers terrorized the people. The Cheyenne and the Ute and Blackfoot and Pawnee came from the north and the west, and even the Iroquois and the Creek and the Delaware of the east sent representatives to hear the wisdom of Gray Owl, and each night the council fires grew bigger.

More than once white men arrived, soldiers of rank and politicians from Washington. They wanted to know more about the Uk'tena enemy, and Gray Wolf shared what he may.

Badly dispersed by the flying machines and under siege in a dozen places by ground forces of the Uk, the Calvary was mostly busy protecting important cities like Washington and Philadelphia and Denver and San Francisco. But, and as a courtesy perhaps, a small company had been moved from Fort Gibson to Muskogee and a platoon to Tahlequah to aid in the event of open attack.

It was a historic time in the history of a young America when Apache warriors and their old adversary, the 7th Calvary, rode together across the plain; when outlaws and lawmen mended their differences and began to address a common threat, a more dangerous enemy. There were hundreds of reports, many of them real and many were rumors about brazen attacks on cities and towns and settlements all across the nation. One rumor was that Mexico City had fallen into the hands of the 'star aliens' and a massive invasion was preparing to flood Texas. Texas Rangers were teaming with Mexican banditos and Methodists were convening with Baptists as Americans everywhere turned to face a threat larger than any they had ever known.

Word had arrived from Ridley Willard from New Orleans that his search for the Uk'tena command center had narrowed to only two places across the city. Alex was summoned to the Gulf city as was Jonah, who elected to delay his journey until he could afford to ride south with a contingent of Wolf Clan warriors. Molly remained with Jonah in Tahlequah spending many of her days with Marela learning more of the language and culture of the Cherokee, and the history of the Wolf Clan, which both fascinated and frightened her.

On the eighth day after the first general council meeting, just as the sun was beginning to set, the first wave of Uk ground troops assaulted nearby Muskogee, the largest city in the region. Cherokee and Osage and Caddo cultures coexisted with Creek, Seminole and others there, but because there was such a strong population of both Indian and white settlers, the Wolf Clan warriors had concentrated their efforts in the south where the bulk of the Cherokee dwelled, leaving Muskogee subject to quick occupation. With superior fire power, stronger soldiers and sufficient numbers, the Uks quickly gained control of the city in spite of numbering less than a hundred. Their technology had won the day, and from there they set their sights on Tahlequah, the ancestral home of Gray Wolf.

There was a noticeable absence of flying airships and Jonah could only assume they had been intentionally kept out of the battle as a result of the Cherokees being in possession of the star guns. Though he could not know it, they had too few airships in service to risk losing one in battle.

Jonah had ordered a contingent of thirty shape changers to assist warriors from a half dozen tribes to set up a defensive line ten miles south of Muskogee to stop the advance of the Uks. The first night after the occupation of Muskogee, a dozen Wolf Clan warriors, assuming the shape of the beast, filtered into town under the cover of darkness and like assassins in the night massacred thirty four Uk warriors and four Kriegers before the enemy could rally enough force to defend themselves using blasters and light sticks. The Wolf Clan warriors were gone as quickly as they came, suffering only two casualties, neither of them serious, and the dozen Comanche warriors that followed them into town were successful in collecting no less than nine star guns before heading back to the Indian line of defense. This greatly enhanced the tribes' ability to hold their defensive position in the days ahead, and three days following that a massive tribal raid completely routed the Uk, who narrowly escaped in their flying machines which were called in as transport.. Muskogee had been liberated.

The following night nearly a dozen specially trained Krieger assassins attempted to enter Tahlequah from the south having been dropped into the heavy forest by a smaller flying airship. But Jonah's warriors, as they were to become called in times thereafter, repelled the attack and killed six of them before they could escape Indian Territory. Jonah participated in this action as a transformed warrior and would long remember the taste of that victory.

Two days later, satisfied his defenses were holding and with the addition of the new star guns and the quick ability of the Comanche to become proficient in their use, Jonah made plans to catch the train south to New Orleans accompanied by Catsu, Jaygokwe and seven other of his best shape changers. Word had arrived from Alex that Willard and his agents had positively located the Uk operation center and had it under constant surveillance. It was located in one of the French Quarter's older structures and they discovered it sat on top of a large subterranean complex where an unknown number of Indian prisoners were being held. Willard knew that the Apache Geronimo was one of them, and he knew the complex was heavily fortified by dozens of the blood seekers and a large contingent of reptilian warriors. With the help of an escaped New Orleans *"lady in waiting"*, Willard was able to determine that a man calling himself Fanchon Harleaux had been building a small empire of odd characters over the last year and was responsible for establishing Grima House as a place of covert activity. Willard reported an assault on the center was being planned in two days time.

Jonah's plan was to take the Katy south to Galveston then east to New Orleans. In spite of his arguments against it, Molly insisted on accompanying him. Eventually relenting, they caught the Katy in Muskogee and were nearly a day into the trip when Catsu, who had acquired the habit of riding on top of the passenger car, spotted twin War Birds in the distance hovering side-by-side above the tracks. A large section of track had been blasted away and when the engineer spotted the airships, he engaged the emergency brake so quickly that unsuspecting passengers throughout several cars were jolted out of their seats. Catsu was catapulted off the train and managed to change to wolf form before hitting the ground, landing instead on all fours.

The train was navigating a slight curve in the track at the time and Jonah, looking out the window, spied the War Birds, now moving slowly in their direction. Shouting orders, his contingent started bolting out of open windows and exiting the rear door of the car to the left side of the train near a bayou, across which heavy brush lined the banks and offered cover.

Passengers were beginning to exit other cars of the train when the airship swooped down along the length of the train and opened fire, striking first the engine, which exploded the moment the boiler was ruptured causing it to jump the tracks. In a domino effect other cars began turning over, more than one sliding into the bayou. Continuing their strafing run, several other cars were hit and Jonah, crawling out of the water of the bayou on the opposite bank, motioned his men into the brush and returned fire with the star gun, striking one of the airships as it flew past his position. It wobbled, but continued its flight down the length of the train, sweeping wide over the plain in an effort to make another run at the train. The War Bird in the lead veered to the left and was hovering near the rear car, blasting it completely into pieces, then hovered a moment before lighting gently on the ground. Almost immediately the door and ramp opened on the underside and a column of giant Uk reptilian warriors began filtering out, armed with star guns and opening fire on confused passengers who were exiting cars and scrambling for what cover they could find.

Regrouping, Jonah, Molly and the Cherokee warriors watched as the two other airships, still in the sky, continued to systematically destroy the last of the rail cars while the ground troops quickly and ruthlessly disposed the last of the passengers.

Jonah and the his Cherokee warriors felt helpless, they had to fight the urge to rush into the fracas, but their inferior numbers were no match for the airships in flight and the large number of troops on the ground in spite of the two star guns they carried with them, and Jonah ordered they not be used again lest the airships glean their position.

The Reptilians on the ground were well armed and were still searching through the debris, obviously looking for something specific for there was no movement among the passengers now. Jonah realized then that the attack had not been random or accidental. The enemy must have known Jonah and his team were on board the train and they were searching for their bodies, and he realized they must quickly escape if they hoped to survive.

Taking a head count, Catsu accounted for all of the Cherokee and an additional twelve passengers who were lucky enough to find their way across the bayou and into the brush without being detected. With as much stealth as possible they quietly worked their way deeper into the brush and into a swampy area heavily covered with brush and trees. Soon they were a few miles away from the rail massacre and heading east across a country thick with growth and marked by frequent ponds of brackish water.

They finally reached more solid ground and shortly they came upon an opening in the brush and looked across a field at a farm house on the edge of a pine forest. Standing on the porch was a large man brandishing what looked like a shotgun from this distance, and a smaller man, perhaps a child, standing with him. Jonah stepped into the opening of the field and waved across to him.

"Are you sure about this," Molly asked, still shaken by the attack on the train.

"I don't think we have a choice."

The larger figure on the porch spotted him cross the yard in his direction. Molly joined Jonah in the field, but motioned for the Cherokee to remain concealed. Crossing the field, they met the farmer about half way.

"Davis Campbell's the name. Who might you folks be and what in the name of Moses is going on? We could hear the explosions," the farmer asked, holding his shotgun at the ready.

"Jonah Montana...this is Molly Langtry. We're federal agents who were on the Katy that was attacked by flying airships..."

"Damn aliens! I knew it!" Campbell lowered the shotgun and was joined by another young man. "This here is my cousin, Jebidiah Campbell. We've been hearing a lot about these space invaders, but we haven't seen any of them this far out in the bayou country. But we were ready if we did." He patted the shotgun. "You got others with you?"

He scanned the brush line across the field.

"Yes, actually we do. I have a few Cherokee, special deputies, and a dozen or so passengers who managed to escape the train before the airship totally destroyed it and just about everyone on it. There are…alien soldiers on the ground not far behind us."

Campbell was alarmed and raised the shotgun again.

"They aren't immediately behind us. We managed to escape, but I think they have been looking for us, so they could initiate a more intense search. My men and I are headed to New Orleans for an operation against these aliens. But the survivors, the other passengers, are going to need shelter, and a way to reach civilization."

Campbell lowered the shotgun again a second time.

"Well, we can help you with that. Bring them along, but quickly."
Molly turned and placing her fingers to her mouth, whistled loudly. The Cherokee came out of the brush along with the frightened survivors, and closed the distance between them.

"Well, looks like we're going to have to put the soup on," Campbell remarked as he turned toward the farm house.

Campbell's wife, as promised, prepared a large caldron of crawfish stew and was serving it up to the wet and cold survivors. Blankets were circulated among them, as many as were available, and the younger Campbell opened the barn for them as shelter. The Cherokee remained grouped together in the yard while Jonah and Molly were talking with the farmer, who spoke with a slight Scottish accent.

"You can tell your Indian friends there to relax. I am friend to the local Indians about these parts, a few Caddo, a few Cherokee and a couple of rough looking Delaware trappers. You are all welcome here. Now, how you plan on getting to New Orleans?"

"I'm working on that."

It turned out the farmer was the nephew of James Campbell, a renowned ship captain that served in the clandestine fleet of Jean Lafitte in the early part of the century. A noted privateer, his uncle amassed a great deal of knowledge about the navigable waterways of southern Louisiana and southeast Texas, and young Davis had acquired his uncles skills at sailing and navigating. He suggested that he could provide transportation aboard an old schooner he had acquired from his uncle.

"She's not much to look at, but I have navigated her from Caddo country all the way down the Sabine to the Gulf. I've taken her to New Orleans a few times over the last few years in fact. She's a worthy craft if you ignore the rats in the hole."

Molly didn't like the sound of that, but Jonah accepted the offer and plans were made to leave after the meal. Campbell promised his nearest neighbors would help to move the surviving passengers to a nearby community.

CHAPTER SEVENTEEN
PRELUDE TO INVASION

"It's not the end of the world, but you can see it from here..."

–Pierre Elliot Trudeau

Culper Ring agent Ridley Willard was getting concerned about the elevated activity at Grima House. After first identifying the place as the Uk stronghold and headquarters of their operations he had maintained constant surveillance. But over the past 36 hours there was much more coming and going from the compound, including a large influx of eerie looking men he feared were the notorious blood seekers – the vampyres. They were a nasty sort and difficult to kill he had been told, for they could take a bullet and still manage to fight. But Alex had told him they weren't impervious to injury. Enough firepower could bring them down, but they were hard to keep down, to kill.

They were also subject to damage or death by a wooden stake driven through the heart. Alex told him that the Cherokee sage, Gray Wolf, believed that certain types of wood, Cottonwood, cherry, live oak and cedar among them, were most effective, but it was actually the natural oils in the wood that worked like a fast acting poison on their alien systems. He had spent the last several days having a local munitions company fashion wooden bullets made from green cedar that he passed among his agents.

Still, the last thing Willard wanted was a close-quarter battle with these monsters, who were said to have the ability to expose an enormous set of incisors that could rip the flesh out of a man's neck or body. And worse, could animate a dead man and turn him into a slave warrior.

Willard watched through the window of the empty second story office across the boulevard from Grima house as more of what he suspected were vampyres filtered into the complex. He lowered the looking glass and reminisced of the days when life was more simple and the greatest threat to man was man himself.

Alex meanwhile was busy on his talking machine behind him and had just concluded a conversation with Grover Cleveland. Sighing, he lowered the receiver.

"Bad news I'm afraid Professor. Jonah and his team were attacked on the train near Galveston two days ago. The train was totally destroyed, but not a single Cherokee body was found. Thankfully he and his men must have escaped. Word has it that they were spotted among a few train survivors at a farm house a few miles away, but the farmer's wife says Jonah and his team were being transported by ship down the Sabine and up the coast to New Orleans. She says it's a three day trip with good weather, and that would put them here sometime tonight or tomorrow if the weather was favorable."

Willard considered it.

"Then it looks like we can't move until they arrive."

"Also professor, Captain Bolgers and his artillery unit report they are in place a few blocks away. But keeping those canons out of sight is going to be increasingly difficult without raising suspicion. Edgars and his infantry are still on the outskirts by the river, and Cleveland says another two dozen Ring agents will be here tonight on the train. How's it going across the way there?" Alex nodded at Grima House.

"There's a lot of activity out there. I have counted no less than a dozen new blood suckers just today. I think Jonah should have brought more Cherokee."

"Well, I haven't seen what they can do, but I heard that when those vampyres tried to infiltrate the Tahlequah defense line a few days back, the shape changers tore them into pieces. They took casualties as well, but from what I hear, I would just as soon face a vampyre than a werewolf."

Willard looked at Alex.

"So you really believe these shape changers can turn into werewolves? I am familiar with the legends, but in all my years of working with the Cherokee, I have never heard of such a thing. I believe it of course, but I tell you Alex, it's a much stranger world than I ever knew possible."

"Well, for what it's worth, I have never seen them change. But Molly, the agent who travels with Jonah, she saw three of them change, including Jonah, and she said it was the most frightening thing she has ever seen."

"Well – and I can't believe I am saying this – but I hope you're right. By the looks of things, we're going to need whatever help we can muster."

In spite of the rats in the hole, Molly had to admit she was enjoying the voyage on the "Victory". She had never experienced the sea before and she immediately fell in love with it. They fed on fresh fish and drank wine from a barrel throughout the journey and the weather was perfect for the cruise. Campbell was a character, perhaps a little odd, but Molly liked him.

It was mid afternoon when the Victory sailed up the Mississippi and into the channel at New Orleans. Alex had provided Jonah with instructions on how to find the safe house used as central command by the Ring, just off Jackson Square and around the block from Grima House and Willard's stake out location. Leaving all but Molly and Chatsu behind, the trio arrived just as Willard and Alex were returning from their surveillance shift.

"You're a sight for sore eyes Jonah. I understand you had a few obstacles to cross during your journey," Alex was genuinely glad to see Jonah.

"But we made it. You look well," turning to Ridley Willard. "Professor, it's really good to see you again."

"Well Jonah Tenkiller Montana, you look…wind blown," he chuckled. But the smile left his face and he was stern now. "I hope you have arrived with your special contingent, and I hope they are as talented as I hear they are."

"I think you'll be pleased with their ability…Professor this is…"

"Molly Langtry, the Beloved Woman," Willard said. Molly blushed. "Your reputation proceeds you. I understand you're one of us now?"

"One of...oh, yes...I was recruited by Jonah," she flashed a look at Alex. "After agent Bell passed me over for the job."

She smiled at Alex and he shrugged.

"Well, I'm glad you made it safely. I'm afraid we're in for a fight. As far as I know we still have the element of surprise, but there has been a great deal of activity over the last 72 hours and our task will be anything but easy. Are your men fit for a fight?"

"The *i-na-ge-hi wa hya* are always ready for a fight Professor. When do we move?"

"The blood seekers..."

"Vampyres," Jonah made it simple.

"The vampyres are most powerful by the cover of darkness as I'm sure you know. I think first light would be our optimum time for assault."

"Frankly Professor, the *i-na-ge-hi wa hya* are better suited for a night fight. Their night vision is better even than the blood thirsty vampyres, and it will put the big lizards at a disadvantage. What numbers are we looking at?"

"We have no idea how many...lizards as you call them...may be inside. They don't move around in the city, so how ever many there are, they have been there for some time, or they have a way in that we haven't discovered. The vampyres, that's a different story. We have counted as many as two dozen, maybe thirty that have come and gone. At least four of them seem to be special, perhaps commanders. They're larger, I would say stronger and more dangerous, and seem to order the others. These may be part of a group that arrived by steam ship. We believe they are directly connected with the flying airships. But other than a few random reports, we haven't been able to confirm any of those in the general vicinity. But we're surrounded by some pretty wild country Jonah. They could be flying in and out under the cover of night and we would never know it. I suspect this may be the case. As far as on our side, we have a company of infantry on the outskirts of town, a platoon of light artillery a few blocks away and they are capable of moving up as needed. We have two dozen Ring agents on hand plus your contingent."

"We have brought ten *i-na-ge-hi wa hya* counting myself. We will lead the assault by infiltrating the Grima compound with stealth. Once inside, if we can get that far, you can launch an assault once you hear weapons fire. We won't be armed, so if you hear weapons fire inside, you know we are involved in open conflict and could use the help."

Willard nodded.

"Then we're set Jonah. I say we move just past midnight tonight - agree?"

"Midnight it is. Now, I'll ask before Molly has the chance, where can get we get something to eat around here that isn't fish?

The clock was closing in on midnight when Jonah addressed his warriors. He had little experience as a field commander, but he knew he didn't need to say much to prepare them for the fight that was coming.

They had assembled in the room across from Grima House where Willard conducted his surveillance. Ring agents were stationed on the first floor and the building had been vacated of everyone not associated with the operation. Molly, Alex, Willard and a handful of Ring agents accompanied the Cherokee to the first floor. All the oil lamps were out in the building and Willard had New Orleans officials cut the gas to the block, making certain there were no street lamps burning. In the dim light of the lobby Jonah and the Clan transformed, and fear filled the room causing Alex, Willard and the handful of agents to leap back at the sight. Ten large, beastly creatures filled the room and they were breathing heavily, a few snapping their jaws as if limbering them up for the fight. Only Molly stood her ground, standing next to Jonah's side. She reached up timorously and stroked the coal black hair of his cheek. Slobbering slightly from the enormous incisors of his lower jaw, he looked at her with the intense deep eyes of a wolf. She couldn't be certain, but it seemed those eyes were smiling.

When the double doors were opened wide it was an amazing sight to see the band drop to all fours and rush across the paved street in blinding speed. They leapt up to the second story balcony that fronted the length of Grima House, a pair of wolves slipping through one of five different windows that lead to rooms inside. Maintaining their stealth, they entered the dark building. In a moment they were all inside.

With no light streaming through the windows, it was pitch black inside the house. Jonah strained to hear noises and could detect a few,

188

including a low hum that was emanating from far beneath them, he assumed from the lower levels of the building. The room he had entered was empty except for the furnishings and crossing to the door he listened before opening it and stepping out into a hallway. There were a number of other clansmen emerging from similar rooms down the hallway, but so far there had been no contact with the enemy.

Jonah detected a subtle noise from above that only his enhanced hearing could detect. He wasn't the only wolf to hear it. Communicating with body language and eye movements, he dispatched a trio of clansmen to investigate. Shortly there were sounds of a scuffle above, then silence, and a moment later three wolves returned panting slightly. Jaygokwe quickly transformed to half human form and whispered in Jonah's ear.

"Three blood seekers on the roof, guards I think, never saw us coming." Blood dripping from the corner of his mouth, he smiled and quickly transformed back to the face of the wolf.

There were two staircases that led to the first floor. Jonah took three clansmen with him and descended the rear stairs slowly listening for movement below and entered the kitchen area which was quiet and unoccupied. The remaining six werewolves were going to use the larger stairs near the front of the building, but when they made the turn in the staircase half way down, a pair of Kriegers were standing in the hall below. Catsu, a lieutenant among the clansmen, immediately jumped down from above, followed by more of the wolves, and surprised the vampyres. It was a ferocious fight, but Catsu and his team quickly dispatched them and silently began a systematic search of the rooms that led off of the long lower level hallway, including a parlor, a dining room and a pair of bedrooms.

Jonah's party, coming from the kitchen, entered the lower hallway just as the last of Catsu's team were returning from their search. Jonah transformed back to human form.

"These two can't be the only occupants of the house. If they're not upstairs or on the main floor, they must be in the slave quarters out back, or underneath us. I did hear movement below. There is a stairway leading down from one of the pantries in the kitchen. But first, let's check the slave quarters out back."

Transforming back into beastly form, he and all but two of *the i-na-ge-hi wa hya* quietly exited the rear door of the building from the kitchen to discover another pair of Kriegers standing guard in the garden outside. In spite of their superior sight and hearing, the Kriegers never saw the werewolves approach. With swinging claws and gnashing teeth, they dispatched the vampyres with haste.

Turning their attention to the slave quarters near the garden, they quietly entered through the only door and found a number of the giants, the reptilians, slumbering on tables and chairs or sitting on the floor with their backs to the wall. One of them wrested from his sleep and let out a gurgling cry of alarm, but it was too late. The room had become a killing field. With the element of surprise and the natural tools to inflict fatal injuries quickly and efficiently, the majority of the reptilians lay heaped and dead on the floor within seconds. There was a yelp, then another and a third. By the time the wolves converged on the final three Uk warriors, two of the clansmen had suffered injuries, none of which were serious. The last three Uks were cornered and still groggy from their slumber. Too large to stand in the room, cutting their throats was an easy task for the Cherokee. When it was over, Jonah counted seven giant bodies on the floor.

That made the total enemy death count an even dozen, but Jonah knew the bulk of the enemy was holed up in the subterranean operations center below the house. So far the element of surprise had been maintained, but re-entering the Kitchen and regrouping to begin their descent down the stairs, a large figure started lumbering up from below, and because of its height it spotted the wolves before they could react, firing off a single blast that wounded the wolf next to Jonah and put a gaping hole in the roof of the pantry.

Knowing he who hesitates is often dead, Jonah lurched down the stairs and ripped the neck out of the reptilian giant before he could get off a second shot, but that brought a volley of activity from the Kriegers and Uk soldiers in the room below who realized now they were under attack. The clan had lost the cover of darkness as the command center was brightly illuminated by an eerie red light streaming from multiple control panels and electronic equipment scattered across the walls. A quick scan of the room revealed at least a two dozen Kriegers and perhaps twenty Reptilian soldiers and technicians spread across it. The control room was massive, at least as large as the house overhead.

The Kriegers were the first to respond using their superior speed, and these appeared to be stronger and faster than the ones they had already encountered. They were joined by the reptilians who began firing volleys across the room at the stairwell, striking equipment panels on a nearby wall causing one of the Kriegers, obviously one of rank, to scream orders at the others.

"Stop firing! You'll damage the equipment!"

Jonah and the three wolves that had made it to the bottom of the landing were quickly confronted by more of the enemy than they could defend against, forcing them back onto the lower steps of the stairs, dropping two reptilians and a pair of Kriegers in the process. Jonah could see and hear a smaller reptilian, obviously a technician and not one of the large fighting class, sitting at what appeared to be the largest console in the room, shouting orders into a head device, he assumed communicating with either nearby troops or with the flying airships. He guessed the Uk must be calling for reinforcements, but there was no way to prevent it for he was slowly backing up the steps and fighting for his life.

At the top of the stairs the Cherokee scrambled back into the kitchen, hoping to bottleneck the enemy's advance in the narrow pantry, but the Reptilians had taken the lead in the rapid charge up the steps, and in a moment's time were streaming out and into the open kitchen where the hand to hand fight intensified. But the Kriegers behind them started firing with their weapons again without fear of hitting the reptilians and the clan was forced to retreat quickly into the main hallway.

Once there, and with their backs to the front door of the house, the enemy rushed out of the kitchen and into the hallways and began filing up the stairs that led to the second floor of the house. Only two of the Kriegers stood their ground in the hallway, and these two set up cover fire while the remainder of the enemy contingent that had been in the basement war room filtered past to the rear of them and scrambled up quickly, obviously attempting to escape instead of stand and fight. The Cherokee were forced to seek cover just inside the doors of the parlor and bedrooms that led off the hallway, and each time they tried to exit these doors in hopes of rushing the enemy, another volley of cover fire from the Kriegers would send them dodging back inside. Jonah realized then why the enemy were in retreat, for Ring agents burst through the front door of Grima House suddenly and into the hallway about the same time that Jonah heard rapid fire from conventional weapons, shotgun blasts and the unmistakable sound of Winchester rifles coming from the kitchen, and he knew that Ring agents must have sealed off the back door that led out of the kitchen. Indeed, Fanchon Harleaux, who wasn't the first or last Uk to scramble out of the basement, screamed orders for a full retreat, realizing that he was grossly outnumbered by Ring agents who had surrounded the house. The Uks were on the run up the stairs, but where they were headed Jonah could only guess. Another of the clansmen was hit by a blaster in the leg, and several Ring agents had taken hits from the Kriegers providing the cover fire. It was then that Jonah and the werewolves regrouped and rushed the Krieger gunmen. Two more wolves were wounded, but with their numbers and speed they overpowered the gunmen and destroyed them. It was just then that a small, round metal explosive device bounced down the stairs and Jonah was almost too late transforming enough to human form to scream a warning to his team.

Leaping for cover, the concussion from the blast rocked the hallway, but their quickness and agility was enough for most of them to reach the rooms leading off of the hallway and only three of the wolves were injured, but two Ring agents were killed and three were badly injured by the blast.

When his ears stopped ringing, Jonah detected a whir and hum of one of the War Birds over head and realized where the enemy was headed. The control operator had apparently been successful in calling for transport before abandoning the war room, and in a head long rush up the stairs Jonah bolted up to the second floor landing and then down the upstairs hallway and up a metal ladder that lead to the roof, emerging just in time to see the last of the enemy loading into the airship. The ramp was retracting and the door was closing before Ring agents had time to make it to the roof with the blaster Jonah had loaned them just in case an airship got involved in the battle. The War Bird lifted rapidly and sped away at great speed, but there was a second ship behind it, and instead of landing on the roof it barreled down toward Jonah and tried to blast him off the roof.

Willard had just jumped off the top ladder rung brandishing Jonah's star gun. Jonah transformed to human form again and reached out for the blaster. Willard handed it to him and Jonah used the switch to intensify the power and fired off a round, which quickly found its target. The airship wavered and wobbled and immediately lost altitude, clipping the corner of Grima House on the way down, preventing it from righting itself and taking back to the sky. The airship hit the ground hard and the leading edge bounced once and crashed into the building across the street, the same building where they had mustered before the assault.

Jonah bounded off the roof to the second floor balcony and from there to the street below. The airship sat slightly tilted, so when the ramp extended the door only opened slightly, making it difficult for the three lumbering reptilian warriors to stoop low and exit the ship with blasters in their hands. Still running across the street Jonah raised his own blaster and opened fire, striking all three Uks in order. Bounding past them and up the ramp and rushing into the ship without stopping he found another small reptilian creature at the controls. Holding his blaster to its temple, Jonah ordered him to turn the power off. Reluctantly, fearfully, the creature complied.

Jonah turned the Uk pilot over to Willard and immediately assessed the injuries to his team. Five had sustained minor injuries, one had serious injuries and another was significantly wounded. The two with the most serious injuries remained in wolf form to speed the healing process.

Jonah then headed back into Grima House. He wanted to take a look at that control room. Molly accompanied him and he explained along the way that when he was in the lower room earlier he experienced a tingling that foretold of something more than the immediate danger. He wanted to investigate. Once inside he surveyed several of the screens on the walls and finally stationed himself in the chair before the main control panel.

"I can see your thoughts working. What is it Jonah?" Molly asked.

He was slow to answer.

"Tell me, does this screen look familiar to you?"

"Yeah. It looks like the little screen on our box, the one with the grids."

"That's what I was thinking."

Molly reached across him and tentatively fumbled with a switch on the side panel. Immediately a grid formed across the screen. Toggling a switch next to the first, the grid went from large to small, and a small green light displayed on the screen.

"That looks very familiar doesn't it Jonah?" She asked. "This is a map of the area, just like on our little box. The light there, that must be your airship, the one they used for the escape."

She toggled the switch back to show the larger grid, but Jonah immediately toggled it off.

"Wait, Molly, look…not at the light that is flashing, but here," he pointed with his finger. "These little lights, what do you think those are?"

"I see," there were three of them in the upper left of the screen, but the lights weren't flashing, just a steady glow. "More ships?"

"Exactly. Three not flashing, one flashing. Why?

"Because the one flashing…"

"Is flying…"

They looked at each other.

"So they have five ships now, counting the one outside?" Molly asked.

"Yes, but more importantly, the flashing light, the ship in the air, it's heading toward the others."

"And?"

"And, if you look carefully, this line, I think," he pointed at the screen. "Represents the Illinois River, meaning…"

"My gosh. They are in Tahlequah, or close to it."

Molly fumbled in her pocket and pulled out one of the talking box. Engaging the button, she excitedly called for an answer on the other end.

"Marela, Marela…Molly calling. Can you hear me?"

A moment later she repeated it.

Again, there was no answer.

"You gave Marela the other box?"

"I thought we might need to communicate with someone in Tahlequah if Gray Wolf…"

She was interrupted by Marela's voice coming from the box in her hand.

"Molly…can hear you…"

There were background noises that were making it difficult to understand her. Like a light in his head, Jonah realized what was happening. It was the sound of gunfire and explosions.

"…attack…airships…the star guns are not work…" the box went silent.

"They're under attack. Look…" Molly pointed at the screen. The lights that were solid were now flashing. "They're all in the air now. What did she say, the star guns aren't working? They'll be slaughtered."

Jonah jumped up from the console and started for the door, but suddenly stopped, listening intently.

"Tingling again?

"Yes, shhh…"

Jonah detected a sound, coming from below their feet. He scanned the room, as large as it was, and in a moment headed to the far corner.

"Here…" he studied another electronic panel on the wall and followed a conduit that stretched down to the floor. He tentatively pushed first one button then the next. The third button toggled a switch and a panel in the wall slide open revealing a staircase that led down. He looked at Molly and headed down. At the bottom there was a dimly lit hallway with several doors that led off to each side. Slowly, carefully, he walked down the hallway to the first door. There was a small window in it with vertical bars. It was a jail cell. He reached down and slide the bolt unlocking it and slowly opened it. It was dark inside.

"Hello. "

A voice, weak but human, responded.

"Are you the one that caused the noise above?"

"Yes… I am Jonah Montana."

"Are you friend or enemy?"

"Well, if the lizard men have you locked up, then I must be a friend. We would share the same enemy."

"Good…then help me up."

Jonah entered the small cell and nearly tripped over a figure laying on the floor. Helping him rise, the prisoner offered his name.

"I am Touch the Clouds," Jonah should have known by his height. Standing he was too tall to fit into the room. "In the other cells you will find more prisoners."

Molly was in the hallway now and started opening cell doors. Slowly prisoners began emerging from all but one of the cells. Out in the hallway now, Jonah looked at the others.

"Tenskwatawa.." said one.

"Geronimo." Said another.

Two of the prisoners nodded. One was unable to talk but the fourth pointed at his chest.

"Chalpultemec."

Jonah nodded and motioned for them to follow him up the stairs. All of them were able to navigate the stairs except Touch the Clouds who required assistance. Half way up Jaygokwe met them and assisted in bringing Touch the Clouds to the top and into the kitchen beyond. Once there Geronimo headed to first one window and then the next.

"They are gone?" He asked.

Jonah answered in crude Apache, but Geronimo shook his head.

"I speak the language of the White man. Where are the snake eyes?"

"They have fled. But we have killed many," Jonah told him. Geronimo nodded in approval. "But now they attack my people, the Cherokee, and I must finish the fight."

Geronimo liked that idea.

"I have waited for just a fight. Geronimo will fight with you."

Jonah looked at him. Who could resist an Apache wanting revenge on the Uks?

"Then follow me," he replied just as Willard entered the room. "This is Ridley Willard. He is friend to the Cherokee and all our brothers. He will help each of you to return to your people."

"Jonah, it will take days…" Molly started.

"No, it won't. I'm going to catch a really fast ride," he said and headed out the door.

"A really…what? Oh, you must be kidding…" Molly was quick on his heels and behind her came Geronimo.

Walking into the street in front of Grima House Jonah approached the Uk pilot, now being watched by Chatsu.

"Do you speak English?" Jonah asked the Uk.

"A little," clicked the reptilian.

"How damaged is the flying ship?"

The Uk didn't answer, but as quick as lightning Geronimo relieved Chatsu of the knife he carried in his waist band, wrapped an arm around the Uk's neck and placed the blade sharply against the scales of his face.

"Answer the question," he demanded.

With eyes wild with fear the Uk complied.

"It requires some repair."

"What kind of repairs? Serious repairs?"

Geronimo tightened the choke hold.

"Not serious."

"Will it fly?"

"Yes."

"Then get up and lets go."

Geronimo dragged the pilot to his feet as Jonah explained to Chatsu what was happening in Tahlequah. He ordered him to gather the able bodied clan warriors, except for the injured, and to report back to the flying ship. He turned to Molly and Alex who had joined them.

"Don't even think about it. I am going," Molly informed him.

Without arguing Jonah turned and headed to the War Bird. The ramp was still down but because of the way the ship was tilted it was a couple of feet short of touching the ground. Leaping on to the platform he offered Molly a hand and then helped Geronimo lift the Uk up. Inside they discovered the ship's interior was smaller than it looked from the outside. Jonah pushed the Uk into what was obviously the pilot's chair. Geronimo made certain he didn't move by keeping the knife to his neck. Checking the control panel, the Uk looked back at Jonah for instructions.

"Get us in the air," he barked.

Looking around the interior of the craft Jonah spotted another control panel with a screen he recognized. Small lights that represented the ships around Tahlequah were still moving around. All were flashing except one.

"Molly. You're the one that understands these maps. Sit here and make certain snake eyes doesn't take us in the wrong direction, and keep up with these other ships. Geronimo, if he tries to pull anything that looks wrong, cut off his nose."

The Apache offered a rare smile.

Chatsu, Jaygokwe and three other of the *i-na-ge-hi wa hya* clambered on board and looked wildly around the inside. Jaygokwe flashed his usual smile.

"Let's go," Jonah shouted at the Uk and immediately the hum of the engines sounded and the floor began to shake. Lifting slightly off the ground, the ramp retracted and the bottom door closed. They were airborne.

Jonah watched the Uk carefully and took note of how he steered the ship and what controls he used to increase and decrease power. It didn't seem that complicated. Higher and higher they rose into the night air and the lights of New Orleans slowly became smaller below them. The control panel in front of the Uk came alive with a larger version of the screen that Molly was watching at her station. Jonah leaned over the Uk and pointed at the flashing lights.

"This is where I want to go. Take us there."

Though the War Bird tilted to navigate a turn, Jonah noticed the floor seemed to remain level. Occasionally he could feel the ship shutter.

"Why is it doing that?" He demanded of the Uk.

"Stabilizer is damaged. It is not a problem."

"Then make this ship go fast and get us there quickly, understand?"

The Uk nodded and the ship lurched forward. In moments they were cruising across the night sky at speeds Jonah could not comprehend. It must have been the floor or some technology he could not understand, but in spite of the speed and occasional sharp turn, Jonah never lost his footing.

Molly was watching the map screen closely and informed Jonah when they were about half the distance to the flashing lights. It had only taken a few minutes.

Addressing the pilot, Jonah asked about the onboard weapon system. The Uk was slow replying until the Apache placed the edge of the knife on the scales of his nose.

"Behind you."

Jonah turned and saw another screen, motioning for Geronimo to watch the Uk, and sat down in the chair in front of it. He played with several switches and the screen changed various colors. With a small control on the right he learned he could cause a small square on the screen to move from side to side and up and down. There were two red buttons and he tried each of them, discovering they were indeed triggers that fired the weapons.

Gray Wolf scrambled from the telegraph office to the stable just ahead of a blast from a passing War Bird. Inside, One Owl was barking orders to a group of *i-na-ge-hi wa hya* as a pair of Comanche women were wrapping the wounds of a fallen Cheyenne warrior.

"There are Uk warriors heading up the street from the west," Gray Wolf yelled above the sounds of the explosions.

One Owl nodded and sent his warriors to engage them. Nearby a couple of the Comanche were firing Winchesters at Uks near the post office. It was chaos on the streets of Tahlequah, and Gray Wolf knew the superior firepower of the enemy was taking its toll on his defenses.

Nearby Two Bears was helping the wounded into a wagon while Marela suddenly changed to wolf form and darted off in the direction of the council house where she ravaged a Krieger who was leading a charge at a group of elderly and children who were barricaded in the school house.. There were Creek warriors on the roof of the trading post firing rapidly up the street and across a field a second War Bird was setting down, Uk soldiers offloading down the ramp.

Gray Wolf had counted four ships in the sky at one time and knew that each was powered by a crystal. That meant only his crystal, the one hidden by Wovaka, and a third from one of the missing Keepers remained. If they were acquired by the Uks, the war would be lost and the world subject to total domination. He could not allow that to happen, for once all the crystals were in their possession, they would unleash the full power of the ancient machines and the world would fall into slavery. If only the Thunderbird clan, the star people of Pleiades were still on Earth to lend their superior fire power. But he knew they were gone now, called far away to distant corners of the Galaxy where other conflicts, bigger battles demanded their attention, for war had spread to the far reaches of infinite space and their numbers had dwindled through the centuries. So the hope of earth's people depended on Jonah now, the last to carry the Thunderbird bloodline, and he was miles and miles away.

Gray Wolf considered his options. He lad lived a long life. If the Uks won the day he knew what he must do. He must take his own life to prevent them from finding the master crystal, for it was the power crystal that unified the others. It was true that all the crystals were powerful. But the power crystal was the key to them all, the one crystal that greatly intensified the power of all the others. With it the Uk'tena could power the larger star ships that were buried deep beneath the oceans. Then they could rejoin the Galactic conflict – and with a power so great even the Thunderbird would be challenged where ever they might be, and all the people of all the galaxies of all the worlds could suffer.

All hope, he feared, was quickly waning.

He looked into the sky, the dawn was just now touching the horizon, and he prayed to the Great Spirit to save the people. Slowly he pulled the knife from his waistband and prepared to meet his fate.

It was then a third War Bird landed in Two Bear's field and Uk troops were offloading down the ramp and headed into the city, and a fourth ship hovered over the edge of town and was firing blasts now at homes and buildings along Tahlequah's main street. Smoke filled the air and Gray Wolf Knew the end was near. But for reasons unknown, Gray Wolf hesitated before using the blade to slice his throat. He did not know why, but something inside compelled him to watch as yet a fifth airship arrived on the scene, high in the morning sky, and suddenly its great guns sounded and an array of blasts struck the hovering airship that had been randomly targeting buildings in the village.

Gray Wolf rubbed smoke from his eyes not believing what he was seeing. The War Bird that had been hovering shuttered and wobbled and burst into flames just as another volley erupted from above it. With a deafening explosion the damaged airship exploded in mid air sending metal debris raining down upon the village. It took a moment for him to understand what he was happening, but suddenly he realized that it must be Jonah who was controlling this fifth airship. His hope was confirmed when it turned its fire on one of the three airships that had landed in the field.

A cheer suddenly erupted from the ground for Gray Wolf was not the only one to see it. The besieged people of Tahlequah and their allies realized that miraculously help had arrived from a most unexpected source. Jonah's War Bird opened fire again and again, this time striking not only the ship on the ground but a large contingent of Uk'tena warriors who were now scattering in every direction. Swinging sharply to the side, Jonah fired on the other two ships that had landed. Volley after volley of fire spewed from the his War Bird and many of the blasts connected as smoke billowed high into the morning sky.

The Uks, taken by surprise, were confused and now at a disadvantage. Perhaps they were too involved in unloading troops or personnel on board had sustained casualties, but for whatever the reason, the three ships that had landed simply sat silent on the ground like wounded birds and they became easy targets as Jonah's ship riddled them with blasts again and again causing massive damage and destruction.

The third ship on the ground, the first to land, was trying to lift off to engage Jonah's War Bird. But as quickly as it rose, Jonah's ship unloaded a volley of fire that struck the top of the vessel sending it crashing back to the ground with such a force that two of the legs that were still extended crumpled, forcing the leading edge of the disk to tip and burrow into the field.

I-na-ge-hi wa hya warriors recognized the opportunity and ran onto the field and engaged the scattering Uk warriors. Their numbers were reduced by Jonah's fire, but one of the Clan's warriors who carried a blaster that had not worked before pointed the gun and squeezed the trigger anyway, and to his surprise it fired suddenly, striking a reptilian square in the head. Apparently the Uks were able to prevent the blasters the Cherokee had captured from working, perhaps by remote control, and until Jonah exacted damage to one or more of the airships, they had become useless. The exceptions were the star gun grandfather had given to Jonah and the blaster he and Molly had taken from the Uk warrior on the bluff that they took with them to New Orleans. No one knew the why or how of it, they only realized that now all of them were working again, and those that had them started firing, and suddenly the Cherokee and their allies were gaining control of the ground battle as a result. A few of the Wolf Clan transformed to beasts while those with blasters rained fire on the enemy.

It was easy pickings now. With one ship destroyed and three crippled or disabled on the ground, Jonah had won the sky. The tide was turning and Kriegers and Uks were being cut down on the streets and fields by the dozen. The Indians were still taking casualties as well, but slowly and systematically that changed as *i-na-ge-hi wa hya* ripped and tore into the enemy with such fierceness that songs would later be written about their courage and rage.

Jonah would have kept up the fight in the sky but his damaged ship was slowly losing power. It had served him well, but the damage it suffered in New Orleans and the fire it had taken from the ground in this battle were too much. And when he looked at Molly, and then back at the pilot's console he gasped, for the Reptilian pilot now laid slumped on the control deck with blood oozing from a deep wound in his neck. It was Geronimo, the Apache, that sat at the controls, for who knew how long now, and he was piloting the craft on his own, obviously having watched the Uk pilot enough to know how to make the bird respond, and he had done a great job of it that would ensure his name would long be remembered.

But heavily damaged and losing power, the controls unresponsive, Geronimo simply looked at Jonah and shrugged his shoulders. They were going down. They were near the open field and very low in the sky and Geronimo miraculously managed to get a last puff of life from the engine just as they hit. It was enough to ease their landing greatly. It was a hard jolt, but they survived and the ship remained intact.

The ramp lowered and Jonah rushed down and on to the field just in time to see the damaged War Bird, the one with the crumpled legs - the same one that carried Fanchon Harleaux on board - managed to shake violently and rise slowly out of the dirt and gain altitude. Taking ground fire from the Cherokee blasters however, Fanchon Harleaux ordered the War Bird to fly instead of fight, and it fled as quickly as the damaged ship would go, disappearing over the near horizon, wobbling and smoking along the way.

Watching the last War Bird flee from the battle, a few of the Uk'tena warriors began laying down their blasters, recognizing they had lost the battle. Where could a Uk run when trapped in the middle of Indian Territory? Soon they all either fought to the death or surrendered in numbers. Only a few of the Kriegers resisted, but they were mercilessly dispatched by the *i-na-ge-hi wa hya* where they stood.

Thick smoke filled the air, but as the first full rays of the morning sun spread across the field and painted the sky a beautiful shade of coral, a cool breeze from the northwest began to blow, and where there had been a landscape of conflict and turmoil, a beautiful autumn morning was beginning to spread.

Molly stepped down from the ramp and Geronimo and Chatsu and the other Wolf Clan warriors followed, and a new day was dawning on the Clans and the many tribes of the Americas. The joy of victory was tempered by the loss of many warriors, but amid the solemn sorrow rose a cacophony of yelps and hollers in typical Indian fashion. For every victory there is a price, but celebrating was as much to honor the dead as for those that survived. Even a contingent of Calvary who had fought beside the Apache and Comanche and Creek and Ute began to shout and fire their rifles into the air, embracing their native brothers in the spirit of victory.

Molly reached for Jonah's hand and squeezed it, and he placed an arm around her shoulder and smiled. Geronimo spotted a group of Apache, and when they saw him they scampered up on their ponies and in their native language lauded his efforts, and he told them the story of how he had flown the great War Bird in the sky and they were humbled and glad.

By late afternoon the dead had been gathered and buried and the task of putting out fires and clearing debris was taking place at remarkable speed, a tribute to the resourcefulness of the native cultures. Using a captured Uk technician from one of the damaged ships, Alex and Gray Wolf supervised the recovery of the sacred crystals that were used to power the airships. With great labor the ships were pulled by large teams of horses and by the sweat and muscle of hundreds of men to the center of the last field of battle and completely destroyed using first the captured star guns and then massive bonfires made with the rubble of homes and buildings that had been destroyed. Days later Alex politely protested the destruction of such advanced technology, but it was too late. A joint tribal council had made the decision and what was done was done. The star guns had been secretly gathered by Gray Wolf however, who said that Jonah would decide where they were to be hidden in the event the need to use them should ever arise again.

While Harleaux had escaped with a War Bird and the crystal that powered it, and while there were other hidden airships far away, some even larger and more advanced, Gray Wolf reasoned they could not be used in great numbers so long as the remaining crystals were again hidden and kept safe.

In Washington, Grover Cleveland sat at his large oak desk in his New York office and discussed the recent events with Ridley Willard and Alex Bell, and after their reports were filed Alex was sent back to Indian Territory to work with Gray Wolf and other tribal leaders in opening an avenue of better communication with the government. There was still much that could be learned from them.

The discovery of and the threat of alien intervention would forever change the Nation, including its political structure. Already his party was touting Cleveland as the next American president, a plan that eventually came to fruition. The Culper Ring, and the newly formed agency headed by Willard that was charged with keeping tabs on fringe science and investigating more mysteries in the years ahead, both performed admirably. Willard and Bell and Montana and Langtry would get medals for their work, and the Council of Keepers and the Cherokee General Council would receive special recognition for their contribution to American Society, as would leaders of every major tribe across the Americas.

Gray Wolf hoped it would represent a better understanding and degree of cooperation between the Native cultures and the white man's government. But Geronimo wondered why the technology was not kept and used to expel the 'white eyes' from Indian lands. But for the moment at least, a new found peace and a willingness for cross-culture understanding and cooperation appeared to be blossoming, and Gray Wolf hoped it would survive the test of time.

Jonah Tenkiller Montana would spend most of the autumn helping to rebuild and reorganize the Cherokee nation and he and Molly traveled to Missouri to proudly present a Presidential directive that set her uncle, Jim Lumley, free. By mid November they returned to Tahlequah where Molly found a permanent home in the Sunday House of Two Bears and Marela, and she spent her days and evenings conspiring with Jonah on the steady stream of new assignments they regularly received from Alex Bell.

Alex was content after being provided free reign and a sizable budget to work on inventions based upon alien technology he had seen, and over the course of several years his name found a permanent place in the history books of America. He remained a friend and was active in the many assignments that fell to Jonah and Molly to investigate – and there were many.

Geronimo was pardoned and allowed to return to Arizona territory until he and a group of renegades raided livestock from an Arizona military post. Eventually he was captured again and became a ward of the state.

The other Keepers and representatives of the many tribes made their long journeys back to their home lands after the Last Great Battle – as it would come to be known - and vowed to keep the channels of communication open, especially with the principle people, the *Aniyvwiya;* the Cherokee.

The Wolf Clan and the *i-na-ge-hi wa hya* prayed the day would never come again for them to hunt like wolves, though they vowed to remain ever ready if the need should arise, and often they could be seen running in the forest practicing their skills and preserving their heritage as the protectors of the Cherokee.

Deep in an undersea base off the coast of Cuba at the primary Uk'tena Earth base, Fanchon Harleaux suffered a fate worse than death. Supreme Planetary Commander Thet had his head surgically removed and placed on display as an example of the price for failure. Thet considered the ill conceived offensive a terrible set back, but like an expert chess player, he knew that losing a single game was little more than a lesson learned.

He reasoned that if Earth could not be subjugated then it should be destroyed, and the only thing that kept him from proceeding with that plan was a way off the planet for him and his remaining surviving contingent of the Uk'tena. Already his best scientists were working on a way to intensify the energy of the sacred crystal that was still in his possession. That enhanced power would give him the ability to send a message across the light years of space and make the Uk'tena galactic council aware that his remnant society of Draconians were still alive on Earth, and soon afterward, he hoped, they would send a Mother Ship to rescue them, and then the Earth would fall.

PREFACE TO APPENDIX

America – the New World - must have been a frightening place to early explorers and settlers who traveled from Europe and beyond in search freedom, hope, fame and fortune. To begin with, they were coming from a world that was densely populated and well ordered – civilized by their standards – to a place that was full of dark swamps, dense forests and smoky mountains. Imagine the first non-native American to look at the splendor and magnificence of Niagara Falls, or depths and majesty of the great Grand Canyon.

There were mountains so tall a wagon couldn't cross them. There were no roads through the Badlands. There were miles and miles of relentless and unforgiving deserts, rattlesnakes and grizzly bears. Think of the painted desert of Utah or vast plains of the Midwest and the impact they must have made on the first settlers to push west across the continent. And then there were dark-skinned natives who often painted their faces and beat their drums throughout the night, who danced away the night and perform rituals foreign to the European eye. The had strange stories to tell about giant Thunderbirds and of skin walkers that could transform from human to animal and back again at will. Some of the tribesmen talked about coming from the stars; places like the Pleiades cluster and Sirius and Ursa Minor and other star systems. They worshiped feathered serpents and spoke of fierce water creatures that could steal a man's soul and a few would chew on strange plants that would allow them to fly or talk to their Gods.

America was a very frightening place.

The following appendix features but a few of the many historical reports of close encounters of the Old West.

HISTORICAL APPENDIX

Before the Wright brothers made their virgin voyage and before Henry Ford sold his first automobile there were abundant reports of strange flying machines in America's Old West. When reports of such flying craft were made in the 1800s, often adorned with flashing lights and traveling at incredible speeds, the likely excuse of misidentification could not be used by skeptics. Whatever witnesses were seeing in the sky was anything but a plane or satellite. Examination of some of these aerial sightings in America's frontier West offer substantial evidence that something truly strange and unknown was at work. - **LH**

Saucer Crash and Alien Burial At Aurora, Texas – April 1897

The 1897 flying disk that crashed in the sleepy agriculture community of Aurora, Texas, is an example of an incredible story of a close encounter of the Old West. Located west of Fort Worth, the chief local commodity in Aurora at the time was cotton and flour. The community's 300-plus residents were mostly farmers and the community sported two cotton gins and two schools at the time. The tallest structure was a windmill that served to bring water from a shallow well.

On April 18 that year S. E. Hayden, an Aurora cotton buyer, reported a flying disk that was trailing smoke and crashed into a windmill on the property of local Judge J.S. Proctor. The Dallas Morning News published an article that alleged the remains of a small, non-human body was recovered along with pieces of an "unrecognized metal", believed to be fragments from the craft. An officer of a U.S. Army outpost in nearby Fort Worth was called in to examine and identify the body, and concluded it was "not of this world", and speculated the remains may have been of "an entity from Mars".

Not knowing what to do with the strange body or the remaining wreckage scattered across the field near the windmill, reports indicate the wreckage was collected and tossed down a well and the small humanoid body was "given a Christian burial" in the local Mason's cemetery. A grave marker was erected, but disappeared years later after a contemporary report attracted a large number of curiosity seekers. Today a Texas State

Historical Marker can be found at the cemetery that mentions the alien grave.

UFO Crash and Artifact Recovery, Dublin, Texas - June, 1891

Was the crash at Aurora, which predated the Roswell incident by 50 years, the first reported UFO crash in America? Apparently not. Preceding the UFO crash in Aurora a remarkably similar incident occurred in the summer of 1891 in the town of Dublin, Texas - birthplace of the Dr Pepper bottling company. At the time, Dublin was little more than a farming community. Cotton was its largest commodity and life centered around farming and ginning operations.

On June 13, 1891, a remarkable incident occurred on a Saturday as many of the small community's townsfolk were actively milling around the town visiting with friends, stopping at the local mercantile, and casually taking a day off from the rigors of farm life. Newspaper accounts indicate a large number of local residents spotted a "flaming object" in the sky. According to reports, the object was brilliantly lighted "like flames but even brighter" and began to slow and eventually hover over the local cotton mill, suddenly exploding and sending debris across much of the town. Witnesses claim the explosion rattled windows and captured the attention of the entire community, scattering residents who sought shelter from what some thought was the "end of the world".

The following day a more careful search turned up a most unusual discovery, chunks of rock that were described as similar to what might be found following a volcano. In addition, several small fragments of a paper-like substance were found with printing on them. On close examination, the written characters on these pieces were in an unknown language, the likes of which no one had ever seen.

A newspaper account of the incident attracted a great deal of attention from scholars in nearby Fort Worth and Dallas. But when inquiring reporters and researchers arrived in Dublin a few days later, a local flour mill operator who collected the many pieces of paper-like fragments reported they had mysteriously disappeared. Many of the metallic fragments were still available as several of the towns people had collected them. But the prize artifacts, the paper with the writing on them, were mysteriously gone forever.

Interestingly, between April 13 and 17, 1897, following the crash at Aurora, there were 38 reported sightings of "airships" in 23 counties, mostly in North Central Texas, in the vicinity of Erath County. In contemporary times, the area is noted as a hot bed of UFO activity. In January, 2008, a remarkable sighting occurred in nearby Stephenville, Texas, and was witnessed by hundreds of credible witnesses, including police officers and store owners in the community. The celebrated sighting is proving to be one of the most remarkable in recent years and received widespread press coverage including eye witness interviews on national televisions news and talk shows.

According to a report in the Fort Worth Star-Telegram, an area including Aurora, Dublin and Stephenville is an area with high concentrations of UFO sightings and incidents over many decades, dating back to the days of Comanche occupation of the area.

Messages From The Stars, Great Falls, Montana, October 1864

James Lumley was a trapper in the mid 19th century spending much of his adult life plying his trade in the upper Rocky Mountains of Montana. A simple man and a loner by trade, you can imagine the impact a celestial event must have made on his life while camping in a remote area near the Great Falls of the Upper Missouri River.

According to a published report in the Cincinnati Democrat, Lumley was sitting in his mountain camp near Cadotte Pass when, just after sunset, he witnessed a bright luminous body in the heavens moving at a great speed in an easterly direction. Visible for at least five seconds, the airborne object suddenly separated into particles, resembling, as Mr. Lumley describes it, 'the bursting of a sky-rocket in the air.' The newspaper report appeared many months after the incident occurred when Lumley had traveled to Cincinnati to sell his load of furs.

According to the report, Lumley "heard a heavy explosion, which jarred the earth perceptibly, and this was shortly followed by a rushing sound, like a tornado sweeping through the forest. A strong wind sprang up about the same time, but suddenly subsided."

Lumley claims the following day he headed out towards where he believed the "meteor" might have crash landed and soon discovered a wide path that had been cut through the forest. Trees had been uprooted and broken off near the ground. The tops of hills were shaved off and the earth plowed up in many places. Following the path through the forest, he stumbled upon an area littered with stone fragments, still warm to the touch. A little further along he claims he found several very large stone fragments carved with "etchings", or hieroglyphics. Lumley said he also discovered fragments of a substance resembling glass, and here and there dark stains, as though caused by a liquid.

Mysterious Airship of Galisteo (Lamy), New Mexico, March, 1880

March 26, 1880 was a quiet Friday night in tiny Galisteo Junction, New Mexico (now the town of Lamy). The train from nearby Santa Fe had come and gone and the railroad agent, his day's work finished, routinely locked up the depot and set out with a couple of friends for a short walk.

Suddenly the group heard what they described as voices speaking in an unknown language, which seemed to be coming from the sky. The men looked up to see an object, "monstrous in size," rapidly approaching from the west, flying so low that elegantly-drawn characters could be seen on the outside of the peculiar vehicle. Inside, occupants could also be seen, appearing to be ordinary humans. The witnesses described what they called laughter and also heard "some type of music" coming from the craft. The craft itself was described as "fish-shaped" -- like a cigar with a tail.

As the object passed overhead the group reported something fell from the "air ship". The depot agent said he immediately recovered an item that resembled "a beautiful flower with a slip of fine silk-like paper containing characters". Almost immediately the aerial machine ascended and sailed away toward the east at a remarkable high speed. The next morning searchers found what they described as a cup, which they believed also may have fallen from the aircraft.

"It is of very peculiar workmanship," the Santa Fe New Mexican reported, "entirely different to anything used in this country." The depot agent took the cup and the flower and put them on display. Before the day was over, however, this physical evidence was sold to a "traveler". It was in the evening of the day after the sighting that a "mysterious gentleman" identified only as a "collector of curiosities" appeared in town, examined the finds, suggested they were Asiatic in origin and offered such a large sum of money for them that the agent had no choice but to accept. The "collector" scooped up his purchases and never was seen again.

Falling Object Startles Cowhands, Max, Nebraska, June 6, 1884

John W. Ellis was a southwest Nebraska livestock breeder and an ordinary cowboy according to his friends. Hard work, an honest day's living and down home honesty were said to be his creed. It must have made it hard for Ellis to tell the story of how he and two of his wranglers working in the field experienced a very strange phenomena on warm summer day in June of 1884.

Newspaper accounts from the Nebraska Nugget, the nearest newspaper to the frontier town of Max, says Ellis and his herdsmen were engaged in a summer roundup when they spied an object high in the sky hurtling down toward the Nebraska plain at an unbelievable speed. Ellis described the object as "on fire" with a trailing tail of smoke and flame. As it neared the ground, a short rolling bank in the ground hid the actual impact from them, but when the object hit an audible explosion shook the ground and could be "felt through our boots".

Running across the field and over the bank, the wranglers must have had a hard time determining what they were looking at in the field below. The object apparently had skidded across the ground for some distance leaving behind a charred rut as it dragged to a stop. One of the cowboys, identified as Alf Williamson, received burns to his hands when he attempted to touch wreckage from the craft. He was taken back to the ranch house and treated.

What wreckage remained of the craft was "unusual" according to the Nebraska Journal. The largest piece remaining was metallic - like brass - about 16 inches wide, three inches thick and three-and-a-half feet long, but weighing "very little". More material of the same type was collected by area cattle brand district manager E.W. Rawlins, who could offer no explanation for the crashed object.

The Strange Light of Shreveport, La., 1860

Nineteenth Century reports of unidentified flying objects were many, but perhaps because of a lack of modern record keeping and adequate document storage, most reports are short and often vague. Combined with non-technical witnesses who were seeing something odd rarely seen before, many stories and reports of the era can be confusing.

Such is the case of the unusual light spotted in the skies over Shreveport, Louisiana in 1860. The exact date is unknown, but multiple witnesses report a rare phenomena that made a lasting impression on the residents of this sleepy river town in the northwestern part of the state.

The best report of record comes from a family journal - author unknown - that resided for years in a local museum. It reads: "Our attention was called to a strange light in the heavens. On going out into the gallery we had a magnificent view of it. It appeared to the naked eye about 300 yards in length, extending from North to West appearing just above the tallest trees. Its color was that of a red hot stove from the center, beautiful rays resembling those of the sun drawing water would ascend to a considerable height, the whole presenting a very beautiful and sublime appearance. We watched it for about an hour without perceiving it to change any."

While little has been written about the incident, it's fair to speculate that the sighting happened near the beginning of the Civil War when tensions were running high with the expectation of the war reaching Louisiana soil. Confederate recruiters were actively soliciting volunteers, and there were rumors that Northern forces were in possession of new and destructive war inventions. Such rumors may have been fresh on the minds of Shreveport residents who witnessed the strange light in the sky. But whatever it may have been, there are no reports of its return, and few details about its origin.

A Fiery Vortex at Ashland, Tn., 1889

Reports of unexplained phenomenon are often offered by witnesses with an untrained eye. In some instances, the cause and effect of the incidents take precedence over what may have caused them. Such is the strange case of the fiery vortex, or tornado, of Ashland, Tennessee.

Though well documented (a report of the incident can be found on the NOAA, National Weather Service Web site), the story tells of a frightening fiery wind that caused wide spread destruction across the countryside, but lacks in attributing the incident to a specific cause. Perhaps reporting aerial "airships" was too racy for the times, or perhaps the many witnesses to the incident simply didn't know how or could not discern the source. Whatever may have caused it, the damages left behind are terribly impressive.

A published report in an 1869 Symon's Monthly Meteorological Magazine reads as follows:

"A whirlwind came along over the neighboring woods, taking up small branches and leaves of trees and burring them in a sort of flaming cylinder that traveled at a rate of about five miles an hour, developing size as it traveled. It passed directly over the spot where a team of horses were feeding and singed their manes and tails up to the roots; it then swept towards the house, taking a stack of hay in its course. It seemed to increase in heat as it went, and by the time it reached the house it immediately fired the shingles from end to end of the building, so that in ten minutes the whole dwelling was wrapped in flames. The tall column of traveling caloric then continued its course over a wheat field that had been recently cradled, setting fire to all the stacks that happened to be in its course. Passing from the field, its path lay over a stretch of woods, which reached the river. The green leaves on the trees were crisped to a cinder for a breadth of 20 yards, in a straight line to the Cumberland (river). When the "pillar of fire" reached the water, it suddenly changed its route down the river, raising a column of steam which went up to the clouds for about half-a-mile, when it finally died out. Not less than 200 people witnessed this strangest of strange phenomena, and all of them tell substantially the same story about it."

Modern UFO investigators speculate that what witnesses actually saw could have been a spacecraft hidden in clouds, intentional or not. The heat, which may have caused the fire, may have been generated by a propulsion engine or because the spacecraft was experiencing mechanical difficulty.

While the National Weather Service fails to offer a reasonable meteorological explanation for the event, they admit no known weather condition could have caused it, leaving the incident in the realm of mystery.

Spaceship South of Tombstone, Arizona, 1889

South of Arizona's Superstition Mountains in the town of Nogales just across the Mexican border, a published story surfaced in the 1970s about an Arizona lawman who chased a crippled UFO into Mexico before occupants of the craft abducted a member of the posse. The incident was alleged to happen in 1889. The report claimed the incident was reported by an eyewitness, Jorge Hernandez, who later retold the story to a Catholic priest, Father Joel de Mola, before he died in 1971 at the age of 107. He claims his father was a member of that posse and he said he grew up hearing the story many times over down through the years.

According to the priest, Hernandez said he joined the posse after a rancher spotted a strange flying craft that had landed on his ranch in Arizona, near the Mexican border. The rancher sent his son to the nearest settlement for help. A U.S. Marshal hastily assembled a posse of 12, which included Hernandez. Arriving at the ranch, they watched in shock and disbelief as the silver, saucer-shaped craft lifted straight up off the ground and flew a few miles at rooftop level before it landed again.

This happened a number of times as the craft continued flying south, landing as if experiencing mechanical problems. Each time the posse would catch up, the craft would rise in the air again and travel farther south, a game of stop and go that allowed the ship to stay a step ahead of the lawmen. By now the strange craft and the posse had entered the fabled Zone of Silence in the Chihuahua Desert where, in modern times, aircraft have been known to lose power and U.S. controlled V-2 rockets and an Athena missile crashed. Could the strange space craft of the 1800s have experienced similar problems trying to fly across the area?

Finally, after a long and hard chase that lasted more a day's ride, the posse caught up with the craft one last time. As they neared, a U.S. Marshall identified in the report only as "Morton" approached the craft with stealth. As the story goes, when he closed in, he simply disappeared into thin air right before the eyes of the posse without a trace. Almost at once the craft lifted and departed at great speed. Morton was never heard from again.

Native American Mythology, Superstition Mountain Region

Deep in arid Southwestern Arizona the Superstition Mountains rise above the desert floor, a mysterious place of legend, Native American lore and tales of strange encounters with an unknown race.

As strange as it may sound, such stories abounded in 19th century Arizona when prospectors traveled west and first heard that within the fabled mountains were riches of unmined gold, tales of ancient treasures, and far-flung legends of underground tunnels and caves where a race of unknown people protected hidden secrets and coveted treasures from the world above. Even today the stories are still told around campfires, in taverns, and among the few and hardy that venture into the desolate land.

Some of the more popular stories are those of strange lights, sometimes called ghost lights, that appear on the mountain tops and in the canyons of the rugged and isolated countryside, that often appear under the cover of night and then, mysteriously, disappear "under the mountains".

An old Apache legends hints of a "Lady Below the Mountain" and a "White Stallion" that guard the many underground secrets hidden there. The infamous Apache renegade Geronimo was said to use the mountains as a hiding place, and there have been many reports of him "stepping into rock walls" and disappearing from pursuers, then mysteriously surfacing hundreds of miles away in an area of New Mexico where today White Sands Proving Grounds stand. The strange tale is supported by Native American beliefs that the "underworld" is the place of origin of America's native peoples, and that eventually they emerged from their "sipapu", a hole in the ground that connects the underworld with the surface world above.

Indeed, Pueblo, Hopi, Anasazi and other North American cultures share a common belief with many of the Mesoamerican cultures - the Maya, Zapotec, Toltec and Aztec - that "Star People" traveled to Earth thousands of years ago and established underground cities because the Earth's surface was a harsh environment to their kind. Here they gave birth to the human race, the Indians, who were created to govern the affairs of the surface world and to commune with the sun. Tales of little men and giants abound in both historic and modern Arizona history. Could these beings be the Star People of Native American mythology?

From the Apache Creation Story: *In the beginning nothing existed. Suddenly from the darkness emerged a thin disc, one side yellow and the other side white, appearing suspended in midair. Within the disc sat a small bearded man, Creator, the One Who Lives Above.*

Jicarilla Apache Legend: *In the beginning the earth was covered with water, and all living things were below in the underworld...It was dark in the underworld, and eagle plumes were used for torches...the people didn't see much because they were underground...But the sun was high enough to look through a hole and discover that there was another world - this earth. He told the people, and they all wanted to go up there. They built four mounds to help them reach the upper world.*

Hopi Belief: *Two separate realms exist in the Hopi cosmology, the surface of the earth as the site of human activity and a combined sky/underground region as the home of the sky spirits.*

The Lakota Sioux of the northern plains were dedicated followers of the stars. In modern times, we could liken their 'sky science' to modern astrology. They believed all answers to life's questions lie within the stars. For generations on end, the spiritual leaders of proud Lakota studied the night sky and charted the various sky signs.

According to their Star Legends, there was the Big Dipper, which signified the Seven Council Fires of the Lakota. In the Seven Council Fires Legend, a Lakota woman went into the sky to marry a star, but she fell to her death through a hole in the constellation trying to return to her village. The Lakota belief demonstrates their uncanny understanding of the vastness of space, for it took a long time for the woman to fall, representing the great distance involved. During the long journey down from the stars, she gave birth to a son, and he was named Fallen Star.

For generations of Lakota, Fallen Star was known to be half Lakota, and half star man, who became a legend among the people. His deeds were great and many and he was often attributed with possessing great knowledge and wisdom like his father, the Star.

Another tale from the Lakota Star Legends is the story of brother and sister who guided by Fallen Star, climbed upon a low hill to escape a ravaging bear. But the bear was far too large for the hill to provide adequate refuge. But in his wisdom, Fallen Star caused the hill to rise above the plains so that brother and sister were above the bear's reach. The angry bear used his powerful claws to ascend the hill, but it was far too steep, and each time he would slide down the hill to try again, leaving behind enormous scratches on the slopes. To this day the Lakota can point to the sacred hill with its claw marks, a place they call the Devil's Tower in modern day Wyoming.

The Lakota sky watchers developed a star chart that illustrates a full array of sacred constellations symbols. While the ancient Greek's followed a star configuration they named Betelgeuse, and a six star cluster (Pleiades) they called Taurus, or the bull. But the Lakota, according to the star legend, charted a great constellation represented by a bison, which included both Pleiades and Betelgeuse. The Bison was a part of a larger star system the Lakota considered a racetrack. It was on this racetrack, according to the legends, that animals of every variety competed to determine which one would direct the future of the Lakota people. The lowly magpie was the winning creature, and still today the magpie is considered sacred among the people for upon winning the great sky race, decided as his prize to allow the Lakota to remain on the earth in their native lands.

Many believe the Lakota Star Legends represent a native mythology based upon a connection with actual beings that came to earth from the stars thousands of years ago and interacted with the native people. Ancient astronaut theorists suggest the Lakota's knowledge of the constellations and their star charts hint at such a connection.

In modern times the Hopi Indians of Arizona, and many of their North American kinsmen, speak of star warriors and sky beings as central figures of their belief systems. In our minds, we might think of such terms being used to explain a mythological concept. But the more we understand the complexities involved in their cosmology, the deeper we see into their meaning. Ask any Hopi and they will tell you, the star cluster known as Pleiades is the home of their ancestors. "We come as clouds to bless the Hopi people" is a quote passed from generation to generation among the Hopi, and refers to the star people of the southern sky.

In the mid 1800s the push was on to spread civilization's borders Westward. The "New Americans" called it manifest destiny, believing they were the new stewards of the land bordered in the east by the Atlantic and to the West by the Great Pacific. Wagon trains of immigrants and settlers loaded up their possessions and headed West looking for a land of milk and honey and often seeking fame, fortune, gold and silver, and their rightful place in history. More often than not what they encountered was anything but good fortune or fame, and occasionally, they discovered events beyond their understanding.

As incredible as it may seem to us, many Pueblo-dwellers, including the Ancient Anasazi, the Hopi and the Navajo, believe the Star Beings once nurtured them in a kingdom beneath the ground, the inner-world, or underworld. Evolving into varying physical states through the years, these forerunners to modern Native Americans would graduate from the innermost layer of the Earth to the upper levels, four of them in all, to eventually escape through a hole in the ground known as a Sipapu. They emerged in a transitional state, part animal and part human, learned to walk upright on two legs and finally claimed dominion over the surface, or outer layer of the planet. Even in modern times, the Native Americans at San Ildefonso Pueblo in northern New Mexico, and in many of the other Pueblo communities of the region, demonstrate this 'historical emergence' through periodic ceremonial animal dances held at special times throughout the year. In a dance of both drama and artistic expression, dancers emerge from a modern Kiva, a ceremonial pit in the ground, usually central to the center of the Pueblo, dressed in costumes of animal fur and carrying crooked sticks in each hand to represent their front legs.

As the dance evolves, the participants slowly rise from their bent over and crooked positions and stand firmly on two legs, casting aside their sticks, representing their transition from animal to human form.

Among these Pueblo dwellers is a belief that such power of evolution was given to them by the star people, their stewards, in what we might call magic in modern terms. Many theories suggest something more may have be at work however, perhaps genetic manipulation that helped transform a lower life form , such as a Neanderthal-like humans, into a modern man.

Among these Hopi and Navajo and Pueblo people there is a belief that some tribal members still have the ability to change back to an earlier physical form. They are known as skin walkers. Often compared to the mythical lycanthropes, or werewolves of European lore, these skin walkers are believed to be members of the native community who did not evolve completely, or have embraced their inner nature and periodically return to animal form. They are greatly feared among today's Navajo people, who will not even speak of them openly. A few and perhaps daring members of this culture who are refer to these skin walkers, suggest they are 'throw-backs', individuals who failed in making a successful transition to permanent human form. Perhaps they consider them to be failures of the evolutionary process, bad experiments of the Star Being stewards. Some even suggest that these skin walkers are hybrid humans with mixed genetics of other star people not from the Pleiades system, but from star clusters where life forms are more dramatic, perhaps less human in nature, and anything but benevolent.

For whatever reason, there are myriad tales of skin walkers in historical times who interacted with settlers heading westward in the 1800s. These 'witches', as they were often called, would walk in human form to approach a settler's cabin and spy the family inside, perhaps eating a comfortable dinner by the fire, and the envy inside of them would swell and cause a metamorphosis to animal form. They would then unsuspectingly enter the cabin to ravage the occupants. It is said they could take the form of a bear or wolf, or some other animal of their choosing, but the change would leave them part human and part animal, fierce, relentless and unmerciful.

Many stories of the Old West about animal attacks were believed to be skin walkers, and many times it was innocent tribal members who were wrongly accused of the heinous crimes. Even among the Indians skin walkers were greatly feared, and steps were taken to avoid them. Even in the modern Navajo world, children are instructed to never leave their shoes outside, and if they should urinate outdoors, they are to cover it with dirt lest a skin walker pick up the scent and after nightfall and return to pay an unwelcome visit.

But it wasn't just shape changers that were to be feared in the Old West. Even when settlers and Native Americans peacefully co-existed in the same region, there was a great deal of fear and distrust between them. The 'civilized' westerners were wary of their Indian neighbors, often because they practiced ritual dances late into the night, and as such were considered pagan and dangerous. In addition, many Native cultures spoke of their mysterious encounters with Star Beings, a concept difficult for the settlers to understand, much the same as it is today.

According to a Lakota belief, some 2,000 years ago a mystical being came to the them on the Dakota plains. Her name was White Buffalo Calf Woman.

Other Native American Indian tribes reportedly have similar legends.

According to Chasing Horse, a descendent of Crazy Horse, the great Lakota war chief, White Buffalo Calf Woman came in a cloud that descended from the sky, and off of the cloud stepped the white buffalo calf. As it rolled onto the earth, the calf stood up and became this beautiful young woman who was carrying a sacred bundle in her hand. She spent four days among the Lakota people and taught them about the sacred bundle, the meaning of it.

When she was done teaching, she left the way she came. She went out of the circle, and as she was leaving she turned and told the Lakota that she would return one day for the sacred bundle. And she left the sacred bundle, which the Lakota claim they still have today.

It was also in a similar cloud that War Chief Crazy Horse said he heard the "supreme being" speak and told him how to defeat the White man's army.

He was instructed to visit the elder chiefs of the Lakota and Cheyenne and to unite them and teach them to fight using the White man's methods. The rest is actual history. Crazy Horse's efforts were successful and against all odds, the warriors won decisive battles over the U.S. Calvary, including the deciding battle at the Little Big Horn where George Custer fell. Did Crazy Horse receive instructions from one of the Star Beings?

A Church Ordered By Star Beings?

Ancient Astronaut theorists believe that American religious reformation of the early 1800s provides evidence of alien visitation in the early days of American history. Unknown to many yet widely accepted by millions are the teachings of two American religious reformists of the period, Joseph Smith and his predecessor Brigham Young, founders of the Mormon Church.

Of all recorded alien encounters in America's 19th century Old West, the little know tale of how off world beings visited the Mormon founder at a very young age and delivered a mandate that formed the cornerstone of a religious movement and the founding of one of America's most successful churches.

Founded in 1830 by the then twenty-four year old Joseph Smith, the Church of Jesus Christ of Latter-day Saints (as it is formally named) has emerged to become a world-wide movement now numbering nine million members.

The Church's connection to ancient astronaut theory may have started in 1820. Smith later related that two otherworldly beings appeared and told him to join no church because all were corrupt. Other heavenly beings afterward told him to establish a new church.

In writing about the incident, Smith said *"On September 21, 1823 after retiring to bed,...I discovered a light appearing in my room, which continued to increase until the room was lighter than at noonday, when immediately a personage appeared at my bedside, standing in the air, for his feet did not touch the floor. His whole person was glorious beyond description, and his countenance truly like lightning...I saw, as it were, a conduit open right up into heaven, and he ascended till he entirely disappeared, and the room was left as it had been before this heavenly light had made its appearance.*"

Smith identified this being as "Moroni", who revealed to him the location of two "golden plates containing Native American prehistory" that told how these first Americans built a flourishing and advanced civilization. Moroni instructed Smith where these plates were to be found and further told him of "two stones" he would also find there that would empower him to translate the ancient text on the plates.

Smith did indeed find the plates where the "heavenly being" instructed, and using the stones was able to translate the text and incorporate it into what has come to be known as The Book of Mormon. According to this book, Moses (of Biblical reference) "beheld many lands; and each land was called earth, and there were inhabitants on the face thereof." Then the Lord explained to Moses "there are many worlds that have passed away by the word of my power. And there are many that now stand, and innumerable are they unto man." (Book of Moses 1:28-35)

His translation also stated that many sought "the city of Enoch which God had before taken, separating it from the earth, having reserved it unto the latter days, or the end of the world." (Inspired Version, Genesis 14:34) Joseph Smith's grand-nephew, apostle Joseph Fielding Smith (future president of the church) affirmed this idea in 1954, "we are taught that portions of this earth have been taken from it."

In 1835 Joseph Smith purchased some ancient Egyptian papyri which he translated into the Latter-day Saint scripture, *The Book of Abraham*. It describes a star named Kolob which is near the throne of God. The star (possibly a planet) governed others "which belong to the same order as that upon which thou standest" (Abraham 3:3). Many Latter-day Saints believe Kolob is the planet where God and other celestial beings live.

As further support of ancient astronaut theory, Smith wrote in his translations: ""And I saw the stars, that they were very great, and that one of them was nearest unto the throne of God; and there were many stars which were near unto it; And the Lord said unto me; These are the governing ones; and the name of the great one is Kolob, because it is near unto me, for I am the Lord thy God; I have set this one to govern all those which belong to the same order as that upon which thou standest."

In 1989, Mormon leader Neal A. Maxwell said the Mormons do not know how many inhabited worlds there are, or where they are. But they believe "we are certainly not alone."

In 1852 Brigham Young, who took over the leadership of the Mormon Church after a vigilante mob killed founder Joseph Smith, taught that Adam and Eve lived on another planet before coming to earth. He believed the moon and sun were inhabited. Joseph Fielding Smith echoed this idea in 1954, a descendant of the founder later said "It is my opinion that the great stars that we see, including our sun, are celestial worlds; at least worlds that have passed on to their exaltation."

In the popular Internet Blog Spot, "UFO Experiences", the editors report that in a written interview with a a senior member of the church, Garth Batty, the Church leader says the Mormons' late president Joseph Fielding Smith is quoted by saying "The Lord is not restricted in giving invitations to other creations to visit this earth so you need not be surprised if some visitors from other worlds do visit this one."

Batty wrote: "True religion, unblemished by the doctrines of men, founded upon revelation directly from God, would of course have to give information which is both reasonable and which gives knowledge that God truly has created innumerable worlds which are inhabited."

The Mormon Church and its founders and leaders have been the subject of ridicule and consternation since its early American beginnings in America's Old West. But in the modern world, most agree they are a respected and admirable Church that strongly promotes family values. History tells that with the guidance of Brigham Young, the followers of the Church were successful in moving west to a Valley in Utah and established what is today the modern city of Salt Lake City. The great Mormon Temple is central to the city and is a testament to the successes of the Church and its lasting influence on American society.

CHEROKEE LANGUAGE & CULTURE

Throughout 'Close Encounters of the Old West" you were introduced to a number of words, phrases and sentences written in the phonetic Cherokee language. The Cherokee language, with its multiple dialects, is a beautiful and complex language system. With several "groups" of Cherokee in existence, only three are federally recognized, the Cherokee Nation with headquarters in Tahlequah, Oklahoma, the United Keetoowah Band of Cherokee also with headquarters in Tahlequah, also known as the Nighthawk Society, and the Eastern Band of Cherokee located on the Qualla Boundary in western North Carolina.

There are numerous other groups and organizations that make claim to their Cherokee heritage, including State-recognized Cherokee tribes have headquarters in Texas, Georgia, Missouri and Alabama. Other large and small non-recognized Cherokee organizations are located in Arkansas, Missouri, Tennessee, and other locations in the United States.

Another group, unorganized but arguably of true Cherokee heritage, are descendants of what was referred to as the "old Settlers" of northern Arkansas and Southern Missouri, Cherokees who moved west prior to the infamous Trail of Tears and who later resisted federal registration.

My intent in providing this information is to help the reader understand the Cherokee people are and have long been diverse, widespread and multicultural. The Cherokee Nation of Oklahoma is the largest tribe of Native Americans in the United States with over 300,000 members in the 2000 census. But estimates of at least one million Americans can trace their ancestral lineage to the proud Cherokee people.

Needless to say the language of the Cherokee has become as diverse as those that claim to be blood related, therefore words and phrases used throughout this book may be recognized by one group while others may use a completely different word or phrase to express the same meaning. In other words, this work of fiction should not be used as a Cherokee language lesson or as representative of any one particular dialect of this remarkable language. Over the last year or so I have been involved in language classes offered by the Cherokee Nation in Tahlequah. My very proficient language instructor, Ed Fields, would most probably be horrified at some of the terms used in this novel, while others may be right on the mark by his standards (obviously, I have much to learn). But since the novel is intended to be a work of fiction with the intent of providing entertainment, I have not taken the time or effort to present it for language review. It is my hope that it may spark an interest in you to consider learning more about the language and you can do that by visiting the Cherokee Nation Web site at www.cherokee.org, and click on the free language lesson link.

Many of you may be interested in hearing the spoken language. You can do this easily by watching a number of popular movies, such as Avatar and Geronimo, the later featuring my favorite Cherokee actor Wes Studi.

Language Background

Cherokee has three major dialects. The Lower dialect became extinct around 1900. The Middle or Kituhwa dialect is spoken by the Eastern band on the Qualla Boundary. The Overhill or Western dialect is spoken in Oklahoma. The Overhill dialect has an estimated 9000 speakers. The Lower dialect spoken by the inhabitants of the Lower Towns in the vicinity of the South Carolina–Georgia border had *r* as the liquid consonant in its inventory, while both the contemporary Kituhwa or Ani-kituwah dialect spoken in North Carolina and the Overhill dialects contain *l*. As such, the word "Cherokee" when spoken in the language is expressed as Tsalagi (pronounced Jah-la-gee, Cha-la-gee, or Cha-la-g or TSA la gi by giduwa dialect speakers) by native speakers.

The Cherokee speak a Southern Iroquoian language, which is polysynthetic and is written in a syllabary invented by Sequoyah. According to Wikipedia, Because of the polysynthetic nature of the Cherokee language, new and descriptive words in Cherokee are easily constructed to reflect or express modern concepts. Examples include *ditiyohihi*, which means "he argues repeatedly and on purpose with a purpose," meaning "attorney."

Sequoyah, or *Ssiquoya*, as he signed his name, or S*e-quo-ya* as his name is often spelled today in Cherokee, is credited with developing the popular Cherokee syllabary. **George Gist** or Guess as he was known by speakers of English, was a Cherokee silversmith who in 1821 completed his independent creation of the syllabary, making reading and writing in Cherokee possible. This was the only time in recorded history that a member of an illiterate people independently created an effective writing system. However, there are legitimate critics who believe the written form of the Cherokee language existed for many centuries before it was abandoned in or around the 16th century, and Sequoah's version of the syllabary may have been based on the original. This can not be supported by evidence.

In short, the Cherokee language, both written and spoken, is a powerful language of a powerful and proud people. Arguably it could be said that its preservation is paramount to saving ancient American language in its truest form, and lovers of American history and culture should take the time to become familiar with the language and, hopefully, to take an interest in learning at least the basics.

The following glossary of terms is but a glimpse into some of the terms referenced in this volume and a few more common terms not found in the novel's text. I hope you enjoy them.

CHEROKEE WORDS AND PHRASES

NOTE:

Vowel Sounds
a: as in father
e: as in plate
i: as in pit
o: as in note
u: as (oo) in fool
v: as (u) in put

Consonant Sounds
g: nearly as in English
d: nearly as in English, but close to t
h, k, l, m, n, q, s, t, w, and y as in English

Various Nouns

act ... i-ya-dv-ne-di

actor or actress ... a-dv-ne-li-s-gi

addict ... u-ga-na-si-s-gi

address ... na-na ge-sv wa-se-s-di

adventure ... a-ne-(lv)-to-di

agent ... a-tsi-nv-si-da-s-di

agriculture ... di-ga-lo-go-di

air ... u-no-le

alarm ... a-da-s-ga-s-da-ne-di<

alcohol ... a-ma a-su-yv-di wi-s-gi

ally ... a-li-(go)-di

ancestor ... tsu-ni-ga-yv-li-i-yu-(li)-s-ta-nv

angel ... a-ni-da-we-hi

apostle ... a-da-s-da-wa-di-to-hi

apparel ... di-nu-wo-s-di

appetite ... o-yo-si-s-gv

apple ... sv-(ga)-ta

apricot ... ka-wo-ni

argument ... di-go-si-so-di

Arkansas ... yo-wa-ne-gv

beads ... a-de-la-di-ya-tso-di

beauty ... u-wo-du

blame ... a-da-du-hi-s-to-di

blessing ... a-da-do-li-gi

bridge ... a-sv-`tlv-i

brook ... u-de-ya-di-s-di

camp ... a-le-wi-s-to-di

candy ... ka-(li)-se-tsi

canoe ... tsi-yu u-s-ti

cap ... a-(li)-s-du-lo

carcass ... u-li-wo-tsv-hi

cash ... a-de-lv

center ... a-ye-li

century ... s-go-hi-(tsu)-qui tsu-de-ti-yv-di

chain ... u-(na)-da-de-sv-da

chair ... ga-s-gi-lo

chapter ... a-ya-to-lv

cheese ... u-nv-di ga-du-nv

circle ... a-de-yo-ha

city ... ga-du-`hv-i

country ... s-ga-`du-gi

dawn ... u-gi-tsi-s-gv

death of an animal ... u-li-wo-s-di

death of a person ... a-yo-hu-hi-s-di

delivery ... a-da-ne-di

dirt ... ga-da

disgrace ... u-de-ho-hi-s-di

door ... a-s-`du-di

dream ... a-s-gi-(ti)-s-di

drum ... a-hu-li

dust ... ko-s-du

ear my ear ... tsi-le-ni

ear, his/her ... ga-le-ni

earring ... a-tli-i-do

earth ... e-lo-hi-no

eternity ... i-go-hi-da

eyes, his/her ... di-(ga)-to-li

eyes, my ... di-tsi-ga-to-li

faith ... go-hi-yu-di

family ... du-da-ti-h-na?v?i

feather ... u-gi-da-li

fever ... u-di-le-hv-s-gi

field ... tso-ge-si

fire ... a-tsi-la

floor ... ya-te-no-ha

flower ... hu-tsi-lv-ha or a-ji-lv-s-gi

flyer, something that flies ... a-h-la-wi-di-s-gi

forest ... a-do-hi

freedom ... a-du-da-le-s-di

friend, his/hers ... u-na-li

friend, my ... o-gi-na-li

gain ... u-ne-quo-i-s-di

garden ... a-wi-sv-nv

grass ... ga-`nu-lv

happiness ... a-li-he-li-tsi-da-s-di

hair ... u-gi-tli

haven safe place ... ni-ga-na-ve-gv-na na-hna-i

hay ... ka-ne-s-ga

health ... a-ye-lv nu-dv-na-de-gv

heart ... a-da-nv-to

hill ... ga-du-si

home ... o-we-`nv-`sv

honesty ... du-yu-(yo)-dv

hope ... u-tu-gi

horn ... u-yo-na

hours .. i-tsu-tli-lo-dv

house ... gal-`tso-de

House my house ... a-que-nv-sv

Honeysuckle ... gv-na-gi-tlv-ge-i

hunter ... ga-no-ha-li-do-hi

ice cream ... a-(ga)-da-tlv-da-u-ne-s-da-la

Indian ... a-yv-wi-ya

individual ... a-si-yv-wi-ha

infant ... a-yo-li

iron pot ... tsu-la-s-gi

Island ... u-hna-lu-dv-i

it ... na -s-gi

jar ... gu-gu tsu-la-s-ga

jelly ... u-lo-sv-i

joke ... ga-we-(tlv)-di

journal ... de-go-we-lv

journey ... vi-s-vi

joy ... u-li-he-li-s-di

juice ... u-da-ne-nv-hi

justice ... du-yu-(gu)-dv

keeper ... u-(ga)-se-di

king ... u-gv-wi-yu-hi

knife ... ha-yel-`sdi

lake, ... v-da-li

land ... ga-to-hi

leaves ... tsu-ga-lo-ga

legend ... nu-(li)-s-ta-ni-to-lv

life ... v-le-ni-to-hv

light ... a-tsv-s-dv

mate ... u-na-li-go-hi

miracle ... u-s-qua-ni-(go)-di

mist ... ka-nu-yo-la-di?a

moon ... sv-no-yi e-hi nv-da or nv-da

mountain ... o-da-lv?i

music ... di-ka-nu-gi-dv

near by, place ... e-s-ga-ni

oneself ... o-wa-sa

other ... so-i

others ... a-ni-so-i

pain ... e-hi-s-dv

pasture ... wa-ka di-yv-to-di

path ... u-s-di nv-no-hi u-lo-hi-s-di

peace ... nv-wa-do-hi-ya-da

people ... yu-wi

person ... si-yv-wi

place ... na-hna-i

plate ... `a-se-li-do

praise ... ga-lv-quo-do-di

presence ... e-do-hv-i

pride ... a-tlv-quo-dv

rain ... a-ga-s-ga

rainbow ... u-nv-quo-la-da

rider ... a-gi-lv-di-s-gi

river ... u-we-yv?i OR e-quo-ni

road ... nv-~no-`hi

rock ... nv-ya

scout ... a-ya-(wa)-s-gi

shadow ... tsa-da-yv-la-dv

shell ... u-ya-s-ga

shirt ... a-s-ga-yv u-nu-wo-hi

snow ... v-(na)-tsi

song ... ka-no-gi-s-di

soul ... a-da-(nv)-to

spirit ... a-da-nv-do

spring (water) ... ga-nu-go-gv?i

star ... no-qui-si

stone ... nv-ya

strawberry ... a-nv, ani

stream ... u-we-yv-i

strength ... nu-li-ne-gv-gv

success ... a-s-gwa-di-s-di

sugar ... ga-li-se-tsi

sun ... nv-do-i-ga-e-hi or nv-da

sunset ... wu-de-li-gv

sunshine ... a-ga-li-ha

teacher ... di-de-yo-hv-s-gi

tears (cry) ... tsu-ga-sa-wo-dv

thunder ... ah-yv-da-gwa-lo-s-gi

tongue ... ga-(nv)-go

town ... ga-du-hv?-i

trees ... de-tlu-`gv

truth ... du-yu-(yo)-dv

valley ... u-ge-da-li-yv

vision ... a-go-(wa)-dv-di

water ... a-ma

wealth ... nu-we-hna-v-i

weight ... nu-da-ge-sv

wind ... u-no-le

window ... tso-`la-`na

world ... e-`lo-`hi

PHRASES

You listen ... hi-tsa-tv-da-s-da
You all get up and listen ... ha-tv-da-s-da
what are they doing? ... ga-do-a-na-du-ne
I believe ... a-quo-`hi-yu
I will believe ... da-`go-hi-yu-`ni
I'm going ... `ge-`ga
I was going ... `ge-gv-`i
I will be going ... `ge-ges-`ti

I hear ... ga-`tv-gi
I heard ... ak-dv-`ga-nv
I will hear ... ga-`ga-dv-`ga-ni
I see ... `tsi-go-`ti
I saw ... a-gi-go-`hv
I will see him or her ... da-`tsi-go-`i

I am speaking ... Tsi-wo-ni-hu.
I'm talking ... tsi-`wo-ni
I talked ... gi-`wo-ni-`sv
I will talk ... da-tsi-`wo-ni-`si
I'm thankful ... ga li `e li `ga
I was thankful ... a qua li `he li tsv
I'll be thankful ... ga li `e li `ges `ti

I think ... ge-`li
I thought ... ge-`lis gv
I will think ... ge-`lis-ges-`ti
I'm tired ... da gi yo `we ga
I was tired ... da gi yo `we gv

I want ... a-qua-du-`li
I will want ... a-qua-du-`lis-ge-sti
I wanted(two or more items) ... `da-qua-du-`li
I will want(two or more items) ... da-qua-`lis-`ge-sti

I'm working ... da-gi-`lv-wi-sta-`ne
I was working ... da-gi-`lv-wi-sta-ne-`hv
I will be working ... da-gi-`lv-wi-sta-ne-`he sti
I don't understand ... `tla-i-`go-li-`ga
I didn't understand ... tla-ya-quol-`tsi-i

I'm hungry ... a-gi-`yo-si
I'm going to eat ... da-ga-li-sta-yvn
I will eat later ... go hi u da ga li sta yv ni
I am eating ... ga li sta yv hv sga
I have eaten ... a qual sta yv nu
I was hungry ... a gi `yo sis gv i
I'll be hungry ... a gi `yo sis `ges ti

You eat ... ha-li-s-ta-yv hv-s-ga
He/she will eat ... da-li-s-ta-yv-ni
They are eating ... a-nv-li-s-ta yv-hv-s-ga
Do you want to eat? ... tsadulis tsaldati
What am I eating ... ga-do-u-s-ti-tsi-gi
Pass me (food item) ... de-skv-si (this is used for solid foods)
Pass me(drink, gravy) ... e-s-gi-ne-hv-si
Are you hungry? ... ja-yo-si-ha-s?

I'm going home ... dv ge `si-di `quenv `sv i
I will go home ... a `qua ni gi ses `ti
Today I'm going ... ko `hi i ga-ge `ga
I went yesterday ... sv `hi-wa qua do `lv
I will go tomorrow ... su na `le-da ge `si
I'm going to town ... di`ga du `hv-ge `ga
I've been to town ... di`ga du hv-wi ge `da
I will go to town ... di`ga du`hv-a qua `nv ses `ti
I'm going to work ... da gi `lv wi sta `le `ga
I went to work ... da ge `lv wi sta ne `le `sv
I will be working ... da gi `lv wi sta ne `he `sti
I'm going to eat ... da-ga-`lis-`ta-yv-`ni

I'm riding with him ... tsi`tsa-ne
I rode with him ... tsi`tsa-ne-lv
I will ride with him ... da-tsi`tsa-ne-`li

We are going(two people) ... o-`ste-`ga
We have been(two people) ... wo-`ste-`da
We will go(2 people) ... o `ste ge `sti
We didn't understand ... tla-yo gi nol 'tse i
We will be working ... do gi ni`lv wi sta ne 'hes `ti
We are going to move(two people) ... da `yo sta da nv `si
We are going(3 or more people) ... o`tse `ga
You stay home (1 person) ... tso `le `sti
Go with me(one person) ... kstaqua du `ga

He/she ate ... ul-`sta-yv-`nv
He/she believes ... u-`wo-hi`yu
He/she is eating ... al-`sta-yv-`hv-sga
He/she is hunting ... ga-no-ha-li-do-ha
He/she is laughing ... u-yets-`ga
He/she was laughing ... u-yets-`ga-`i
He/she sees ... a-go-`ti
He/she will see ... u-go-`hv
He/she is singing ... de-ka-no-`gi
He/she is talking ... ga-`wo-ni
He/she thinks ... e-`li
He/she thought ... e-`li-sgv

That is mine ... is `na-a-qua-`tse-`li
This is my house ... hi `ya-gal tso `de aqua `tse `li
This is my car ... hi `ya-a tso do `di-a qua `tse `li
This is my wife ... hi `ya-ak sta `yv hv `sga
This is my son/daughter ... hi `ya-a que `tsi
This is ours ... a gi na `tse `li
This is our house ... hi `ya-gal tso`de-o gi na `tse `li
This is our car ... hi `ya-a tso do `di o gi na `tse `li

This is our child ... hi `ya-ogi `ne tsi
Is this yours? ... hi `yas-tsa `tse `li
Is this where you live? ... hi `yas-di `ste nv `sv

CHEROKEE CLANS

There are seven clans in Cherokee Society: *a ni gi lo hi* (Long Hair), *a ni sa* ho ni (Blue), *a ni wa ya* (Wolf), *a ni go te ge wi* (Wild Potato), *a ni a wi* (Deer), *a ni tsi s qua* (Bird), and **a ni wo di** (Paint).

According to the Cherokee Nation Web site:

a ni gi lo hi

The Long Hair Clan, whose subdivisions are Twister, Wind and Strangers, are known to be a very peaceful clan. In the times of the Peace Chief and War Chief government, the Peace Chief would come from this clan. Prisoners of war, orphans of other tribes, and others with no Cherokee tribe were often adopted into this clan, thus the name 'Strangers.' At some Cherokee ceremonial grounds, the Long Hair arbor is on the East side, and also houses the Chiefs and other leaders of the ground.

a ni sa ho ni

The Blue Clan's subdivisions are Panther, or Wildcat and Bear (which is considered the oldest clan). Historically, this clan produced many people who were able to make special medicines for the children. At some Cherokee ceremonial grounds, the Blue arbor is to the left of the Long Hair arbor.

a ni wa ya

The Wolf has been known throughout time to be the largest clan. During the time of the Peace Chief and War Chief government setting, the War Chief would come from this clan. Wolves are known as protectors. At some Cherokee ceremonial grounds, the Wolf arbor is to the left of the Blue arbor.

a ni go te ge wi

The Wild Potato Clan's subdivision is Blind Savannah . Historically, members of this clan were known to be 'keepers of the land,' and gatherers The wild potato was a main staple of the older Cherokee life back east (*Tsa-la-gi U-we-ti*). At some Cherokee ceremonial grounds, the Wild Potato arbor is to the left of the Wolf arbor.

a ni a wi

Members of the Deer Clan were historically known as fast runners and hunters. Even though they hunted game for subsistence, they respected and cared for the animals while they were living amongst them. They were also known as messengers on an earthly level, delivering messages from village to village, or person to person. At some Cherokee ceremonial grounds, the Deer arbor is to the left of the Wild Potato arbor.

a ni tsi s qua

Members of the Bird Clan were historically known as messengers. The belief that birds are messengers between earth and heaven, or the People and Creator, gave the members of this clan the responsibility of caring for the birds. The subdivisions are Raven, Turtle Dove and Eagle. Our earned Eagle feathers were originally presented by the members of this clan, as they were the only ones able to collect them. At some Cherokee ceremonial grounds, the Bird arbor is to the left of the Deer arbor.

a ni wo di

Members of the Paint Clan were historically known as a prominent medicine people. Medicine is often 'painted' on a patient after harvesting, mixing and performing other aspects of the ceremony. At some Cherokee ceremonial grounds, the Paint arbor is to the left of the Bird arbor.

TRADITIONAL BELIEF SYSTEM
(According to the Cherokee Nation Cultural Resource Center)

In the search for order and then to sustain that order, the Cherokee of old devised a belief system that, while appearing at first to be complex, is actually quite simple. Many of the elements of the original system remain in place with traditional Cherokee today. Although some of these elements have evolved or otherwise been modified, this belief system is an integral part of day-to-day life for many.

Certain numbers play an important role in the ceremonies of the Cherokee. The numbers four and seven repeatedly occur in myths, stories and ceremonies. The number four represents all the familiar forces, also represented in the four cardinal directions. These directions are east, west, north and south. Certain colors are also associated with these directions. The number seven represents the seven clans of the Cherokee, and are also associated with directions. In addition to the four cardinal directions, three others exist. Up (the Upper World), down (the Lower World) and center (where we live and where you always are).

The number seven also represents the height of purity and sacredness, a difficult level to attain. In olden times it was believed that only the owl and cougar had attained this level and thus have always had a special meaning to the Cherokee. The pine, cedar, spruce, holly and laurel also attained this level and play a very important role in Cherokee ceremonies. Cedar is the most sacred of all, and the distinguishing colors of red and white set it off from all others. The wood from the tree is considered very sacred, and in ancient days it was used to carry the honored dead.

Because of these early beliefs, the traditional Cherokee have a special regard for the owl and cougar. They are honored in some versions of the Creation story because they were the only two animals who were able to stay awake for the seven nights of Creation, the others having fallen asleep. Today, because of this, they are nocturnal in their habits and both have exceptional night vision.

The owl is seemingly different from other birds, resembling an old man as he walks. Sometimes the owl can be mistaken for a cat with his feather tufts and the silhouette of his head. This resemblance honors his nocturnal brother, the cougar. The owls eyes are quite large and are set directly in front like humans, and he can close one eye independently of the other. The cougar screams resemble those of a woman; further, he is an animal possessing secretive and unpredictable habits.

Cedar, pine, spruce, laurel and holly trees carry leaves all year long. These plants, too, stayed awake seven nights during the Creation. Because of this they were given special power and they are among the most important plants in Cherokee medicine and ceremonies.

Traditionally the Cherokee are deeply concerned with keeping things separated and in the proper classification or category. For example, when sacred items are not in use they are wrapped in deerskin or white cloth, and kept in a special box or other place.

The circle is another symbol familiar to traditional Cherokee. The Stomp Dance and other ceremonies involve movements in a circular pattern. In ancient times, the fire in the council house was built by arranging the wood in a continuous "X" so that the fire would burn in a circular path.

The river, or "Long Man," was always believed to be sacred, and the practice of going to water for purification and other ceremonies was at one time very common. Today the river or any other body of moving water, such as a creek, is considered a sacred site and going to water is still a respected practice by some Cherokees.

The everyday cultural world of the Cherokee includes spiritual beings. Even though the beings are different from people and animals, they are not considered "supernatural", but are very much a part of the natural, real world. Most Cherokee at some point in their lives will relate having had an experience with these spiritual beings.

A group of spiritual beings still spoken of by many Cherokee is the Little People. They cannot be seen by man unless they wish it. When they allow themselves to be seen, they appear very much like any other Cherokee, except they are very small, and have long hair, sometimes reaching all the way to the ground.

The Little People live in various places; rocky shelters, caves in the mountains or laurel thickets. They like drumming and dancing and they often help children who appear to be lost. Not just those geographically lost, but children who appear saddened and confused. They are also known to be quite mischievous at times. The Little People should be dealt with carefully, and it is necessary to observe some traditional rules regarding them.

They don't like being disturbed and may cause a person who continually bothers them to become "puzzled" throughout life. Because of this, traditional Cherokees will not investigate or look when they believe they hear Little People. If one of the Little People is accidentally seen, or if he or she chooses to show himself, it is not to be discussed or told of for at least seven years. It is common practice to not speak about the Little People after nightfall.

Traditional Cherokees also believe that after a person dies, his soul often continues to live on as a ghost. Ghosts are believed to have the ability to materialize where some, but not all people, can see them.

Very basic to the Cherokee belief system is the premise that good is rewarded and evil is punished. Even though the Cherokee have a strict belief in this type of justice, there are times when things happen that the system just does not explain. It is often believed that these events are caused by someone using medicine for evil purposes.

Witchcraft among the Cherokee does not resemble that of non-Indian cultures. To understand and respect the beliefs of traditional Cherokee about using medicine, conjuring, and witchcraft you must first consider early Indian societies and consider how this has remained an integral part of Cherokee culture even up to the present day. There are ordinary witches and then there are killer witches. Ordinary witches are actually considered the more dangerous since a person can never be sure he is dealing with one and they are more difficult to counteract. They may even deceive a medicine person and cause them to prescribe the wrong cure if not they aren't careful. One killer witch still spoken of often by traditionalists today is the Raven Mocker.

Today, although many Cherokee still consult with medicine people regarding problems, both mental and physical, some will not see a medicine man for any reason and refuse to acknowledge their powers. Some believe in using both Cherokee medicine and licensed medical doctors and the health care systems.

The knowledge held by the medicine men or women is very broad. They work and study for years committing to memory the syllabary manuscripts passed on by the ones who taught them. Many formulas have been documented in Cherokee syllabary writing in books ranging from small notebooks to full-blown ledgers. If the words are not spoken or sung in the Cherokee language, they have no affect. Until the words have been memorized the medicine person may refer to his book. This does not compromise his abilities, after all; modern medical practitioners often refer back to their medical texts and other reference books as well. The writings in these traditional books are strictly guarded and anyone who is not "in training" is forbidden to study or even read the books.

The spoken words are usually accompanied by some physical procedure, such as the use of a specially prepared tobacco, or drink. Medicine people themselves must be, and remain in perfect health for their powers to be at peak.

ABOUT THE AUTHOR

Logan Hawkes is a writer, broadcaster, and dual resident of Santa Fe, New Mexico, and Padre Island, Texas, reflecting his equal passion for the alluring mountainous west and a deep appreciation and fascination for the ancient sea and the natural histories of the two regions. Hawkes is an award winning writer, journalist and recurring guest on numerous radio programs and popular History Channel programs including *Ancient Aliens*, whose knowledge of ancient American history, myths and legends provide an insight into America's mysterious past. Winner of the Hearst Award and an author of an audio docu-drama series about Ancient American mysteries, he brings years of storytelling experience and knowledge of Native American tales to life for the reader. His own Cherokee heritage provides the backdrop for this rollicking adventure into America's Old West. When not living on the Pojoaque Pueblo Reservation North of Santa Fe, he spends his time on Padre Island with his partner and wife Carla and his youngest son who serves the gaming industry as a voice actor.

CPSIA information can be obtained at www.ICGtesting.com
Printed in the USA
LVOW061607290512

283776LV00003B/14/P